J.R.

# BLOOD RELATIONS

**BLAKE**

# FOR R.W.S.
# WITH MY LOVE

This edition first published by
Blake Publishing Ltd.
98-100 Great North Road, London N2 0NL, England, 1994.

First published in 1991 by Barrie & Jenkins Ltd

BRITISH LIBRARY CATALOGUING IN PUBLICATION DATA
A catalogue record for this book is available from the British Library.

ISBN 185782-0509

Phototypeset by Spectrum City, London E2

Printed and bound in Great Britain by Cox and Wyman, Reading, Berkshire

# Winter 1970

# Prologue

It was early November, and the morning had dawned as clear and sharply etched as a spring day. Even the dull urban vista from her window, of rooftops and pavements, seemed as brightly inviting as a travel poster. Like an ad on the telly, she told herself delightedly, throwing off her niggling apprehensions and welcoming the good omen. For today she was getting out.

'Today,' she solemnly informed her closest friend – who of course would miss her terribly – 'is the first day of the rest of my life. It won't ever be the same without you.' There was room in her triumph to make that acknowledgement and she felt mildly uplifted at having done so. It left her free to concentrate on herself.

After breakfast she waved to the others, a mixture of excitement and easy contempt, for she would soon be free while they – poor mutts – were stuck where they were. They expected her back, to tell them all what it was like out there; but of course she'd never go back. She settled into the car and their deliciously imagined envy of her status gave her a warm feeling of confidence and even of casual generosity towards them all. They hadn't been a bad bunch. Then she surrendered to a pleasurable vision of herself, wrapped in furs and jewels; beautiful, mysterious, desired, sweeping away in a chauffeur-driven limo with her attendants. They'd be dismissed at her destination – no doubt tearfully, for they loved her. But that was life.

But for once fantasy couldn't improve on reality. This was her day, her big chance. A brave new day in a new place. A new beginning. New friends too, in time, who'd know her at last as she truly was and who'd love her for herself. There'd be men, and she the centre of their attention but properly valued, for once. But today – now – was the start of her new life.

When the car had set her down and driven away she went out into the sunshine after a while to enjoy the thrill of real freedom, to confirm it now that her chance had come. She'd worked bloody hard for it, she reminded herself. I'm a free woman, she exulted, a grown-up. I've put away childish things.

She inspected the local shops with a consciously independent eye but was uncritically pleased with everything she saw – although, of course, she'd soon be moving on to better things. She could almost feel herself filling out to fit her adult image, expanding in her self-satisfaction and conscious of being noticed. She imagined her inner glow lighting her up, like one of those ads on the telly for breakfast cereal. Inexpertly she ogled and pouted in return, as she'd seen them do on the telly, and was encouraged by the reaction.

Beyond the shops lay open land, green space in which to lose herself. She was sick of supervision, however much for her own good. They'd never realised how unlike she was to the others; more in need of love than supervision, more sinned against than sinning. And that was God's truth – the story of her life.

She'd already proved another truth, the truth of all that preaching that had stuck in her throat at the time and made her want to puke in their faces: Blest are the meek,

4

the pure in heart, those that suffer, for they'll be rewarded. Grin and bear it, she paraphrased with a sudden giggle, and you'll two-finger them all one day. Even Beth herself. Beth was loaded down with the sins of others and she'd only be a burden. Poor Beth should be cut adrift with the old life of childish things. With Sandra. Sandra made enemies like jam attracted wasps. But she'd stick to Carole. Carole was anyway more in her new, sophisticated style.

Almost without warning the late afternoon blew cold and clouds swarmed across the sun. The light drained from the heathland and left skeletal trees in stark relief against the sky like the spars of ancient shipwrecks. As though someone had pulled the plug from the bottom of the world, she thought uneasily, dismayed by a wave of loneliness yet just then suspicious of any company.

Rightly suspicious, for her murderer had waited for such a moment and it was just then she died. After all, it had been the last day of her life.

# Summer 1989

# One

Beth wilted in the heat and angrily reviewed the various aspects of hell she'd suffered since morning. The sun blazed down on the dignified English garden, as it had done for days in a way that pre-empted the attraction of foreign holidays; but because she felt antisocial Beth sweltered in the car, rather than join the other early parents who waited on the shaded lawn for the end of afternoon school. She'd come from a miserable lunch that had crowned a wasted morning helping Jane Mallinson entertain her grotesque old aunt.

Jane had warned her – casually – but Beth knew she'd have gone even if the old woman's disgusting attributes had been spelled out for her. Self-contempt further fuelled her anger, as usual a secret boiling of emotions that rarely found expression even when she was alone. For it was never easy to refuse Jane, and certainly not when her invitation was coupled with a gratifying one for Penny.

'So when Jonquil suggested that Penny might come for the weekend,' Jane had tempted over the phone, 'with Sherry, naturally – '

'Naturally,' Beth murmured, and they both laughed. Weekends were for riding and the Mallinsons' spread easily accommodated a second pony.

'Well, anyway. Rob thought it was a splendid idea. It'll give Aunt Grace some added interest and see her happily off for another year. Jonquil's probably talking it over with Penny now, but why not come for lunch today and meet my aunt yourself? She'd like that. She's blind, you see, and doesn't get much out of life, poor dear. Yes – diabetes. How about it?' She'd only be slumped at home in the oppressive heat, Beth knew. She might just as well slump at Jane's. So, all unwitting –

'Of course I'll come, and thank you, but I'd better talk to Penny first about the weekend. She and Duncan may have some paddock ploy in mind.'

Weekend invitations from the Mallinsons were always accepted, but Beth never answered for either of her daughters without checking first. It was one of several self-imposed principles she observed on their behalf, remembering the depersonalising lack of such consideration in her own childhood.

Beth dressed in sleeveless sky-blue cotton, crisp and simple, that darkened her eyes and suited her pale skin better than the usual summer wear of white or cream. She wasn't one of those lucky blondes who tan to a seductive honey, but burned a raw and painful scarlet. In her late thirties, however, her skin was still smooth and supple, with the dim sheen of magnolia petals.

She left the house satisfied with her appearance, always carefully presented, from her burnished cap of fine, pale hair to her neat hands and feet. Beth was about five foot four or five, slender but not angular, and with good legs. Her features weren't particularly memorable but she never dressed as though to counteract their deficiency. She merely clothed what she had to its best advantage in a quiet neatness that had a style of its own. Her social manner was as retiring, although never awkwardly so; never too cautious, but restful.

Men found Beth comfortably undemanding company, and in their wives her inoffensive personality inspired at least a tepid friendliness. Beth didn't ask for more. Acceptance and peaceful coexistence were all her social ambitions. So she was available, in a neighbourly way, for baby-sitting or school lifts; she politely accepted and conscientiously returned social invitations and pleasantly entertained Duncan's colleagues. It wasn't easy to fault her, and even the suspicion that Beth sometimes actually preferred her own company was put down to her blameless diffidence or, alternatively, an (almost) admirable enthusiasm.

For since her marriage to Duncan, nearly eleven years earlier, Beth had developed a passion for gardening. This was as well since Duncan, an actuary in a busy finance house, had allowed the large garden pretty well to run wild. Beth regarded the labour as a sort of freedom, an activity that didn't necessitate joining any club, so she hired no help. Even more of an oddity, given the size of the place, she did her own housework. Others might have their dailies or their au pairs, like the Mallinsons' Renata, but the work was no hardship to Beth who loved the house. She didn't 'do household chores', she cherished; yet without imposing the irritating restrictions from which families of house-proud women sometimes suffer. Duncan's home had become her castle, and Beth felt at her safest and happiest within its boundary walls.

She needed all her acquired confidence to survive the company of Jane's aunt, for the lunch invitation proved far more of a strain than she'd anticipated. Jane introduced her merely as 'Aunt Grace', a name that seemed more sickeningly inappropriate by the minute. For a start, Beth was physically repelled by the woman; by her gross white body, by her sparse hair that left exposed unlovely expanses of scalp, and by the even more sickening wiry white tufts that sprouted at the sides of her mouth and gave her the look of having insufficiently boned a meal of herring. She wore the conventional dark glasses, but more as a badge than a discretion, it seemed, and turned their unresponsive black glitter on Beth as she asked persistent questions about her family.

Then, Beth's over-fastidious soul was disturbed by the expectation of spills and breakages during lunch – unnecessarily so, since the meal had been tailored to suit the aunt's disability. However, it was soon clear that one of the pleasures she still found in life was her food. The woman ate like a mechanical grab, Beth noticed disgustedly.

Only by keeping her eyes on her own plate could Beth concentrate on eating enough to avoid comment, and she despised herself again for being edged off-balance. Beth prided herself on her social poise. Ostensibly at ease among the Mallinsons' self-consciously *Homes and Gardens* furnishings, she managed to parry the worst of the old woman's inquisitive questioning in her quiet voice and left as soon as she decently could. She only hoped that her conversation hadn't been noticeably more colourless than usual.

Beth arrived far too early, therefore, at her younger daughter's private prep. school and paid for it with an extended broil in the car; a sort of self-punishment. And there was more irritation ahead before she could relax. Altogether a hellish day.

12

She had three girls to return to their homes: Penny, Jonquil Mallinson and a younger child who was dropped off first and whose going didn't noticeably reduce the clamour in the car. The afternoon lifts, accompanied by a noise as of trampled bagpipes, were understandably less inhibited than the morning runs to school.

'Thank you, Mrs Masters.' Jonquil slammed the car door and waved perfunctorily before disappearing round the side of the house. Beth roused herself from a sense of battered submission and drove back through the Mallinsons' vestigial park.

'Had a good day?' she asked Penny, who replied as ritually,

'It was OK' and pitched her summer boater on to the back seat. 'The Top Form gave us a questionnaire to find out how apathetic we are. They're always saying we're apathetic.'

'Oh, dear! So what was decided?'

'Nothing. Nobody could be bothered to fill it in.' Beth gave a grunt of laughter. It was sometimes difficult to decide whether Penny's straight-faced stories were recounted in all seriousness or intended to amuse. 'Er – this seems to be Ewell,' Penny pointed out, anxious to be reunited with Sherry before he pined entirely away. 'Why aren't we going home?'

'We're meeting Jennetta. It's her last exam today and she'll have stuff to bring home.' Penny settled back resignedly.

'Eight more years and you'll be doing this for me. Sutton won't seem too much like a new school next year, there'll still be people who knew Jennetta. And Jonk's coming too, did you know?'

13

'Mm. Actually I was over at The Lodge today. Lady Mallinson wants you to spend the weekend with them.'

'Jonk told me this morning. Did you see Jonk's Mum's aunt? I met her when she came last year. Pretty grisly, I thought.'

'She can't help it, darling,' Beth's gentle reproof came automatically.

She slid a glance sideways. Penny's short sandy hair had followed her discarded boater upwards and now stood in soft tufts above tawny eyebrows drawn down almost to meet her freckled snub nose. Naturally she'd be unenthusiastic about meeting the aunt again. Beth wondered if she was actually in two minds about the visit. She hoped an unlooked-for refusal wouldn't make too many waves.

Jonquil had been Penny's best friend ever since she'd come new to Greenbanks two years before, when Penny took her under her wing. It had seemed an unlikely pairing at eight and was even more so now, their only apparent interest in common being a passion for riding. Yet perhaps it wasn't so strange, Beth reflected. Penny's sturdy self-reliance was a good foil for Jonquil's flighty brilliance. She did sometimes wonder if Penny squandered herself in her friend's interest, but otherwise their friendship had her approval – although she didn't herself much care for Jonquil. The word 'pert' flitted through Beth's head.

Without telegraphing her gratification, Beth had always been delighted that, through their daughters, the two families had grown so close. She was still a little in awe of Sir Robert (privately so in her thoughts but Rob to his face), however often she reminded herself that his

14

knighthood was 'only' for services rendered before his retirement – from the City or Industry or something; but Jane Mallinson was her kind of person.

Jane was Beth's closest friend, in the sense that they met often; because Jane's company was offered without the demands of shared confidences. Beth was easily embarrassed or offended with that kind of tit for tat relationship, but hers wasn't a naturally introverted personality and reclusiveness among her family interests had largely been self-imposed. Now, as Jane's friend, she enjoyed her cautious forays into local society.

Before her marriage to a man twenty years her senior, Jane had been a teacher – in quite ordinary schools (Beth caught herself up with a self-conscious grin when she found herself thinking like that) – and her husband's late elevation left her unchanged. At forty-three, Jane remained the kind, intelligent, forthright woman with a resilient sense of humour that Beth could imagine in the classroom. Still able, too, to keep one jump ahead of her erratic daughter, something Sir Robert signally failed to do. Beth pictured his spine as a vertebral corkscrew twisted firmly round Jonquil's little finger. He had two much older children from his previous marriage, and so the Mallinsons' family situation a little paralleled Beth's own, but Jonquil was the adored child of Rob's old age.

By comparison with the Masterses the Mallinsons were *nouveaux,* having moved from one of the London suburbs to the outskirts of Epsom only a little over two years earlier. But whatever the services for which Sir Robert had been rewarded, they'd enabled him to buy up a fair chunk of the old Rosebery estate; and that, together with his knighthood, naturally made the Mallinsons

15

socially desirable – not to say useful. There were seats on local committees to be filled. And because of Penny the Masterses had become acceptable to the Mallinsons.

It was a compliment of which Duncan was cheerfully oblivious. His Viking looks hid the heart of a gentle teddy-bear that cared for none of these things. For Duncan, Rob was a pleasant enough chap with the mildly amusing habit of taking out his shooting-stick to show friends round his garden but who didn't play golf. Duncan's astigmatism resulted from an equally unconscious and enviable sense of security that Beth could only imitate, and for the real lack of which she despised herself.

Jennetta was waiting with a noisy group of newly emancipated friends, A-levels and school ten minutes into their past. She wound up her enthusiastic plans to meet 'after Results' and bundled herself and her school bags into the back of the Polo.

'How did it go?' Beth's expression warmed as she turned to her elder daughter.

'A doddle!' Jennetta laughed with the happy confidence that always flipped Beth's heart over. Fortune had a way of turning malign. Jennetta leaned forward between the seats as Beth headed back through Cheam. 'Now we just sweat it out 'til August, but don't worry, Mum. And talking of sweat – you must've had a pretty torrid games lesson on a day like this,' she remarked to Penny, catching sight of her games-bag.

'Tennis,' Penny grunted dispiritedly.

'But you like tennis.'

'Not with Miss Jorgensen, I don't. And she's worse than ever now with Wimbledon on.'

16

'It is a truth universally acknowledged,' Jennetta began primly, 'that games teachers are always popular. What's wrong with Miss Jorgensen?'

'Some people like her, actually,' Penny admitted fairly, slewing round to face Jennetta. 'Because she's Swedish. And because she once played at Wimbledon. But she was beaten by a Brit., you know, and she's never got over the disgrace. So she stayed in England to take it out on the rest of us.'

'The imagination you kids have!' Jennetta grinned. 'What does Jonk think of her?'

'Jonk's good at tennis,' Penny replied defensively, as if her friend's loyalty had been questioned. 'Her Dad coaches her on their own court, so she can't help it.'

'Why don't you take your racquet with you this weekend?' Beth suggested as they swung round the perimeter of Nonsuch Park. 'Get some practice with Jonquil. Penny's been asked to stay,' she explained to Jennetta.

'No big deal,' Penny shrugged, as if a hint of Beth's satisfaction had sounded through her words. 'There's a spooky old aunt who keeps touching you.'

'Eh?' Beth was startled out of her complacency.

'Because she's blind. Didn't she do it to you? She feels you to see what you're like. And if she likes you she keeps hugging you.' Beth's gorge rose in sympathy with Penny's disgust. At least she'd been spared that form of investigation over lunch.

'Penny met her last year.' Beth caught Jennetta's eye in the driving-mirror and silently pleaded for tact. 'She liked you, did she, darling?'

'Mm. Because, Jonk says, she was terribly pleased I was "such a nice friend",' Penny quoted savagely, flushing with the bottomless shame of being tagged with such a label. 'That shows you. But she worked in a prison, you see, before this disease turned her blind –'

'Penny!' Jennetta interrupted as Beth fluffed a gear-change. 'Is that another of your imaginative thumbnail sketches?'

'No. And anyway, Mrs Woolcombe says I haven't *got* any imagination,' Penny retorted. 'Miss Parker used to work in a prison and she's got a hang-up about "nice friends". She used to nag Jonk's Mum about Jonk's friends where they lived before, and that's why Jonk wants to trot me round the ring now.'

Beth braked outside their double garage and went ahead to the back door while the girls cleared the car.

'Tell Jonk you can't go and she'd better invite one of her other nice friends instead, if you don't like the idea,' Jennetta made the obvious suggestion as they followed Beth into the kitchen.

'They've all heard too much about her,' Penny snorted. 'And anyway, Jonk says she can't trust anyone else. It's a *rotten* responsibility.' It seemed to Beth that at that moment Penny's childhood withered and fell away, leaving her more vulnerable than before.

'So what shall I tell Lady Mallinson?' she asked. 'I'll have to phone her soon.'

'Tell her it's on, of course,' Penny said glumly. 'I've already said yes to Jonk.' They heard her trudge upstairs to change before going down to the paddock.

'Poor Penny!' Beth smiled uneasily at Jennetta. 'Should I have found her a reason to cry off?'

'She wasn't looking for that. This aunt sounds like a prize drag, but don't worry, Mum. Penny'll do a good PR

18

job for Jonk. Anyway, I'm for a flop in the garden while this lasts. The weather's sure to break now that exams are over.'

It occurred to Beth that Jennetta quite often told her not to worry. She was at the same time grateful and uneasy that, for all her ebullience, Jennetta recognised her mother's secret need for reassurance. They were on the same wavelength, Jennetta would say, although in this instance it wasn't Penny's behaviour at the Mallinsons' that disturbed Beth. She knew she'd miss Jennetta almost unbearably when she went away to college – and there could be no 'don't worry' that could soothe that.

Beth waited until Jennetta too had changed – undressed, rather – and gone outside, before she phoned Jane with Penny's formal acceptance of an invitation more self-interested than had at first appeared.

'Penny remembers your aunt from last year,' she added. 'Jane, *did* she work in a prison, or is that just kids' talk?'

'In a girls' hostel, actually,' Jane replied comfortably but not expansively. 'Much the same thing to these children, I suppose.' *Not* a college hostel or the YWCA, Beth deduced grimly. 'Oh, by the way – you'll have one less on your lift tomorrow afternoon. I'll bring Aunt Grace in to collect Jonquil. She likes to feel involved. Bring Penny over to talk to her then. Isn't this weather *absolute heaven*?'

'Heaven,' Beth echoed limply. Her dress was pasted to her back. She found the heat oppressive and its tacky by-products and sheer inconvenience offended her. No joy for Beth to hear that the summer of 1989 bid fair to rival that of 1976. Already the lawns were turning straw-coloured and brittle, and the proposed hosepipe ban could mean death to Surrey's sandy gardens.

Beth rang off and went slowly upstairs, feeling now almost a winter's chill that wasn't entirely caused by the damp cotton clinging to her body. From past experience she knew that the next stage was likely to be a blinding headache others called a migraine. It seemed to enable them to suffer more gracefully.

A glance through the bedroom curtains, drawn closed since the morning in an attempt to keep the room cool, showed Penny defying the temperature with Sherry in the paddock where a few jumps were set up. Her face glowed like a beacon but she never seemed to wilt in the heat. Nor had it bothered herself as a child, Beth remembered; her thermostat seemed to have packed up during puberty, for some reason. But Penny was a tough little nut. Jennetta, face down on an air-bed, more purposefully courted the sun. She was lucky. With her dark colouring Jennetta tanned an even honey-bronze without burning; her father's legacy.

Beth refocused her gaze on the paddock. Sherry really was a bit of a dobbin, she reflected with a smile. A Thelwell sort of pony tending to fluffiness round his ankles when he grew his winter coat. Not a patch on Jonquil's Tyrone for breeding and elegance, but he was bomb-proof on the roads and Penny adored him. It would never cross her mind to compare him with Tyrone. Sherry was incomparable. Beth felt her usual twinge of uneasiness at the prospect of trauma ahead for them all when Penny eventually outgrew her pony. She wasn't *that* tough, and it wouldn't be possible to keep

Sherry on as a sort of pet with her new one.

Beth had been nervous about Penny having her own pony. She'd never been within even touching distance of one herself, but Duncan had been right. Sherry was a huge success and Penny had blossomed in her uniquely gruff and self-contained way. It had startled Beth to hear her talking so unselfconsciously about trust and responsibility, but presumably those were qualities she'd learnt with her pony. Penny had already matured, almost unnoticed (whereas Jonquil, for all her comparative sophistication, was only a precocious child), but did Penny nevertheless have to cope with an ordeal by neurotic aunt? There was still time to arrange an urgent visit to Duncan's parents in Weymouth.

Not that she'd get any thanks for intervening on Penny's behalf, Beth reminded herself as she turned away. Penny resented being babied, a result of the age difference between herself and Jennetta, Beth supposed. If she were to spot a manufactured escape Beth would lose her trust, perhaps even her future friendship when Penny's interests extended beyond the paddock. But this weekend could be a crunching mistake, her nerve-ends warned as Beth stripped and showered briefly. For the next hour she lay on the bed in the darkened room, her thoughts colliding like moths around a candle-flame; in her imagination she saw Penny – her whole family – drawn into an orbit possibly as destructive.

At three-fifteen the following afternoon, Friday, Beth watched the Mallinsons' green Range Rover drive past the side road where she waited. It was followed by the Sandersons', the Farrars', the Havergals' and the

Breakspeares' second cars before she eventually pulled out into the traffic. By the time she turned in at the school gates there were already a few of Greenbanks' too-dis-inctive uniforms out on the pavement and running the gauntlet of early arrivals at the bus-stop from the nearby comprehensive.

Inside the gates the semicircular drive around the cedar shaded lawn was lined with cars, the Range Rover half a dozen ahead of Beth's Polo. The raised terrace before the main door, of what was once a large Victorian private house, was grouped with mothers waiting to field their young. Beth saw Jane Mallinson cross the gravel to join them and fall prey to the school thruster. The price you paid for carrying clout, Beth grinned to herself, even if you chose not to wield it.

Instead of heading for the terrace herself she walked around the edge of the lawn within the line of parked cars, her sandals silent on the grass, until she was level with the Range Rover. Its windows were open, and for a second Beth hesitated before continuing past the pas-senger door for a view through the windscreen. The still, shapeless figure stared ahead like a blind Buddha: Miss Parker, who'd worked in a girls' hostel.

This time Beth studied the woman attentively and caught something of the eerie quality that had bothered Penny. The inscrutable puffy face, half hidden behind the extravagant glasses, somehow subtly conveyed a complacent, knowing expression. For a moment Beth had the unnerving feeling that the old woman was secretly inspecting her in return.

She was about to make herself known when there was a sudden flurry of noise and movement. A torrent of

22

children washed out of the main door and down the terrace steps, spilling over the drive and carrying the adults away like flotsam. Glancing past the blind profile, Beth saw Penny peel off from the group around Jonquil and stump away towards the Polo.

'Be *really* early tomorrow!' Jonquil called after her. The blind woman suddenly slanted her head, like some gross bird sounding a grub below ground, and put up a hand to her glasses. On her middle finger a plain gold ring was almost lost in the soft swell of fat that had already swallowed the woman herself. But whatever her disabilities, there was obviously nothing wrong with her hearing; she'd distinguished Jonquil's voice above the hubbub. Beth left unsaid whatever it was she'd intended.

She cut back across the lawn to let her passengers into the car. Jane Mallinson was still buttonholed on the terrace and Beth drove away with an apologetic wave. Blow taking Penny to the aunt for a chat as commanded – what, and stand by watching her touched about by that predatory old bag of tripes? She was less inclined than ever to let her daughter go for the weekend, but it was too late now to fabricate an excuse that would convince either the Mallinsons or Penny herself.

So Beth preserved her reputation for quiet serenity that no one peering into her dreams that night would have agreed she deserved.

# Two

Whatever Beth's secret worries, Penny set out sunnily with Sherry straight after breakfast the next morning, for once formally dressed in jodhpurs, boots and dark-blue jacket instead of her usual jeans. The transformation was always a minor miracle.

'If I'd thought I looked as good as that, I'd have learnt to ride,' Jennetta murmured as they saw Penny off.

'Then thank God it never occurred to you,' Duncan grinned, dropping an arm across her shoulders. 'We have our work cut out as it is, beating off your admirers. Witness the depression in the doorstep.'

Beth persuaded Duncan to take over her usual job of following with Penny's weekend case, after a decent interval, while she went to do some shopping. After lunch, with Jennetta whirled away by her permanent young man and Duncan at the golf course, Beth retreated to the bedroom. Her broken sleep the night before had sapped her as much as the enervating heat, and she thankfully dozed away the suffocating afternoon.

A companionable salad supper – all home-grown, as Beth pointed out with satisfaction – alone with Duncan on the patio in the cool of the evening, was interrupted by a phone call. It was a moment before Beth's concentration caught up with what Jane was saying, so automatically had her reactions flipped to panic stations on Penny's account.

' – know it's later than we usually let her go, but she's

safely on her way and Rob's following with her case. Penny'll fill in the details, but the gist is that we ran into a bit of bother on the way home from Oriel's and it rather unsettled Aunt Grace. A heath fire – the countryside's virtually a bomb waiting to go off; it's so dry. By the time we got home it was obvious poor Penny's weekend was blown. She's been *totally* unflappable but you can't tell what that's hiding, can you, and it wasn't fair to expect her to soldier on. She preferred to ride home rather than be driven and leave Sherry here 'til tomorrow, and it's better to let them establish their own comfortable norms, isn't it. But I'm terribly sorry, Beth. Be forgiving and come for coffee on Monday? Just us. Aunt Grace'll be gone – and my *God* I'll need to unwind!'

That was at once too much and too little information, as Duncan agreed. But although Jane's hurried explanation left Beth bewildered and uneasy, she was also relieved that Penny's visit had been curtailed.

Penny clopped home on Sherry about half an hour later, followed only moments after by Sir Robert as Beth and Duncan hurried out to meet her. Duncan swept Penny down to the paddock, leaving Beth to thank Rob for delivering her case. She hardly had time even for that before he strode back to the Range Rover and accelerated down the drive, squirting gravel. She had the impression that he wasn't alone in the car and that Rob himself was in a barely controlled rage, but she was more concerned about Penny. However, she resisted the temptation to flap down to the paddock in unusually clucking mode and unpacked Penny's things instead.

Beth was waiting impatiently in the kitchen when at last she heard Penny and Duncan coming through the scullery.

'Have you had supper, Penny?' she called, trying to strike a normally welcoming note.

'Yes, but I don't want anything to go to waste,' Penny grinned as she padded, sock-footed, into the kitchen. Beth ran her eyes casually over her and got an equally calm blue look back, to her relief. 'What is there?'

'Garden salad. Pour yourself some juice while I get it ready.' A slight shrug and shake of his head told her that Duncan hadn't questioned Penny yet. 'Sorry your visit's come apart, darling,' Beth went on equably as she assembled the meal. 'Lady Mallinson rang to say you were on your way but she didn't tell us what happened.'

Duncan laid a place at the kitchen table while Beth deftly cut up and arranged tomatoes, cucumber and pepper with the remains of the tossed lettuce and potato salad from their own supper, and a slice of ham. She set the plate in front of Penny and turned away to wash up their earlier supper things. It was over to Duncan now; a manipulative pincer strategy that sometimes worked better with Penny than a frontal cross-examination.

But Penny was quite ready to report the day's events, between mouthfuls, without the need for her parents' guile.

'Well, we were coming back from seeing Jonk's sister's new baby in Sussex somewhere – And *that* was something Jonk hadn't warned me about,' Penny broke off, affronted. 'I'd only just got back into my jeans when suddenly we were all packed into the car with a picnic lunch. But it was OK in the end. They left us alone after we'd looked at the baby. They've got a swimming-pool and spare

27

bathies, so it wasn't too bad,' she conceded temperately.

'Anyway, on the way back we ran into a queue. There was all this smoke from a fire at the side of the road, but it wasn't dangerous. The hold-up was because of the fire engines. Jonk's Dad didn't think we'd be stuck long and we were nearly at our turn-off. Jonk's Mum's aunt was sitting in the front with him and he was explaining where we were and why we'd stopped. You have to do a commentary because she's blind,' Penny explained to Duncan. 'But she got a bit fussy because smoke got into the car before we shut the windows and she could smell it. She thought the fire was worse than it was and wanted Jonk's Dad to find another way home instead of waiting. Is there any more potato salad, Mummy? Kuh! Well, it got very hot with the windows shut and we had to open them again. The smoke came in worse and Miss Parker got worse. Jonk's Dad got very bored with her.

'Then suddenly there were police cars and sirens, and next an ambulance. Jonk's Dad was tired of telling Miss Parker what he didn't know himself and he walked down the line to see what was happening. Jonk wanted to go too but he wouldn't let her, which was a pity. I wouldn't have minded getting out myself.

'Jonk got a bit stroppy after that and Miss Parker kept saying, "Oh, what I wouldn't give for a cup of tea!" It was another pity I remembered a can of lemonade left over from the picnic, because soon after *that* Miss Parker started saying, "I must find a toilet. Is there a toilet?" Toilet!' Penny scoffed. She'd been brought up to use the uncompromising 'lavatory' in polite society. 'As if you'd find one on a golf-course!'

'So it was getting a bit hairy when Jonk's Dad came back –'

'Which golf-course was this?' Duncan asked.

'The ultimate catastrophe!' Beth laughed quietly. She hung up the tea-towel and joined them at the table.

'Not yours, Daddy,' Penny reassured. 'Jonk's Dad told Miss Parker we were on Banstead Downs. That one. Shall I put these things in the washer, Mummy? Mummy!'

'What? No, leave them. Er – the washer takes too much water in this shortage,' Beth explained less curtly. 'Who needs a heatwave!' She wiped a hand across her face. Certainly not Beth, Duncan knew, and he saw with concern that she was looking quite drained.

'You've left us cliff-hanging, Penny,' he reminded with a smile. 'What happened when Sir Robert came back?'

'Actually, Daddy, *you* interrupted me. Well –' Penny yawned, well fed and suddenly exhausted like a healthy puppy. 'He told Jonk's Mum that one of the fire-beaters had found someone dead, but we all heard –'

'Penny!' Beth cut in, horrified. 'Are you sure that's what he said? That someone *died* in that fire?' Duncan tried to catch her eye. Details could be supplied later by the Mallinsons. But Beth's gaze was fixed on her daughter's face, the fluorescent kitchen lights emphasising her pallor.

''Course I'm sure what he said,' Penny retorted in a way that would have earned her a reminder in other circumstances. 'But it wasn't someone who died in the fire, it was only old bones. So *that* reminded Miss Parker of someone who disappeared near there –'

Penny was distracted again as Beth suddenly left the table and hurried to the fridge. After a moment she reappeared from behind its open door with a mug of milk for Penny and went back to pour herself a glass of mineral water.

'Go on,' she said abruptly, slowly sipping her drink with her back to the room.

'And that's why Miss Parker went off her crumb,' Penny accepted her mother's implied rebuke and turned back apologetically to her reduced audience. 'We had to find another way home after all, and all the time she nagged Jonk's Dad to take her to a police station. She said she knew who the bones belonged to. Jonk's Mum kept trying to change the subject and Jonk kept saying how sick she felt. In the end Jonk's Dad blew up and – well, they decided I'd be happier at home. I didn't like to agree but I was glad they thought of it. But how could she recognise *whose* bones they are, Daddy?' Duncan winced and glanced beseechingly at Beth's unresponsive back.

'I – don't really know, Pennikin. All pretty uncomfortable for you, though.'

'Well, it was nothing to do with me,' Penny pointed out calmly. Duncan goggled. 'And actually, the good thing is that Jonk reckons they won't ask her to stay again,' she concluded between cavernous yawns.

Penny golloped down her milk, decorating her face with the inevitable moustache that follows juvenile drinking. In an instant she was recognisably Duncan's engaging child again.

'Looks as if fun in the swimming-pool's catching up with you,' he grinned and got to his feet. 'Come on. A quick shower and then bed. Mummy will come up when she's cleared away.' But when he returned twenty minutes later Beth was still rooted at the sink, staring out over the twilit garden.

Penny was already asleep, flushed pink and gold in the light from her bedside lamp, her hair fluffed like a dandelion-clock after the drier. But for once Beth felt none of her usual delight as she stared down at her daughter's sleeping face, her own its cruel caricature. As sick with shock as if she'd been there herself and listening to that frightful woman piling horror on horror, Beth considered the experience to which her spinelessness had committed Penny. She'd muddled her priorities. Neither the Mallinsons' feelings nor even thought for her own credibility should have smothered her instinct to prevent Penny's visit.

It wasn't any consolation that the child seemed untouched by the experience. 'You can't tell what that's hiding,' Jane had said, and Beth knew enough to agree. For wasn't Penny already a fraction less innocent for her contact, however indirect, with that – *thing* – on the golf-course? In Beth's imagination it was the hairline crack that in the end could gape as wide as the grave. And she had only herself to blame.

The knowledge concentrated Beth's guilt-stricken reflexes. Never one to parade her more uncomfortable emotions, she tried to compose herself and as usual took refuge in – or protective colouring from – routine. Nothing would be gained by rousing Duncan's concern for feelings she couldn't properly explain. She opened the curtains for Penny's instant view of the paddock

31

when she woke in the morning and checked that the windows were set wide enough to cool the room until she came to bed herself. Finally she turned out the lamp above a framed snap of Sherry and went back downstairs like a sleepwalker.

Duncan was sitting on the patio blowing pipe-smoke at occasional midges.

'She's peacefully asleep,' Beth heard herself speak normally as she sank into a chair. The cool anonymity of the dusk braced her to add, 'That must be a good sign.'

'Good God, she isn't remotely disturbed,' Duncan laughed shortly. 'In fact I thought she sounded amazingly callous about the whole business, the aunt as well as the other thing. But I suppose we should be glad it hasn't affected her. It's worried *you* more, on her behalf. Unnecessarily so, I'd say. The Great Anticipator!' he laughed again, more gently, but Beth caught the warning note: she'd over-reacted.

'I'd forgotten how callous kids can be,' she murmured. 'Even little girls.' She leaned her head back and closed her eyes. The headache she'd been trying to will away pounded like a gong.

'And Penny's even got a new subject out of it for her next free-composition homework, if Jonk doesn't mind,' Duncan remarked incredulously. 'She quoted Mrs Woolcombe as saying that her usual subject had lost its freshness.'

'Her usual subject?' Beth wondered vaguely.

'Darling! Sherry, of course!' Duncan peered at her through the dusk. 'I suppose, if you think about it,' he grinned suddenly, 'anyone who can worm a pony without batting an eyelid is likely to be proof against most of

32

the grues and willies of this life.'

Beth dredged up a pale smile and wondered what on earth Duncan could know at first hand of life's grues and willies. There he sat, comfortably clean – clean-minded, clean-living – with never the temptation or the need for anything else during his forty years. As if he'd not only been born with a silver spoon in his mouth but with a corruption-repellent caul over his entire person that had grown with him.

The Mallinsons had been less fortunate in Jonquil's reactions. She'd 'decided to turn sensitive', Jane told Beth acidly when they met for coffee on Monday. Beth had been dreading a rehash of Saturday's dramatics but she had to know if there was more than Penny had recounted; that had kept her on tenterhooks all through Sunday. For Penny might not have been born with Duncan's happy force-field, and worming Sherry was not proper inoculation against every eventuality.

'You've had no nightmares or after-effects with Penny, I hope?' Jane's dark glance that could alternate expressively from mischief, through indulgent, to critical, now too neutrally awaited Beth's reply. Her eyes were always an honest statement of her feelings, whatever her words, and if they gave her rather heavy face animation they also gave her away.

'No ill effects at all.' Beth edged her chair more into the shade, put on her dark glasses and tipped her linen hat further over her face. Even out of the sun the heat was stifling but Jane revelled in it, as her toasted flesh bore witness. 'Penny gave us the barest outline on Saturday but hasn't mentioned it since.'

'Sensible child!' Jane was relieved. 'I could've

33

*smacked* Rob for blurting it all out – and he regretted it too by the end. What with Jonquil trying to hog the limelight and Aunt Grace growing more and more unreasonable, I'm afraid his patience frayed somewhat. But Penny was a *brick*. She's one of those – I suppose she gets it from you – who keeps her head while all around her go doolally.

'Help yourself to shoog and bikkies.' Jane appeared to consider the subject closed. 'I wish I could join you, lucky devil!'

'Do your own gardening and you too can be a muscle-bound eight stone,' Beth suggested with her wry smile.

'You jest!' Jane glanced down comfortably at her generous figure. 'And is that what they call round here an Epsom Sandwich? An indirect compliment between an implied criticism and a delicate reference to one's own virtues? Never mind,' she laughed richly as Beth protested. 'A lissom but exhausted help-meet's less use to Rob than old Cameron's twenty-two-carat green fingers, however. And I need all my surviving athleticism for flopping down on my knees every hour on the hour to give thanks.' Jane waved her hand round at the ancient bricks that walled the garden. Beth was at a loss. 'Well, we were neither of us born to this, you know,' she explained. Beth did know, but she wasn't prepared for the admission or for the look of vulnerability in Jane's eyes. 'It – frightens me sometimes. I pray we never hurt anyone by it.'

Jane's solemnity was embarrassing. After an uncomfortable moment Beth reverted to the less personal topic.

'I don't even know where the fire was.' She raised her cup and sipped. 'Penny just said somewhere on

Banstead Downs.'

'Yes – not far from where the Epsom-Purley road crosses the A217. The worst was over by the time we got there, but the real trouble, you see, was Aunt Grace's conviction that she knew whose the skelly was. *Quite* ludicrous, but in the end we had to trundle her off to see a bobby or go round the bend ourselves,' Jane slipped back into her easier manner.

'You see, a girl from the hostel where she worked went missing after cadging a lift on Banstead Downs – *God* knows how many years ago. We got all the details – *plus* unsolicited encores. Rob kept yelling – she always brings out the worst in him – "But my *dear* Grace, if she got a lift *from* Banstead it can't be *her* bloody bones, *can* it?" And I kept hearing myself saying feebly, "Now, Robert", and Aunt Grace just kept on keeping on. Look, how about a chaser with your coffee? Just the memory's driving me to the bottle. Gin?' Beth shook her head impatiently. 'Sure? Wise girl, but I think I will.' It was a hiatus that stretched Beth's nerves to snapping-point and paralysed her throat muscles so that she could hardly swallow the suddenly foul-tasting coffee.

'And of course,' Jane picked up where she'd left off, clinking a tall glass topped with ice when she reappeared, 'the whole thing ran out in farce. A black farce. When Rob finally got hold of someone who knew about the bones, it transpired that they were from a grown man. Possibly a tramp or someone living rough, poor devil. There but for the grace of God and all that. They found the remains of one of those old-fashioned little primus stoves. The fire'd burnt off the vegetation that'd grown over – Beth! My dear – Are you all right?' Jane paused

35

in full spate as Beth suddenly stumbled to her feet.

'I – It's the heat. Sorry.' She fumbled in her bag for a handkerchief. 'And – I must admit to a little queasiness,' Beth added shakily, dabbing at her mouth.

'*What* a fool I am! Come inside.' Jane hustled her indoors. 'Head-between-the-knees or a bed job?'

'I'm – I'm fine now – really. Sorry – so silly –' Beth sagged on to the sofa, embarrassed and disgusted at herself for such a display. 'Don't worry – *please*,' she added as Jane sped to the decanters, but her cry merely diverted Jane's dash to the kitchen. She returned with a clouded glass of iced water.

'So – so your aunt calmed down after that?' Beth asked politely after a moment, less interested in Jane's reply than in distracting her attention. The pain in her head was obscene. She wished she could pour the cold water gently through her hair.

'She deflated instantly,' Jane laughed as she shrugged off her concern for Beth. 'You can't imagine my relief at not having to see her through hours of irrelevant interviews and statements. I joyfully forgave her for being wrong. But thank God she was due back last evening. Rob couldn't have stood much more of her – and I felt as though I'd a zoo to pacify all weekend. Not Penny, of course, bless her! I wish Jonquil had some of her patience. I mean, artistic temperament's all very fine and interesting, but a little stodginess would be welcome sometimes.'

A compliment that might have been better phrased, Beth considered, beginning to recover her equanimity. The possibly damaging consequences of the golf-course discovery were after all negligible – apart from the curiously unburdening effect it seemed to have had on Jane. Beth's comfortable relationship with her depended on Jane's predictability and her unassailability; qualities which Beth had apparently taken too much for granted. Beth struck her own bargain with the world, of neither saying nor doing anything to upset its balance, and she expected the world to respect hers.

But as for the aunt – she'd been mistaken, hushed up and possibly banished. There'd be no inquiry with Miss Parker, inconveniently near relative of Sir Robert and Lady Mallinson, as chief witness; no avid write-up in the local press; no unwholesome rub-off on Penny via Jonquil, for instance. Beth had much to be thankful for.

'Penny enjoyed her visit to Oriel's,' she murmured, and listened with secret amusement as the conversation turned predictably to Oriel's new baby. But by an unforeseen association it moved on to Jennetta's possible engagement.

'The subject cropped up at the weekend,' Jane replied airily at Beth's bewildered look. 'I mean, she's been going out with that nice boy, Alan Buckingham, for at least a year – and that's commitment at her age. So I wondered if they'd be announcing their engagement before she goes up to Oxford. I'd want to make certain of her, if I were Alan.' It finally dawned on Jane that she might be rushing her fences. 'Erm. Aren't you and Duncan in favour?'

'Actually I am,' Beth admitted, 'although I'm certain the thought hasn't crossed Duncan's mind. And I'd no idea the affair had got as far as speculation. Jennetta's said nothing. I know she likes Alan's family but she hasn't told me much about them and I haven't wanted to seem nosy or as if I'm – pushing things. I've met Mrs Buckingham only once, I think. You know the family, do you?'

'Only in passing. Rob knows the Colonel – well, he's retired now and doesn't insist on it – but you know about him, at least?'

Beth shook her head. 'Duncan plays golf with him but he's only ever referred to him as "Chaz". Retired, is he?'

'Mm. He was given a Golden Bowler when Alan was about ten. He married quite late – a childless young widow – and settled down to writing bird books when he left the Army. There's a couple in the library. They've a younger son at university still.'

'That's not a bad run-down from someone who knows the family only "in passing",' Beth smiled. Jane was an ideal clearing-house for news.

But Jennetta's engagement had associations of its own.

'So, what about the Nichollses?' Jane asked casually. 'Hell, I'm sorry, Beth! That's taboo, is it?' she added quickly, warned by Beth's suddenly stony expression. 'Damn clumsy of me. You've never mentioned Jennetta's father and I'd no business – I was wondering if the family kept in touch, that's all,' she ended in confusion.

'Not taboo, of course not,' Beth spoke slowly, seeing that Jane was genuinely embarrassed and not merely prying. 'After all, Jennetta's kept her father's name. But Jane, it's unbelievable, but until this moment I'd forgotten them. I never met any of Nick's family, you see,' she went on more collectedly. 'Ours was a fairly – whirlwind romance.' She gave a little self-deprecating smile,

38

acknowledging the cliché. 'I was Jennetta's age. Nick's parents were living abroad and didn't come to the wedding. In fact they didn't approve of the marriage. When he died I wrote to them, of course, but I never heard back. Nor when Jennetta was born – '

'My dear, how simply *wicked*!' Jane burst out. She struggled for a moment. 'Words *fail* me!' For which Beth was thankful. She was no longer certain of her own appropriate responses.

'Well, there it is,' she continued briskly. 'Of course, I wrote again with our new address when I married Duncan, but that was more than ten years ago and there's never been a word from them. Naturally I must let them know about Jennetta's engagement – if and when.'

'You don't owe them a *thing!*' Jane commented roundly, her eyes flashing. She folded her lips to show she'd say no more out of deference to Beth's sense of loyalty and poured herself another gin.

But there were still things Beth needed to know.

'Was Penny talking about a likely engagement, then?' That alone would be a surprise. Penny's reaction to Alan's increasingly regular attendance over the past year had been one of morose suspicion, and she wasn't anyway a chatterbox.

'No, Jonquil was – yesterday. Aunt Grace is always terribly interested in Jonquil's friends and she was asking her about Penny's family – you know.' Beth knew. And she wondered what the nosy old bat had made of Jonquil's information. It was an effort not to show her anger. 'Jonquil seems to think Jennetta's father was a racing-driver?' Jane queried tentatively.

'Good heavens, no! She must've misunderstood what

39

Penny'd told her at some time. It's a pity your aunt didn't ask Penny directly. Nick *was* killed in a car smash, though – just a few months after we were married,' Beth told her curtly, remembering.

'Oh, Beth! How *tragic* for you!' Jane's sympathy was sincere. A 'whirlwind romance' – hard enough to associate with her reserved friend – ending in such a disaster, with a baby on the way too and no help from her ghastly in-laws, fully explained Beth's timid approach to life. But Jane had heard the reproof: the tragedy was still a private burden and not for chewing over in a garbled version by third parties.

So when Beth asked, 'Tell me about your aunt. Where does she live?' Jane acknowledged her infringement of Beth's privacy in a fair exchange of forced confidences.

'We've found her a private retirement Home in Wandsworth. It's near enough to some of her old friends, and actually she loves it there. Plenty of people, you see, and some worse off than herself so she feels she can still be useful. She lived with my mother, but when she died – Well, it could *never* work to have her with us,' Jane added defensively. 'She's mentally still terribly active, as you saw, and there simply wouldn't be enough going on here to keep her occupied. But now it's obviously too much of a strain for her to be uprooted for her holidays with us. We'll compromise in future by visiting her more often and taking her for visits.'

Beth deduced from this that Sir Robert had put down his long-suffering foot. A merciful relief for everyone. Aunt Grace had brought ugliness too close to home. Beth couldn't blame Jane for her aunt's idiosyncrasies, but the episode threw an embarrassment over their

40

friendship, nevertheless. Jane's spiritless fatalism, however, irritated Beth. 'There, but for the grace of God –' In Beth's experience, success or failure was a question of personal choice, even for the girl on Banstead Downs, rather than the hand of God.

# Autumn 1966

# Three

Beth was already at the foster-home in Churchill Avenue when Sandra Littlejohn was accepted there too for fostering. The local Children's Department, initially attracted by the credentials of Number 30 – sited on the edge of a respectable suburban estate and within ten minutes' walk of the secondary modern school; the householder a solvent solicitor's clerk and lay preacher – was later impressed by Beth's development in that godly and domestic atmosphere.

When Tom and Lucy offered to foster a second girl, as company for Beth and with a view to adopting them both, the Department gratefully suggested Sandra. She too had no recoverable family and might have been Beth's sister in looks. Both girls were slightly built, with fair hair, blue eyes and pink and white complexions.

So much like Lucy at their age – or so Lucy claimed. Her hair was mouse going on grey by then, her eyes washy and vague (except in the kitchen), while her body had carelessly spread beyond guessing what her build had ever been. By contrast Tom, some years younger than Lucy, was sinewy with naturally ascetic features. Even his baldness resembled a tonsure. His remaining hair was very dark as were his eyes, set deep in the caverns of their sockets; colouring that was repeated in his son who had just started at college.

Sandra's first evening with her new family was not auspicious. Her resentment at leaving her friends at the

Home and her apprehension at changing schools increased her natural bumptiousness. Her belief that Beth was Tom and Lucy's real daughter emphasised her sense of being the odd one out, which the difference between her children's-home acquired manners and what obtained at 30, Churchill Avenue, did nothing to dispel.

There had been a meeting with Tom and Lucy at the Home, when Sandra had not been her usual sunny self but drilled into a glum acceptance of her situation. Everyone else concerned was satisfied, however, and in due course Lucy and Beth collected Sandra in a taxi one Saturday afternoon. Dire warnings about what would happen if she failed to take advantage of her good fortune still rang in her ears, but it was impossible to feel comfortable in the face of Beth's unsmiling and silent detachment and Lucy's equally silent fascination with the fare meter.

'How far is it, Auntie?' Sandra asked tentatively, hoping to be able still to visit her friends at the Home.

'You must call me Lucy,' she was told kindly enough, 'as I'm not your relation. And Dad likes to be called Tom.' Her eyes crawled back to their lack-lustre contemplation of the meter. On their arrival at Number 30, as Sandra quickly learned to think of it since it wasn't a Home and she had no memory of home, Lucy gave Beth the key while she stayed to bicker with the taxi-driver. 'Take Sandy upstairs and make friends,' she suggested absently.

They were to share a room at the head of the stairs.

'Yours are the bottom two drawers and there's space in the wardrobe,' Beth told Sandra indifferently. She sat

46

on her bed and watched in silence as Sandra unpacked her clothes: white school blouses and a navy skirt, a pair of reach-me-down corduroy slacks, some jumpers, pyjamas, socks and under-clothes, a pair of sandals and a dressing-gown. She was wearing a tartan pinafore dress and had left her wellingtons and navy mac downstairs in the hall. Now she changed out of her lace-up shoes into her sandals and inspected the room.

It was small, but the paintwork was cleaner than at the Home. Sandra bounced briefly on the bed. And the bed was bouncier. There was an ornament on the chest of drawers, a blue pottery rabbit.

'Is this yours?' she asked, putting out a hand to it.

'Don't touch it,' Beth retorted with more verve than she'd shown so far.

'I wouldn't have broken it,' Sandra protested. 'I had a china cat – Smokey. I named him after the Meadows cat.' She had given away her treasures to her friends only that morning, partly because they were hers and therefore special gifts to mark her friendship, and partly in the unrecognised belief that by doing so she would retain a more lasting place in their affections. Sandra wished now that she'd at least kept Smokey to put beside the rabbit. 'What do you call him?'

'It's a *she*.'

Be like that, then, thought Sandra crossly. 'Where's the bog?'

'We call it the bathroom,' came the superior reply. 'It's just across the landing. Your towel's got "S" on it.' Sandra found the lavatory in the bathroom, all primrose-yellow with matching wall-tiles. She spent some time admiring it and carefully washing her hands with the scented yellow soap. Her initial had been specially worked on the towel. Sandra was delighted with that.

The bathroom window looked over the back garden, a bit of a lawn running up to a vegetable patch with a couple of climbable fruit trees. Sandra's mood lightened. She was an active child. Immediately below the window was a square of crazy-paving, bounded by the party fence between Number 30 and its next door semi on one side and by the jut of the kitchen on the other. The back door opened from the kitchen on to this little patio where a bench stood against the house wall.

'How long do we have to stay up here?' Sandra went back to the bedroom.

'There's nothing to go down for yet,' Beth shrugged.

'It's sunny. Can't we go in the garden?'

'Sundays we go in the garden. We help Tom in the garden then, if it's fine.' Sandra's spirits sagged again.

'Well, can't we watch telly or something?'

'We don't have one. We don't believe in it,' Beth told her loftily. Sandra stared in disbelief but saw that Beth was quite serious.

'This is *much* worse than the Meadows,' she snapped. 'They *promised* it'd be better.' She flung herself down on the bed.

'Anyone can tell you've come from a Home,' Beth murmured, eyeing her. 'You'll get into trouble here if you put your feet on the counterpane. Can't you read for something to do?' She pointedly picked up one of the books from the table between the beds and turned the pages.

''Course I can read,' said Sandra after a brief struggle with her temper, and she snatched up the other book. It

48

was a Bible. Not even illustrated, she saw with disgust. She pitched it across the room. 'Is this a joke or something?' she stormed.

'There're other books downstairs we can read when we've finished our homework.' Beth hid a smile. She was nearer to laughing aloud than she could remember. 'And you'll find plenty of reading in your schoolwork. If you've bent your Bible you'll lose your pocket-money to pay for a new one.'

Sandra darted over to pick up her Bible.

'How much do we get?'

'*I* get three shillings. I don't know what you'll have. You're younger than me.'

'How old are you?' Sandra was side-tracked.

'You're terribly nosy, aren't you? I'm thirteen.' Sandra was surprised but pleased. She'd thought Beth was much older.

'I'm eleven.'

'I know.'

'Bet you don't know when my birthday is!'

'And I don't care.'

Rude pig, thought Sandra miserably, at last reduced to silence. She spent the rest of the time staring out of the window through the tortured swags of net curtaining that festooned all the front windows at Number 30. There wasn't much happening in the road either. Beth, committed to reading the Bible, found the story of Samson and Delilah and reread it with her usual interest.

'Beth! Sandy! I'm ready for you now!' Lucy called up the stairs.

'Ready for what?' Sandra asked hopefully.

'For us to help get supper ready.' Beth combed her

49

shoulder length hair and adjusted the hairband that made her look like Alice. It was not a coincidence. 'You'd better tidy your hair too,' she warned Sandra. 'Do you cut it yourself?'

'Only the bits that get in the way.' Sandra raked busily. 'We used to help wash up at the Meadows, us big ones,' she volunteered as she followed Beth downstairs, 'but we weren't asked to get the meals ready as well.' There was a tall window set above a tiny landing where the stairs turned sharply, three treads before reaching the hall. Sandra glanced despairingly through it at the garden.

'We make ourselves useful to others as much as we can here,' she heard the dreary warning.

'Come along, girls. That's right,' Lucy glanced up from the stove. 'Show Sandy how we like the table laid, Beth. She mustn't feel left out of things on her first day.'

'I *know* how to lay *tables*,' Sandra muttered grimly when they were in the dining-room. 'Show me where everything is, that's all.'

'The cutlery's in the top drawer,' Beth pointed languidly to the sideboard. 'The table-linen's in the second drawer. Glasses and plates come from the kitchen. I'll show you when you've laid-up.' Sandra dragged open the second drawer and took out the crisp white tablecloth. She flipped it open over the table, pausing to admire the hand-worked border, and laid the cutlery.

'How's that?' she demanded.

'You've laid the cloth cornerwise,' Beth told her gently, 'with the corners dangling. We don't like it looking like a café table. You haven't laid the mats – '

'You didn't tell me where they were,' Sandra reminded through clenched teeth.

'But there they are – on top of the sideboard. Nor have you laid the serviettes that were with the table-cloth. You've forgotten small knives for fruit and cheese, and small forks for the sweet. And what you have laid is all crooked. You'd better do it again.' Sandra did so, ungraciously. 'And the cruet's in the right-hand cupboard,' Beth added.

'The what?'

Beth sighed heavily and set out the pepper and salt. 'Now I'll show you where the plates and glasses are kept.'

'That was very *noisy* table-laying, girls,' Lucy reproved mildly. 'You shouldn't be able to hear kitchen or dining-room preparations. Now, then. Side-plates and glasses? That's right. Show Sandy where we keep the trays for taking them in.' We always carry things on trays, Sandra mimicked silently. Just like a café. She left Beth to carry it in, however, warned by an urgent desire to trip and drop the lot. 'You'll find a water-jug with the glasses,' Lucy told her. 'We fill it and take it in just before we're ready to eat. There, that's right. Now, then. There're potatoes waiting for you in the sink, Sandy, and the peeler's in that drawer to your left. You'll find it an easy one to use if you haven't done this before. And your own special pinny's hanging on the back of the door. Now, then, Beth. Will you get the custard mixed ready while I test the casserole –'

The soft, monotonous voice droned out instructions, admonitions and meaningless repetitive phrases in a stream as clogging to the senses as porridge in the sink-trap. Beth appeared to be immune, in her own detached

51

way, but it filled Sandra with intense irritation. At the same time she was paralysed into a sort of accepting numbness. She had often felt bored to distraction but never without the means of busting somehow out of boredom's grip. This – it was like being sucked shapeless by soft, toothless mouths. It's like a jelly-baby feels, she decided. If it had been left to Lucy alone, Sandra too might have been reduced to Beth's somnambulant state.

The kitchen was Lucy's natural element and her senses were alert to the sound of Tom's arrival home.

'Now, then. There's Dad. That's right. Just on time. Beth, take in the vegetable dishes. Make sure to put them down on mats. I'll bring in the casserole, and Sandy – you can fill the water-jug now. Run the tap a little first, that's right –'

'Sandra!' She threw off the sapping lethargy at last. 'My name's *Sandra*. I'm called Sandra, *not* Sandy!'

'Just as you like, dear,' Lucy agreed mildly. 'There, now, you've let the jug overfill. Dry it off carefully. That's right.'

'How's my family?' Tom asked from the doorway. 'Good evening, Mother. I don't need to ask how you're settling in, Sandra,' he smiled at her. 'This is a happy house and we're all happy people. Ready, Mother?'

'That's right, Dad.' Lucy bore the casserole into the dining-room where Beth was already sitting at the table. 'Sit opposite Beth, Sandra. There, that's right.'

At least the stew smelt good and there were plenty of vegetables, as Sandra knew. She eagerly spooned ruggedly sculpted potatoes and carrots on to her plate and set to, suddenly urgent for food.

'Shall we say grace?' Tom suggested. Sandra swallowed painfully and glanced up. At the Home grace was said before they all sat down: 'Thank you for the world so sweet, thank you for the food we eat. Thank you for the birds that sing, thank you, God, for everything.' But now she saw that although the others had plates of stew in front of them – as yet undecorated with vegetables – they sat with their heads bowed. 'For what we are about to receive, may the Lord make us thankful,' Tom intoned mellifluously. 'Some carrots, Mother? Beth, help yourself to potatoes and pass them to Lucy. You've had all you want, I expect, Sandra? Then I'll help myself. Will you pour us some water, please, Beth. Mother, will you cruet?'

Sandra was quickly left in no doubt as to what had been expected of her. A raised voice and insults could not have made her more conscious of her lapse. And Beth, who knew that Tom had heard Sandra's small outburst in the kitchen, waited with secret excitement to hear her more direct instruction in table manners.

'We always say grace before meals,' Tom began gently, 'because it's courteous to God, from whom all this bounty comes. And we always say grace after meals for the same reason. You can't thank God enough, you see. I'll teach you the words this evening, Sandra, and perhaps you'd like to say grace for us tomorrow.' Sandra sensed that was not intended as a treat. There was no point in telling Tom that she knew all about grace – and a longer one than his, at that – for why, then, was she now at fault?

'And when we've said grace we offer the vegetables to others before helping ourselves. To Lucy first, because she's done the hard work and, after God, deserves our thanks. We always think of ourselves last. And we never take more without asking if we may, nor do we reach across the table. We ask for things to be passed to us. Now, tell me, Beth – do you notice anything wrong with this table?'

'Sandra's serviette's still on her side-plate,' Beth replied clearly.

'*Quite* right. Now, I wonder why the serviettes are laid at all? Can you tell me, Sandra?'

'To mop up spills, I suppose,' Sandra mumbled, flushing scarlet. At the Home only the staff had serviettes; the children wore bibs or bib-aprons.

'To *prevent* spills,' Tom corrected. 'We lay them on our laps to protect our clothes. It's easier and cheaper to wash serviettes than to take clothes to the cleaners. Isn't that so, Mother?'

'That's right, Dad,' Lucy agreed without breaking the rhythm of her eating. She and Beth had placidly browsed their way through Tom's quiet harangue but Sandra, hypnotised by his smooth voice, his gently smiling face, had sat with her knife and fork pointing skywards.

'So, now let us begin our supper,' Tom invited, at last picking up his cutlery. 'We never start eating before everyone else is ready.' Except, thought Sandra mutinously, when there's a slagging-off for someone. It was her last flare of rebellion that evening. She felt sick with suppressed tears but cry she would not, for whose heart would be moved? A lesson learnt early. Even her hunger died and the stalled ox stuck in her throat. But she had to eat all the same because 'It's discourteous to Lucy after all her hard work,' said Tom.

Beth ranked that dressing-down at nine on her private

scale of one to ten. She'd never scored herself so high. Beth had quickly found the virtuous path to approval, but she suspected that Sandra was more rebellious. Sandra would learn in time, but meanwhile life promised to be more interesting. Beth felt she had been alone for long enough and it was time someone else occupied Tom's attention.

'Mother, have you noticed how well Beth's eaten tonight? A good meal indeed! It seems that your stay with us is already having a beneficial effect,' Tom beamed at Sandra. 'Will you send Sandra to me in here when you've all finished washing up, Mother? For what we have received, may the Lord make us grateful.'

Sandra sat at the cleared dining-table and at Tom's dictation wrote out the two almost identical versions of the grace in her neatest hand. That was no problem, her writing was anyway neat; and learning the two lines she found easy compared with learning whole poems at school.

'Very well done indeed, Sandra,' Tom approved. 'I'm very pleased with you.' She smiled back at him, eager now in her relief to be friends. 'Let's go and see what Lucy's found for you to do.' That did not sound encouraging.

'Please, can I write to my friends at the Meadows?' Sandra begged.

'Now that's very thoughtful of you. They're sure to want to know how you're settling in. We write letters on Sundays, but if Lucy hasn't anything for you to do this evening you may write to Mrs Johnson and thank her for the care they've taken of you. That would be only courteous.' But not what Sandra had in mind. It was Mrs

Johnson's fault that Sandra had been forced out of the Meadows. Thank her, indeed! But she had learnt early that when grown-ups offer an inch it is not politic to demand an ell.

Lucy and Beth were in the sitting-room, each silently intent over a piece of sewing.

'Sandra's done very well for me, Mother,' Tom said warmly. 'What have you planned for her now?'

'Well, there – nothing special,' Lucy said doubtfully. 'Do you like sewing?'

'Mending?' Sandra's heart sank. 'I'm not very good at it.'

'I meant embroidery. Look at what Beth's doing and see if you'd like to try something of the sort.'

'It's – belting!' Sandra stared over Beth's shoulder, charmed out of herself by the neatness of her work and the brightly coloured silks. 'How do you do it?'

'Haven't you seen anything like that before?' Lucy asked.

'Only in shops. What will it be, Beth?' Beth screwed a suspicious glance around at her but Sandra was genuinely admiring.

'A traycloth.' She spread it flat on her lap.

'Beth's very handy with her needle,' Lucy observed complacently. 'She embroidered her hairband, look, as well as our initials on the bathroom towels.'

'Honestly? Even on mine?' Sandra was impressed and gratified.

'Come and see what I'm doing,' Lucy invited. 'You see, you can turn quite a cheap, simple thing into something special. This is drawn-thread work, the same as I've done round Beth's traycloth. She'll soon be good

56

enough to do her own.'

'Did you make that lacy edge on the table-cloth?' Sandra was inspired to ask.

'Oh – a long time ago. That's another kind of work.' Lucy looked almost animated. 'Fancy noticing! There, then!'

'I'd like to do these things,' Sandra said firmly. 'Show me how.' She knelt expectantly beside Lucy's chair, quite forgetting the squeaking tedium of Lucy, the kitchen tutor.

'You mustn't try to run before you can walk. You have to learn the stitches first and then practise them before you can use them,' Lucy warned. 'It takes a lot of patience. But if you like, I'll get you some material on Monday for a sampler and we'll see how you get on.' Sandra stifled her impatience. It was something to look forward to at least.

Tom had been rummaging along the bookshelves built into one of the recesses beside the gas fire.

'Why don't you read something about it?' he suggested. 'Look, here's a section about samplers in the encyclopaedia. And may she see one of your sewing books, Mother?'

'That's right, Dad.' It seemed a poor alternative to watching Beth or Lucy at work, but Sandra was soon deep in concentration over the pages of diagrams, patterns and colour-plates. She imagined herself following an intricate map to a magic land of shapes and colours – a chart to hidden treasure. The weaklings never got there.

'Did you make a sampler, Beth?' she asked suddenly.

'It's hanging in the bedroom,' Beth murmured without looking up.

'Do we have sewing at this school?'

'Not this kind.'

Sandra was still engrossed in Lucy's book when, at eight o'clock, Tom carefully folded his newspaper and stood up.

'It's your bedtime, Sandra. We'll have prayers first. Beth, will you play for us, please.' Sandra opened her mouth to protest but a glance at the mantelpiece clock showed that at the Home she would already be in bed. She accepted the hymn-book Tom gave her, listened half-heartedly while he intoned what sounded like impromptu prayers – during which she was very much embarrassed to hear her own name mentioned – and joined in the Lord's Prayer. Then they found the words of 'Abide with me' and silently read the first verse while Beth played the tune on the piano. For the first time the words conveyed their meaning to Sandra, but instead of being encouraged and reassured they made her feel painfully vulnerable.

'Beth will come up in half an hour – because she's older,' Tom explained. 'Lucy will run your bath. Say good-night, now.' He lowered his head close to Sandra's face, almost as if he expected her to whisper the words in his ear. She was taken aback for a moment, but when it dawned on her what he wanted she pecked a kiss on his cheek and fled in embarrassment.

Sandra was admiring the framed sampler hanging above Beth's bed – 'Matthew, Mark, Luke and John, Bless the bed that I lie on', with Beth's full name and date of birth all within a cross-stitch border – when she heard Lucy start running the bath.

'There, that's right. But you must shut the curtains when you get undressed. It's not nice for other people.' Lucy drew a riot of pansies across the looped net. 'Your bath'll be ready now.' She went ahead and turned off the taps. Lucy too invited an unreciprocal kiss. 'Don't bolt the door and remember to clean round the bath. You know how to do that, don't you?' She didn't wait for a reply. Sandra slid under the water, suddenly relieved to be alone.

Shallow, near-tepid baths – all she had been used to – were never for lingering in, however. Sandra was soon meticulously washed and teeth-cleaned; behaviour as instinctive as the activities that often made her grubby.

When she was in bed with the light out she wondered a little at her desire for solitude. At the Home she would have been sharing a bedroom with at least three others. She was used to – expected – a lack of privacy, people around her day and night, and noise. Solitude was the accepted means of punishment. Now she was in a household reduced to four people – not even a pet – where no one had laughed all day and only Tom smiled (such creepy smiles too, that didn't light his eyes), where the loudest burst of sound had been Beth's quiet playing on the piano, and yet she had been happy to be alone. It was the strangest thing of the whole strange day.

But to be alone was not what she consciously wanted and Sandra waited impatiently for Beth to come to bed.

'*Thank* you for embroidering my towel, Beth.' She propped herself on one elbow in the dark.

'Lucy told me to. And anyway, we don't talk in bed,' Beth whispered.

Sandra merely leaned closer and lowered her voice.

'Why do you call her Lucy when she's your mother?'

'*Don't* be so *stupid*!' Beth hissed. 'Of course they're not my parents! '

'How was I to know that?' Sandra squeaked indignantly. 'Who are they?'

'My foster-parents, stupid!'

'*You're* fostered too?' Sandra reached out and clutched at Beth in delight but was roughly brushed away. It was the most wounding of reactions.

'Why do you hate me?'

Beth was enjoying her promotion to assistant torturer and she was silent for a moment composing a cutting reply.

'I don't like being touched, but actually I hardly notice you – except when you leave the bath still white with too much cleaner.' Touching could be nasty, Sandra accepted silently, but it was all right between freinds. They *should* be friends.

'I didn't *ask* to come and spoil things for you, if that's what you're thinking. Why did they want me, with you already here?'

'They wanted *anyone*. They get paid for fostering.'

Sandra fell back on her pillow. Paid. *Liking* didn't come into it, although they obviously liked Beth.

'How long've you been here?' she asked at last.

'Two years,' said Beth out of her loneliness, putting aside the thumbscrews for a moment only. 'And I was in a Home before that, so I know all about people like you. Now shut up and let me sleep.'

Sandra was not a timid child but Beth's positive withdrawal left her fearful. She did not – could never – like that silent house, or Tom and Lucy. It was not solitude

60

she wanted, she realised, but freedom from them back in her own familiar place with her own friends. The prospect of even two years spent at Number 30 intimidated her more than any of the punishments at the Home had achieved. Warm tears slid slowly down the sides of Sandra's face and blotted themselves on her pillow. And Beth, who should be her ally, was on their side. Beth was so clever, with her sewing and her music, so – dignified, thought Sandra, who had all too often been called to account for her undignified behaviour; Beth was so obviously admirable yet so rottenly mean.

She slept only fitfully, weeping silently when she woke and remembered where she was, or thinking furiously about how she could make life more bearable for herself. Sandra was not one to fold her hands and wait – unless waiting was a part of the game.

# Four

Sandra dressed in her corduroy trousers the following morning and dragged a comb through her hair. Her eyes looked as though they had been pressed into their sockets by sooty thumbs.

'You'll be told to change,' Beth warned, covering herself in case she was blamed for allowing Sandra down to breakfast improperly clothed.

'If I get another blowing-up then you'll be happy.' Sandra had come to some conclusions during the night. 'You're one of those who *likes* to see people in trouble because it makes you feel better.' Beth gave her a startled glance and hurried ahead to breakfast.

'Well, there, now – oh, dear!' Lucy was flustered when Sandra came into the kitchen where breakfast was laid.

'Good morning, Lucy,' she said brightly, determined on a pre-emptive strike. 'What shall I do first? Good morning, Tom,' she smiled at him.

'Lucy always gets breakfast for us,' Tom did not return the smile, 'so it's only courteous to be punctual. Sandra, I don't care for my little ladies wearing trousers. We won't wait for her to change, Mother.'

'Oh, but Beth said we always help you in the garden on Sundays. I haven't anything else that'll do.' Tom gazed at her speculatively.

'Did we keep any of Beth's old things, Mother?' Lucy shook her head and mumbled 'Jumble', to Sandra's relief. 'In that case trousers will have to do, but only for gardening. On Sundays we go to worship in God's house and tidy the garden after lunch. Go and put on something proper now.'

'Church? We go to church?' Sandra was genuinely pleased. Here at last was something familiar.

'Church or chapel, it's God's house,' Tom told her solemnly. Sandra heard him start to say grace as she left the kitchen and piously thanked God for the reminder. It seemed that He at least was on her side.

Naturally she had not known about the cords until Beth warned her – and made her determined to wear them. They were accepted wear at the Home, although admittedly not to church. But the explanation she had thought up had worked, so sucks to Beth, Sandra grinned as she changed into her pinafore dress. However, she reminded herself fairly, Beth was a toad only because she was unhappy.

Years in a residential Home had given Sandra an intimate understanding of how other children ticked, and she knew enough to recognise pretty well every symptom of vulnerability. Beth *had* to be miserable after two years in such a miserable place, where they were actually paid to see that you were.

So Beth had worked out a survival plan, Sandra believed, just as anyone would have done. She did the right thing and kept quiet, so they didn't notice her. Sandra knew all about that. So they didn't suspect Beth who, of course, was biding her time. When she was ready she'd run away, like Karen did from the seniors' Home. Abscond. And Sandra would do the same. She'd make them think she liked them and get away with murder. Her (partial) victory over the cords was proof that she could. Grown-ups were suckers for flattery, even if they didn't like you. *Especially* if they didn't like you. Circumventing grownups was a sport Sandra enjoyed.

The others were part-way through their breakfast of cereal, boiled eggs and toast when Sandra returned.

'For what I'm about to receive, may the Lord make me thankful,' she announced clearly, suspecting that Tom might be waiting to catch her out. 'Please can I have the milk, Lucy?' Beth shared her suspicion, but she also knew that Sandra's manner was too pert for Tom to let pass. Pertness in his little ladies was as improper as wearing trousers; but pertness allied with unexpectedly getting things right was almost a declaration of war.

'You should say, "Please may I have the milk",' Tom corrected after a moment. 'Is your bed quite comfortable, Sandra?' She nodded with her mouth full. Her egg was hard-boiled – thank God again – and not nose-blow. She could never have eaten that, whatever the fuss. 'I ask, because it doesn't seem to me that you slept well,' Tom went on smoothly. 'Were you perhaps unwell in the night?'

'No,' Sandra lowered her head.

'Then I hope you weren't wishing yourself back at the Meadows? That would be a very ungrateful return for what Lucy and I have done for you already. Ingratitude is one of the worst sins. You must pray this morning to be free of it. We'll all pray for you.'

'I didn't sleep very well,' Sandra blurted, 'because it was a new place. There were different noises than at the Meadows and they kept me awake.' She looked up and

65

saw that Tom did not believe her.

'You must have an early night tonight to make up for it.' He wasn't going to be so easy to get round. Just don't give anything away, Sandra warned herself fiercely as the frequent accusation, 'You're your own worst enemy, Sandra', suddenly made sense.

Her determination was tested after the morning service. From the outside, 'God's house' resembled nothing so much as one of the de-mountable classrooms at her old school. She did not even realise they had arrived until they were walking up to its door. Sandra felt outraged. Cheated.

The impact of her first church service was lasting although the memory had dimmed: how she had sat entranced by the blaze of coloured glass, the pinpoint candle-flames, the sound of the organ and the choir, the beckoning shapes soaring away into mystery. That was for Sandra truly the House of God. A shrivelled little sprat of a child in reach-me-down clothes, she had curled up against the assistant detailed to keep an eye on her and drowned in this first exposure to delight. The woman had been afraid to move and disturb her until the end. She described afterwards how Sandra, who hardly ever uttered, had timidly asked if they could go there again, and how her little monkey face had been transformed when she heard they would.

Which they did every Sunday, if they were old enough. But however often she went, Sandra discovered something new to hug to herself and gloat wonderingly over – the changing altar frontals and the parson's robes, the brass eagle lectern, carvings in wood and stone, the flowers. Or her eyes would search out old favourites and linger admiringly over details she had overlooked before.

The other children, naturally, thought Sandra's interest peculiar, which encouraged her to keep her enjoyment to herself, but the Sunday services continued to refill her reservoir of pleasure. The language, however, she found almost meaningless, the prayers seemed hardly to apply to herself although she learned to join in the General Confession – and the sermon was a time for gazing and dreaming not listening. The appeal was to her senses.

At Number 30 Sandra was embarrassed by Tom's references to God, and now she was desolated by his miserable version of a church. There was none of the accumulated craft of centuries that she had grown to accept indiscriminately as true beauty and for the expectation of which the day had seemed so briefly brighter. Sandra felt almost drained of the will to fight on. But when they were walking home and Tom said – gloatingly, she believed – 'I expect our service was a little different from what you've been used to,' she recovered enough to reply,

'Yes, but I liked hearing you talk,' instead of screaming her disappointment in his face. She was even able to give a reasonable account of herself when Tom questioned her about his 'talk'. There had not, after all, been anything to distract her from hearing what he'd said.

After lunch Sandra threw herself into raking the leaves and tidying the vegetable beds. It was physical activity and outdoors, and for a while she was almost happy. She also earned Tom's commendation, which she accepted with a secret sneer.

67

She was ready for her tea – always Welsh rarebit and homemade cake in thick, rich slabs on Sundays – after which it was time to write letters. Beth, however, took up her embroidery.

'Aren't you going to write to anyone?' Sandra asked in surprise.

'We're all the family Beth has,' Lucy told her complacently. Neither had Sandra any family; at least, no one had ever mentioned their existence and she had never wanted to ask as some of them did. But still she had friends to write to. The crashing loneliness of Beth's life was suddenly brought home to her.

'I know people at the Meadows you could write to,' Sandra offered, 'and they'd write back. I've got lots of friends there who – '

'Sandra, it's not very pleasant listening to you boast about your friends when you've just been told that Beth has no one but us,' Tom interrupted in his gentle voice. 'Are you jealous of her contentment with us?'

'Jealous?' Sandra asked incredulously. 'I only thought she might like a pen-friend. I wasn't boasting.'

'Jealous and argumentative,' Tom pointed out smoothly. 'Go and write your letter in the dining-room. When you're ready to be civil again, bring your letter to me and I'll give you an envelope for it.' Sandra turned to go. 'There's something you've forgotten to say, Sandra.'

'Thank you?' she suggested dimly.

'And something else.'

'Sorry.' That was usually a safe bet.

'Let me hear you mean it, Sandra.'

'I'm sorry, Tom.' He nodded a dismissal and turned back to his desk.

Sandra thumped down at the dining-table and dug her fingers in her hair. 'Imagine he's watching,' said a small voice inside her head. She sat up and glanced towards the door. She must remember not to show anything, even when she was alone. Doors were never shut at Number 30. For a moment she considered the scene in the sitting-room. She'd been reproved quite noisily and physically at the Meadows but always for a naughtiness of which she'd been aware. Sometimes they'd taken her aside to reason with her and that usually made her feel humble enough to behave better for a while.

But Tom, with his quiet voice and gentle smile that somehow she couldn't blaze back at, found offence even in her best motives; and having done so, ground away at her until she felt limp – though never remorseful. Even his approval was suspect because so often it seemed a prelude to another deadly session in public. Not that that mattered. Sandra cared too little for Lucy and Beth to mind what they saw her being put through. It was different at the Meadows when even a sarcastic comment in front of her friends could fire her up or reduce her to near tears. She couldn't understand Tom, but she'd rather be spanked than listen to his niggling.

In this Sandra was hardier than Beth, who needed to be loved and was easily reduced by the mere threat of favour withdrawn. Until quite recently Beth had found a bearable equilibrium in her loneliness simply because she had felt accepted. Tom knew from her first evening that Sandra was a different proposition entirely and, like her, he too was feeling his way. It was not in his interests to have a rebellious child in the house and he saw that Sandra would not be quietly pushed into compliance.

Misery, however, is a great leveller, like the constant dripping of water on stone.

Sandra finished her letter to Mrs Johnson, the house-mother at the Meadows, taking particular care with the spelling. She realised that in the circumstances it would not be diplomatic to write to any of her friends that evening, but at least there should be nothing to criticise in that letter.

Tom was still at his desk.

'Ready for the envelope?' he beamed, a man generous enough to forget any earlier unpleasantness. He read Sandra's letter aloud.

Dear Mrs Johnson,
Thank you for looking after me. Today we all
went to Tom's Sunday service and after lunch we
made the garden tidy for the winter. Tomorrow I
start at the new school with Beth who lives here
too. Lucy is going to teach me sewing after
school. Please give my love to all my friends and
Smokey. Tell them I'll write soon.
Love from Sandra.

'Yes,' Tom studied the letter, 'I don't think you've left out anything important, Sandra, and it's nicely written. She writes very neatly, Mother, quite as well as Beth,' Tom said, sealing the envelope. 'There. Write the address and I'll post it for you myself.'

'I – don't know the address properly,' Sandra told him, suddenly realising. She had never needed to know it.

'Never mind, I do,' Tom smiled. He turned away to

70

address the envelope, meticulously adding the return address on the back and leaving the envelope face down.

'Now, did you get any pocket-money at the Meadows?' Tom asked. Sandra shook her head expectantly.

'They did in the seniors' Home, though.'

'I see. Come here, Beth.' Wasn't she going to get any, then, Sandra wondered, moving away for Beth to stand beside Tom's desk. There was a tantalising chink of coins and Beth was handed a small booklet. 'Every Sunday I give Beth three shillings pocket-money,' Tom turned back to Sandra, 'and on Monday she pays it in at the post office where they record it in her Savings book. So within two months she'll have saved a whole pound, won't she?' Sandra nodded, wide-eyed. Three shillings – a whole pound! That was wealth beyond the dreams of average. 'And each pound collects interest, a little extra added to it by the Savings people as a reward. So if Beth simply frittered away her pocket-money she wouldn't have the pound or the interest, do you see?' Sandra nodded again, her hopes beginning to revive. Tom smiled widely, preparing her for the climax.

'Well, Sandra, that's what I'm going to do for you. Come and see. Here's your Savings book. I've opened your account with a present of five shillings, just as I did for Beth.' Sandra gloated. 'Now, because you're two years younger than Beth I'm going to give you one shilling. When you're twelve it'll be two shillings, and three when you're thirteen like Beth. So you've no cause here for jealousy or envy, have you?' Tom smiled knowingly, in a way that needled Sandra. She hadn't been jealous of Beth.

71

'So, tomorrow after school Beth will show you what to do. In the evening I'll take your books in again and lock them safely away until next Sunday. Here's your shilling, then, Sandra.' Tom counted out a handful of mixed coppers on the desk and Sandra gleefully stretched out her hand.

'*Thank* you, Tom!'

'Oh – but it's just occurred to me,' he clapped a hand to his forehead. 'You'll need a stamp for your letter. That's threepence-ha'penny.' Tom removed the coins. 'And Mother, didn't you say you were going to buy Sandra materials for a sampler?'

'That's right, Dad.'

'Only eightpence-ha'penny left,' he murmured doubtfully. 'But I don't want you to break into that five shillings. Well, if this doesn't cover it all, Mother, perhaps you could give Sandra the silks?'

'That's right, Dad. We've got –'

'In the same way that I've given her the writing-paper and envelope, in a good cause. So you won't be needing your Savings book tomorrow after all, Sandra, but when you do start using it you'll find it's an excellent way to save up for things you really want.'

Sandra was crushed. All that build-up for nothing. She felt she'd been set up. Like his approval, Tom's gifts were offered merely to be withdrawn, merely as potential punishments. And a whole threepence-ha'penny gone on a measly stamp for Mrs Johnson whom she hadn't even wanted to write to. Letters to the Meadows, even if she could read the address on the envelope that Tom was now stamping, would be few and far between. No wonder Beth had given up her friends. Sandra looked up into Tom's face and saw that he'd won again.

'Thank you, Tom.' She wished she could have managed a careless smile but it was hard enough to talk politely. 'May I have another read of your sewing book, Lucy?'

'*Please* may I have another *look* at your sewing book,' Tom enunciated carefully, reaching it down for her. 'Beth, you'd do Sandra a Christian kindness if you were to correct her slipshod speech. She wouldn't care to be laughed at for want of a timely word of warning.'

Sandra had no expectation of such an outburst of merriment at Number 30, but even the most confident child dreads being laughed at. After that she observed Beth closely for her speech as well as for her behaviour that so cunningly disguised her escape plans and filled her Savings book. Sandra fell asleep that night running a long, rambling scenario in her head in which she confounded the worst efforts of her enemy. It became her nightly pastime.

She and Beth set off for school together the following morning but in her interest at her new surroundings Sandra soon fell behind.

'Hey, wait for me!' she called and ran to catch Beth up. 'Why didn't you wait? I don't know the way, do I? At the Meadows they used to take us in the minibus.'

'You'll have to keep up if you don't want to be late,' Beth hurried on, her longer legs easily outstriding Sandra who was forced to jog-trot the rest of the way. That became their usual progress to school and back.

'Don't you want to be seen with me or something?' Sandra asked once, but in the end it was Sandra who grew wary of being seen with Beth.

'Why do you walk to school with that stuck-up git?' one of her new friends asked; and because she did not yet feel established Sandra would not admit that they lived in the same house.

'We come from the same direction, that's all.'

Later she noticed that Beth was as aloof at school as she was at Number 30 though not, she thought, by intention. Beth could be seen drifting about the edges of groups, within listening distance and certainly within a friendly call to join in, but the invitations never came. There was no overt hostility, merely a calculated blindness. Sandra's enquiries among her friends brought answers ranging from 'She thinks she's too good for anybody', to 'She spies for her father'. On consideration Sandra did not believe Beth was a spy, but Tom's local reputation as God's conscience gave Beth a sort of protection, however unenviable, and Sandra let it alone.

At the end of her first day at the school Sandra followed Beth home at a trot and still had the energy to go out again with her to the post office. She almost regretted taking advantage of the extra half-hour spent away from that joyless house, for conversation was breathless on her part and ungracious on Beth's.

'I'd like a kitten.' Sandra remembered Smokey with a pang as they sped past a pet-shop. 'Shall we ask for a kitten?'

'It would be unhealthy.'

'Not if we didn't *get* an unhealthy one.'

'Their germs are unhealthy. We don't believe in pets.' Sandra saved her breath until they were passing a sweet-shop. She had no real hopes of a kitten but it had been worth a try.

'At the Meadows we were allowed sweets after supper. You could save them up to make decent presents for birthdays. When do we have sweets at Number 30?'

'We don't believe in sweets. They're bad for our teeth.'

'Oh, come on!' Sandra panted impatiently. 'Are you saying you never buy sweets with your pocket-money?'

'I'd rather save it.'

For the absconding, of course, Sandra remembered. You can't abscond with only a couple of bob in your pocket. That's apparently how they'd caught up with Karen from the seniors' Home. And she'd have to save too, Sandra reminded herself. But all the same, she'd manage to buy sweets as well.

'Give us a look at your Savings book,' she asked as they waited in the counter queue. 'You know Tom said I had to learn.'

'You just fill in a form and hand it over with the money,' Beth unwillingly let Sandra see her book.

'Blimey, you've got loads already.' Sandra exclaimed admiringly. 'It's nearly full!' Clearly absconsion wasn't far off. 'How do you get the money out?'

'You fill in another form and they write in what you've taken.' So Tom could keep a check on your spendings, thought Sandra resentfully. There had to be a catch in it somewhere.

'You never seem to take any out,' she went on. 'Don't you buy cards or presents?'

'I make them myself.'

'I've done that – cards, anyway – but only because I've never any money. Does Tom just stop it for that week, then, if you need more sewing stuff?'

'I've never had to pay for it,' Beth admitted after a moment. Sandra watched her glance uncomfortably away. Grown-ups, she knew, had favourites like anyone else, and obviously Beth had worked hard at being one. That was that. She returned to the Savings book.

'Here! Sometimes you've paid in whole pounds at a time!' Sandra noticed with amazement. 'Can't be birthdays –' she flipped the pages back and forth. 'There's one each for May and June, look, and another in October, just before I came –' Beth snatched back the book, her face scarlet.

'Stop *snooping*! Learning how isn't snooping! They're – prizes for competitions,' she added more quietly. 'In newspapers and magazines.' Beth turned her back.

'Let's look around the shops a bit,' Sandra suggested when Beth had finished in the post office. 'I've only got reading homework, how about you?'

'We don't keep people waiting who're expecting us at home,' Beth replied stuffily.

'Oh, for God's sake shut up about "we" this, and "we" that!' Sandra suddenly exploded. 'You know damn well you don't agree with it any more than I do!' But Beth only stared palely for a moment, then ducked her head and hurried home. She had enjoyed pricking at Sandra, under cover of putting her right, and watching her deflate; but there was no sport in her strategically placed darts if Sandra knew what she was about.

That evening Sandra leafed through Lucy's weekly magazines in the sitting-room, but there were no competitions or 'prize letters' that won an exact pound in any of them. Tom's paper, the *Telegraph*, was obviously not

76

the kind that included competitions. It all seemed to confirm Sandra's suspicion in the post office that Beth sneaked odd notes from the house – or, even worse if she were ever caught, from school. However, her 'competition' story had obviously deceived Tom, who must have queried the entries in Beth's Savings book. So he could be outsmarted and that ogred well for herself, Sandra thought triumphantly.

Those first few days were more or less the pattern of Sandra's life for two years – except that she was never again asked to pay for her sewing materials. That did not necessarily mean that she was more affluent. For all her care there were occasional breakages that bankrupted her and put her in debt for weeks. Just as, for all her good intentions, Tom continued to find faults, and for some of these too she was fined.

Sandra always paid greater attention to Beth's behaviour after Tom's critical sessions and she even took to copying her appearance. This was a little forced on her since she was expected to wear Beth's outgrown clothes, and the flowery pastels instead of the bright colours she preferred made her feel uncomfortable at first. 'Cissy.' She bore it, however, since the looks made a better match for the behaviour, and later when she was able to choose her own clothes they were still in Beth's style. Sandra also grew her hair tidier and longer and made herself an Alice band. Although Beth was never more than coolly aloof, she was secretly flattered by the younger girl's apparent admiration.

It did not at first occur to Sandra to transfer her reformed persona to school. Here she was quick enough

77

but willing to exert herself only where her interest was caught – in art, needlework and games lessons. Arriving as she had in mid-term she was more intent on winning and holding her place and making new friends which, together with the atmosphere at Number 30, drove her to over-assertiveness. Sandra took up any challenge and took over whatever raw language came to her ears. She soon had the reputation of being foul-mouthed and aggressive.

In the end a worried note was written to Tom and Lucy and all Sandra's good work at Number 30 was undone. It took her months to recover the ground she had lost.

'A foul mouth,' Tom concluded, after supervising a soap-and-water gargling session that left Sandra's tongue and throat feeling scorched, 'denotes a foul mind and a foul soul. "As the twig is bent, so is the tree inclined." We must straighten you out, Sandra, before it's too late.'

But Sandra did make new friends and she was delighted when one of them invited her home for Saturday tea. Tom quickly quashed that.

'We know nothing about these people, and you must remember my position. How can we invite back, as would be only courteous, someone whose family might turn out to be quite improper for me to know?' Sandra had not thought that far ahead. What suddenly struck her more than Tom's delicate sense of propriety was that a friend visiting at Number 30 would give Tom a weapon against herself he could not resist. She turned down all invitations after that with far less disappointment than he imagined.

And as time went by, even school improved with the

addition of shorthand and typing to her timetable – the one attracted like a secret code, the other a manual skill she naturally enjoyed – and by her participation in school plays. Sandra was already into rehearsals for her first appearance when Tom realised that this was to be a joint production with the boys' school and forbade her taking part.

He reinforced this ban with a note to the Head; who replied with a stiffly worded letter assuring Tom that supervision and discipline during rehearsals was of the strictest, and ending with a reference to the parable of the Talents 'in the interests of Sandra's development'. For Sandra showed an unexpected natural ability on the stage and an even more unexpectedly conscientious commitment to the extra work involved. Realising that he had offended a public figure with whom he was bound to be associated, and was somehow also seen to be failing in his Christian duty towards Sandra, Tom withdrew the ban.

'No one's got a dirtier mind than a righteous Christian,' snarled the drama teacher as the correspondence flew back and forth. Sandra was one of those few in a lifetime who just occasionally lit a rainbow in her back-stage gloom. But as far as Sandra was concerned, acting was an enjoyable form of escape. Since they were generally period plays, she had the bonus of seeing and feeling her sumptuous transformation in costume. The boys didn't count, could Tom only have believed it.

# Summer 1989

# Five

Beth saw less of Jennetta as July wore on, for Alan had finished his postgraduate Civil Service exams and Jennetta spent most of her time with him. One afternoon in July, however, she walked in on Beth as she worked in her sewing-room.

'Hallo, darling!' Beth glanced up, pleased. 'I wasn't expecting you home so early.'

'Alan's got some deadly interview,' Jennetta explained moodily. 'What're you sewing? Hey, these are pretty!' She turned over a couple of new hand-towels Beth had finished with. 'Who're these for?' Beth tilted her head and gazed down consideringly at the intricate knotted border she was working.

'I haven't really decided. I might take them for Gran's gust room next time we go down.'

'Why're you only doing one end?' Needlework wasn't a subject Jennetta usually found stimulating and Beth began to feel interested.

'One end's all that's needed for style and distinction,' she smiled. 'I'll embroider an initial in the corner and even the Queen won't have better.'

'My pyjamas were better than hers, as I remember,' Jennetta laughed and flopped into a basket-chair. 'When I was little you were always sewing or knitting.' So she often was, Beth recalled, and in that same basket-chair. When not making clothes for Jennetta or herself she knocked up things to sell through the local craft-shop for necessary cash. That was before Jennetta started at school, before Beth was released for a part-time job.

'Your memory's surprisingly good,' she murmured.

'Oh, I remember. I thought life would always go on for us like that. You sewing, me watching Magic Roundabout or something. Life was so blissfully uncomplicated.' Was it hell, Beth remembered grimly.

'And you read a lot too,' she reminded Jennetta. 'You were always such a – thinking child. But life's still pretty straightforward, isn't it?' she asked casually, smoothing her work with appreciative fingers as she waited to hear the cause of her daughter's nostalgia.

'Oh – yes, but it's not so simple.' The basket-chair creaked suddenly as Jennetta leaned down to snatch up a length of thread from the carpet. She concentrated for a moment on winding it round her finger.

'Mum, have you ever regretted not going to college?'

'I didn't regret it at the time,' Beth began cautiously, forcing herself not to transfix Jennetta with a too-speculative stare. College could never have entered her head but Jennetta was comfortably academic and it had been natural for her to aim for university, an ambition that pleased Duncan. 'Later, of course, I wished I had proper qualifications, some training for a profession,' she added, loyally toeing the Masters family line.

'What would you've done – if things had been different?' Jennetta asked, suddenly interested to learn something new about one so well known. She unwound the thread from her finger, now purple, and dropped it back on the floor.

'Oh, well. Some branch of the Welfare Service,' Beth mumbled. She was conscious of wading out of her depth

84

but the subject was at least one she knew something about. 'In the end, though, the job I did when you started school fitted very well round you. That's why I took it on.'

'Quite. You couldn't have fitted even the partest-time Welfare job round me,' Jennetta pointed out. 'So even if you'd got a degree and been fully qualified you couldn't have used it, could you? Not as things turned out,' she concluded on an odd note of satisfaction. And Beth, who'd braced herself to discuss her unsuspected ambitions, was left feeling flat. 'You could always go back to it as a mature student, though, couldn't you? When Penny leaves school.'

'When Penny leaves school,' Beth laughed, 'it would be only fair to concentrate on Daddy. Actually it's almost time for her to be home now,' she glanced at her watch. 'I'd better get downstairs.'

Beth was glad to end the uncomfortable conversation. Advance notice of Jennetta's engagement to Alan she was half expecting, but not her unconscious hints that she was considering giving up her university place. Beth wondered if Alan's 'deadly interview' had some bearing on Jennetta's change of direction. With the apparent confirmation that a degree wouldn't have helped her mother in her need – contrary to what was pushed at school – and the comfortable conviction that one could always pick up the threads of early ambition, it seemed that Jennetta wouldn't think twice if she had to choose between Alan and Oxford.

Beth considered warning Duncan, and then wondered if that might pre-empt her neutrality. She didn't want to take sides in this affair. She decided that her safer role would be to pick up any debris afterwards, if there should be a clash. Beth folded away her sewing. And since Jennetta liked them, the hand towels would be part of her own wedding present to her daughter; a selection of good linen, once an unknown luxury to both of them.

Jennetta quickly threw off her uncertain mood when Penny was dropped off from school, and Beth was ready to believe she'd read too much into it. People did consider various possibilities, after all, without actually acting on them.

'Have you heard anything from Jonk's Mum today?' Penny asked when Beth and Jennetta met her in the kitchen. 'They're having their holiday in a friend's catameringue and Jonk wants me to go too.'

'On the good ship *Cream Boat*?' Jennetta asked straight-faced.

'For *three weeks*,' Penny ignored her. Holidays away had been a problem ever since Sherry's arrival. No one had guessed how badly Penny had felt about leaving him that first time until Jennetta reported her crying herself to sleep in their shared room. After that it was understood that Jennetta went with Duncan to his parents at Weymouth or away with schoolfriends, while Beth and Penny stayed with Sherry. Duncan, who only wanted his family happy, knew how much Beth hated leaving the garden, anyway, and she never enjoyed holidays abroad because of the heat, so he cheerfully acquiesced and played more golf.

'I haven't heard from Lady Mallinson yet, but it's very kind of them to think of you, darling,' Beth said. Jonquil's pony would be sent to the local livery stables as usual. 'You know Daddy and I can be trusted to keep

Sherry happy here if you decide to go. Have you got anything planned for the holidays, Jennetta?'

'Mm. I was thinking of a visit to Weymouth, among other things. Alan'll drive me down,' she added carelessly. 'It's time he met Gran and Pops. Well,' Jennetta caught Beth's look, 'I've met heaps of his family recently. Almost every time I go there they've relations staying or visiting.' Inspecting the bride, thought Beth with satisfaction. Let 'em inspect. She had no fears for Jennetta. Perhaps it was time now to get to know Alan's parents better. 'But if you think it'll be too much for Gran, Alan and I can always bed and breakfast nearby,' Jennetta went on. Beth met her gaze over Penny's head and read the message she looked for.

'Of course you must stay with them,' she said positively. 'Gran and Pops would think it most – surprising if you don't. Even wounding.' That settled it. She'd prod Duncan into an introduction to Colonel Buckingham at the next golf-club Social. 'You won't find them at home 'til the end of August, though, darling. They'll be cruising somewhere until Weymouth quietens down again.'

Jennetta's A-level results arrived in early August and thoroughly justified her Oxford place.

'We'll go out and celebrate tonight!' Duncan crowed delightedly. 'Well done indeed, Jennetta! And no more than you deserved. I'll ring and book somewhere from work – a surprise.' Beth left Jennetta on the phone to Alan with her news and went out to the garden before the temperature soared. Jennetta came out to find her, looking harassed.

'Mum, can we postpone tonight's celebration?

Something's cropped up and I have to see Alan. He's calling for me in half an hour.' Beth sat back on her heels.

'Is it really going to take you all day to talk to Alan, darling?'

'Possibly. I'm really sorry, Mum – but it's important.'

'Well, bring him along too. I'm sure Daddy assumed he'd be there.' Highly unlikely. Duncan liked Alan better than some of Jennetta's other 'dummy runs', as he called them, but this was to be a family celebration and he certainly didn't think of Alan as even potentially family. It niggled Beth that Alan should be turning awkward on that of all days. It wouldn't endear him to Duncan.

'I'll try at least to bring him home later tonight. Can you explain to Dad?'

'But explain what?' Beth got up from her knees. 'Is everything all right?' she asked sharply, unlovely possibilities flashing through her mind.

'I hope it will be,' Jennetta answered, but so dismally that Beth couldn't feel reassured.

She rang Duncan and tried her best to sooth his hurt feelings and ruffled feathers although her own were in disarray.

'She'll explain everything tonight, but whatever it is she'll need our support,' Beth warned. 'Not third degree.' She heard Duncan's apologetic laugh with relief. It was easier breaking the news to Penny, for whom 'going out' meant bedding Sherry down early and changing into a dress. That always chipped the gilt off the gingerbread for Penny.

Jennetta arrived home long after Penny was in bed and when Duncan was about at the limit of his patience, but at last they heard her laughing and chattering as she crossed the hall. When she burst into the sitting-room with Alan in her wake her transformation since the morning brought Beth to her feet. Jennetta was alight with happiness. It was Alan who looked battered and hesitant.

'Here we are at last!' Jennetta announced gaily, tripping across to the sofa. She turned with a brilliant smile to Alan, still by the door, and patted the cushion beside her. 'What're you all on? Coffee? Good. We didn't stop for that. What about a liqueur for you, Alan?' But Alan was staring at Duncan like a beaten dog and Beth, puzzled but hopeful, leapt into the silence.

'Did you both have a pleasant day? You can stay a while, I hope, Alan? Duncan, will you see to Alan's drink while I get two more cups?' She threw him a bracing look and sped out.

When Beth returned to pour the coffee, Duncan was listening with a bemused expression to Jennetta's racy account of their meal that seemed to have come straight out of *Fawlty Towers*. Alan appeared no more at ease; his narrow, normally serious face looked positively peaky and pale, Beth thought, and his long fingers were wrapped around his glass as if it was the magic lamp. Beth took over his coffee with her friendliest smile and he half rose, trying to burble something appropriate. Alan had nice manners but apparently too much sense of the occasion.

'Honestly, Dad, I wish you'd been there!' Jennetta unwarily ended her account.

'My hope *was* that we should be together this evening,' Duncan agreed mildly, and Beth saw Jennetta glance at Alan. The look came from Beth's own repertoire and it said quite clearly 'Your turn'. She watched Alan knock back his drink and stand up with a sort of desperation.

'Sir – Mr Masters – Mrs Masters – I, that is, we – Jennetta and I – want to get married.' He looked sick.

'Darling! I'm so pleased!' Beth hurried across the room and hugged her daughter. The suspense – ! 'What lovely news! Alan, I'm delighted!' She reached up to kiss his cheek and found herself clutched at as though for support. 'Duncan, isn't this wonderful news?' Beth twittered, manoeuvring Alan back on to the sofa. It was like repositioning a lamp-post, he was so tense. She turned quickly to intercept Duncan, who was slowly getting to his feet in a state of shock, and slipped an arm through his. 'This calls for a toast, darling!' But Duncan was no less rigid than Alan and Beth gave his arm an understanding squeeze.

'It's no surprise that you want to marry Jennetta,' he managed stiffly, 'but I certainly wasn't prepared for an announcement this evening. Congratulations, but –' Beth gave his arm a tiny shake and leaned a little towards Jennetta. 'And congratulations, Jennetta,' Duncan ended obediently and went over to kiss her.

'Oh – Dad!' She wound her arms around his neck.

'There, there,' said Duncan thickly after a moment, resoundingly thumping her back as Beth became conscious of the loony smirk on her own face. 'Yes, certainly a toast. Champagne, of course.' It had been in the fridge since that morning, waiting to celebrate Jennetta's exam results. He quirked an eyebrow at Beth, inviting her approval. What a good boy am I! She nearly laughed aloud. Laughter, from hollow to hysterical, was never far from Beth that night.

'Well, now!' Toasts gaily drunk, with some relief as well as the usual self-consciousness, Duncan relaxed in his chair and beamed around. 'I think I'm getting used to the idea. Your father didn't give me a hint of this when we played on Saturday, Alan. Your parents do know, I suppose?'

'They know what I had in mind, but – they haven't caught up with this latest instalment.' Alan tried to speak lightly but he was looking nervous again which surprised Beth. She and Duncan had met his parents several times now and she hadn't the impression that they'd found the Masterses unbearable. Their references to Jennetta had been complimentary and, she believed, sincere.

Presumably they had their own ways of learning as much as they needed to about the Masterses, as the Masterses had about them, for they neither volunteered nor required potted autobiographies to Beth's relief. They were people she could feel at ease with. Laura Buckingham was softly spoken and still pretty; much younger than the Colonel, whose rather stilted courtesy towards her at first Beth saw arose from shyness. She could easily imagine him quietly engrossed in his lonely hobby while he was on active service. Both had the same gentle sense of humour that saved them from being dull.

'Well, that's their pleasure in store,' Duncan said comfortably. He didn't doubt that the Buckinghams already saw Jennetta as an ornament in their family. 'I hope you'll both be as happy as we are – though that's given to only a favoured few, I think. When do you propose making the news public?' His eyes fell to Jennetta's ringless left hand. 'We had a very short engagement, but I gather long ones can be pretty stressful and you've three years at Oxford yet.'

Beth heard the pride in Duncan's voice, but Alan was smoothing back his neat dark hair as if preparing for another ordeal. Her thoughts flew back to the conversation with Jennetta in the sewing-room. Poor Duncan. This couldn't have happened on a worse day for him. Beth braced herself again as Alan darted a hunted look at Jennetta, who said easily,

'It won't be a long engagement, Dad. Alan had news of his own to celebrate today. He's being posted to Athens in October.' She reached for Alan's hand. 'So we want to be married before then and spend our honeymoon in Greece.'

'October? So soon? But when does your term start?' was all Duncan could find to say after a startled moment.

'I won't be going to college, Dad.'

There was a longer stunned silence. Glancing again at Alan, Beth saw from his resigned expression that this was to be a confrontation that wouldn't directly involve him. She wondered what Jennetta felt about locking horns with Duncan over an issue that meant so much to him when he'd always given her pretty well anything she'd wanted. Meanwhile she prepared to retire into invisibility. This was Jennetta's business.

Duncan set his champagne glass carefully on the table beside him.

'You can't mean that you're intending to *throw up* your place at Oxford?'

'I already have. Alan's is a plum posting, Dad, and the

chance of a lifetime for me as well. Apart from that, how can I ask him to wait three years for me? And how can I let him go abroad alone? *Anything* might happen.' Jennetta's appeasing smile fell awry at Duncan's expression.

'But good God, you're throwing up your whole future –'

'No,' she interrupted firmly. 'I'm merely postponing my degree. What would that be to me, anyway, if our engagement breaks down because I held out for Oxford? It's with Alan my whole future lies.'

'You can't know your own mind, Jennetta.' Duncan leaned forward urgently. 'You've barely left school – you're only eighteen. How can you even think to take on such decisions that'll affect your whole life? At eighteen –'

'At eighteen I'm legally entitled and *expected* to make responsible decisions. As for marriage – Mum was married at eighteen,' Jennetta reminded quietly. Beth quickly lowered her eyes in case Jennetta – or either of them – beamed her an appeal for support.

Duncan threw up his hands and rounded on Alan who'd sat staring at the floor during this exchange.

'I certainly can't congratulate you on your lack of consideration, young man. How old are you – twenty-two? Yet you propose to intervene in my daughter's career, remove her from her family and keep her in reasonable comfort abroad?'

'Sir, I can assure you –' Alan was beginning unhappily when Jennetta cut across him. The unfamiliar tone of her voice warned Duncan at least to listen.

'Alan was all for waiting. It's taken me the whole day

93

to talk him round. If you put a spoke in my wheel now, Dad, I'll not only *not* go ahead with my degree – and Oxford's out, anyway – but I'll never see you again.'

'Jennetta!' Beth exclaimed, shocked out of her silence. Her eyes flew to Duncan's face. He stared as though he'd been struck.

'I mean it, Mum. And just in case there's any suspicion that I have to get married – forget it. It might have been easier to make Alan see reason if that had been the case.' Alan flushed, but there was a new alertness in his attitude. The worst had been said.

'Reason!' Duncan exploded. 'You're a self-willed, manipulative – *monkey*, Jennetta!' He fought for words but gave up the struggle and turned to Alan. 'My apologies. Obviously I misunderstood your situation. And I withdraw my congratulations. You're more in need of my commiserations. I wash my hands of you, Jennetta – figuratively speaking of course. I can't so easily refuse to see *you* ever again. If only for your poor mother's sake – God rest her nerves,' he added as Jennetta flung herself at him and wept remorsefully on his shirt.

When calm had descended again Duncan worked hard to make his capitulation seem as graceful as possible, and Beth was able to relax – if, she reflected, feeling as limp as wet spaghetti could be relaxation.

'Alan, I'm sorry that what might've been a private discussion between us became a bone to be worried in a family committee – '

'But that's just what he wanted to do,' Jennetta broke in, all smiles again. 'See you alone with his pass-book and his prospects in his hand. I persuaded him not to.'

'For reasons that have now become clear. You're a

minx, Jennetta,' Duncan reproved. 'Tell me more about this posting, Alan. Forget the pass-book.' Beth was always more concerned with how she reacted to people and they to her, than what they actually did or how much they earned – although status impressed her. She'd merely assumed that Alan, with his family behind him, could afford to marry her daughter. She was more interested in the domestic details of what he had to say.

But Alan's immediate prospects were attractive enough to reassure Duncan as well: a fully equipped flat on the outskirts of Athens at a very moderate rent, a salary that with sensible management would enable him to support a wife and save too, and generous terms of leave with paid fares home.

'It sounds like heaven!' Jennetta spoke dreamily. 'And only a few hours from home. I'll love showing you around. It's all air-conditioned, Mum,' she added, as if she heard Beth's spirits expire in anticipation of the heat.

She saw Alan out soon afterwards and Duncan helped Beth clear away the crockery and glasses. They talked quietly about anything but the engagement, tacitly agreeing to wait until after Jennetta had gone to bed.

'I'm *really* sorry about Oxford, Dad,' she joined them in the kitchen. 'No one could've been more pleased than me this morning. But when Alan beat me to it with his news everything turned to worm and gallwood.' She grinned wryly and hitched a hip on to the kitchen table. 'After his interview last month I knew there was a chance he'd be sent straight abroad, but – well, I hoped to have my cake as well. This morning I knew I *had* to go with him. So I wrote to the university and then sweated *blood* trying to convince him. Be happy for me, both of you, and try to understand.'

'Of course we are, and we do,' Beth said quickly. 'But you must understand our – mixed feelings too, darling. About Oxford, I mean, not Alan,' she grinned. 'I've always liked Alan as you must know.'

'None of which alters the fact that it's inconveniently short notice to arrange the wedding.' Duncan glanced at Beth.

'Oh, but in the circs it'll have to be a registry office,' Jennetta said casually.

'Over my dead body!' Beth announced. 'Of course we can be ready.'

'And anyway, I'm looking forward to giving you away, my dear,' Duncan grinned. 'I've still got some Green Shield stamps somewhere.'

'You *are* so good to me and I don't deserve you,' Jennetta came alight again, 'because of course I'd prefer a church wedding. Only one bridesmaid, though. Only Penny. Lord, I'm tired! We'll plan it all tomorrow, Mum,' she promised blithely, kissed her parents and went secure and happy to bed.

'Have you any idea what you've let yourself in for?' Duncan asked Beth. 'Come and have a night-cap. I want to talk to you.' Beth followed him into the sitting-room, feeling free at last to let her happiness lap around her.

'Thank you for not prolonging the agony earlier,' she smiled at Duncan when he sat down beside her. 'I could see how taken aback you were.'

'That's putting it mildly! Did you know this was coming?' Beth shook her head. Jennetta hadn't actually said anything. 'I didn't really have a leg to stand on,' Duncan admitted, 'and you seemed to want this for her. I have got that right, haven't I? I was trying to read your hints,' he added earnestly. Hints. Secret laughter bubbled again like champagne. She'd nearly sent for a loud-hailer.

'Yes, I wanted it, but I wish she could've had both Oxford and Alan,' Beth murmured. 'And he's twenty-four, by the way. He'll do.'

'Poor Alan!' Duncan laughed suddenly. 'She burned her boats at Oxford to force his hand in marriage! Do you think he even popped the question? I bet she simply told him it was all arranged.'

'I'm sure he struggled,' Beth grinned back. 'But I don't know that she meant to force his hand. Jennetta would say it was to prove her serious commitment.'

'So are you sure about the wedding, darling? A full-dress do? We've only got two months,' Duncan reminded.

'Certain sure. Thoroughly white and with all the props,' Beth replied crisply. '*You'll* put the notice in *The Times* and *Telegraph* tomorrow, *they'll* fix a date with the vicar, and the rest'll be easy,' Beth laughed. 'Except for telling Penny. I don't see her in ecstasies at the news.'

Duncan didn't speak for a moment and when he did it wasn't lightly.

'Let Jennetta do her own dirty work. She's proved tonight she could give lessons. Er – do you think she seriously meant that threat? I couldn't believe she liked me so little.'

'No, never that, Duncan,' Beth turned to him quickly. 'She was afraid Alan was still persuadable, that's all. She was truly relieved not to've – forced a breach. We're both grateful to you.'

'You never said a word,' Duncan remembered wonderingly. 'What if it'd all got out of hand?'

'Then my heart would've broken for you both,' said Beth simply.

Her forebodings about Penny were based on her knowledge that she'd certainly miss Jennetta and didn't apparently much care for Alan. Beth couldn't know that Penny had a normal child's rigid image of what constitutes its family, its security. Penny's family consisted of Duncan, Beth, Jennetta and Sherry, in no particular order, and she knew exactly where she stood with them all.

When Jennetta came home the following day with Alan and her sapphire engagement ring, Beth was unprepared for the depth of Penny's hurt. After a frozen moment she shook hands with Alan, who kissed her cautiously, thanked Jennetta in a small voice for appointing her as bridesmaid, and then excused herself politely to get back to the paddock. The stricken look on her face as she left the room reminded Beth of an animal creeping away to die.

She followed Penny down to the paddock a little later and found her sitting on an upturned bucket, listlessly surveying Sherry flicking flies from his flanks.

'It's not the end of the world, darling,' Beth began, feeling inadequate. 'Jennetta'll often be home for holidays.'

'Not as often as if she'd gone to Oxford. I was expecting Oxford,' Penny told her boots.

'And we shall visit her too.' Beth was about to add, 'It's not so far', when she remembered that Penny would hardly be consoled by the thought of leaving Sherry at livery. She tried another tack. 'What about this boating holiday with Jonquil? There's still just time to change your mind about that. I'm sure you'll find it huge fun, darling.'

'How can I leave Sherry *now*?' Penny demanded accusingly, as though Sherry too was distraught at the news of Jennetta's defection. She turned at last to look up at Beth. 'Do you want me to go because you'll be very busy? I won't get in your way.' She returned to her listless contemplation of the pony. It might actually be easier if she was crying, Beth told herself hopelessly.

'Of *course* I don't want to send you away, darling!' Her voice was suddenly ugly with threatened tears and she fought to control it. 'It's just that I can't bear to see you so unhappy – and for the first time in my life I don't know what to do for you. I shall miss her too, you know, but I'll still have you and that keeps *me* happy.' Beth turned and went quickly back to the house. Life's getting too bloody emotional, she told herself wearily.

# Six

It wasn't long before the initial shockwave of Jennetta's engagement subsided to a manageable flood. How much of the emotional demand was submerged in the rush of arrangements, bookings and Beth's private wedding present ploys and how much was due to Penny herself who, after three days of moping in the paddock, suddenly constituted herself Beth's protector, tea-maker and messenger – Sherry's routine permitting – Beth couldn't tell, but she was grateful. At least she didn't have to divide her attention between Penny's unhappiness, and feel guilty about it, and her own pleasure and zest in the whirl of wedding preparations.

Beth consulted Jane Mallinson for help with tips from her experience of Oriel's wedding, but they hadn't otherwise met as often as usual since her aunt's visit and Beth was secretly relieved that Jane was shortly to be away for three weeks. However, although she was glad of any advice Jane could offer to supplement the handbook she was learning practically by heart, no one could stand in for Beth in surveying venues for the reception, in beating up estimates and descriptions or samples of their art from the local florists, caterers, photographers and suppliers of wedding cakes, and in simply being on hand for those who called with good wishes and gifts or rang for ideas on what to give. Even after consultation with Jennetta and Alan, and Laura Buckingham as well, it was difficult to draw up a list, simply to avoid dupli-

101

cation, because the Athens flat was so very well supplied. All the more necessary, Beth believed, that Jennetta should have things entirely of her own. 'B'-embroidered linen was assembling in a respectable pile in the sewing-room, in spite of the calls on her time, and only Penny was let into that secret.

Two evenings were spent at the Buckinghams'; at a dinner just for Beth and Duncan and later at a less formal affair to meet the many relations. All of them were enthusiastic about Alan's choice of bride. Beth purred whenever she remembered. And Duncan too regarded the Colonel with increased approval when he privately offered to share the cost of the reception – 'Because there are such hordes of us and it seems only fair. Besides which, we'd like to feel this is our day too.' That seemed sincerely enough meant to persuade Duncan that the Colonel's wasn't merely a 'social' offer that might later lead to embarrassing haggling.

All the portents were favourable, every prospect pleased, and still the sun beat unrelentingly down.

There was only just time to send out the invitations the conventional six weeks ahead. Beth resigned herself to using preprinted cards and settled down one Saturday morning to filling in along dotted lines and addressing envelopes. Jennetta found her in the dining-room.

'More additions to your guest list?' Beth looked up with a quick smile.

'Don't worry,' Jennetta grinned back. 'Just to say that Gran and Pops have okayed next week. Can you spare me 'til Wednesday? I'd like to go up to Town with you and Penny this afternoon for a couple of major buys but odds and ends I can find in Weymouth, so I'll be killing two birds there.'

'Of course go, darling. Did I hear Alan just now?'

'Mm. We've been finalising the form of service. Dad's got the fair copy for the printers if you want to see it. Alan's down in the paddock now, making up to Penny. Actually he does it quite well,' Jennetta reassured. 'He had a pony himself when they lived on Salisbury Plain and knows about girth-galls and laminitis, whatever they are. Penny hasn't caught him out yet. He's giving her a secret photo of Sherry in a silver frame for her bridesmaid's present – all his own idea. He's really trying, bless him.' Jennetta gazed through the window at the paddock. 'And he seems to be in no hurry to rejoin his betrothed.' She pulled out a chair and sat at the table. 'Are you going to invite my grandparents, Mum?'

Beth gave a small sigh and laid down her pen. She'd been wondering if the subject would arise. 'Grandparents' meant Nick's parents. Jennetta had never met them but she did occasionally want to talk about her father and his family. It was partly out of natural curiosity, Beth knew, and partly because everyone, surely, needs to see their present existence rooted in the past, part of a continuity. She very clearly remembered the painful sense of separateness that occasionally assailed her during her own childhood, passed on as she was through a series of aunts. She'd actually never had any desire to know more about her own family; but she understood enough to realise that Jennetta's instinctive search for something beyond her mother and Duncan wasn't because she felt a lack, precisely, but a need to see herself in a full dimension, particularly at her own wedding.

It was understandable but inconvenient. Perhaps she'd overdone the romance of the Nicholls clan, Beth reflected. And it had possibly been a mistake to insist that Jennetta kept the Nicholls name when Duncan adopted her. Beth had taken a chance there, afraid of wishing an identity crisis on her daughter at what might well have been a twitchy time. Duncan had been hurt but, 'It's the name she's always had', Beth had reminded. 'It's hers.' Jennetta would be changing it now, to Beth's secret relief, but that was her choice.

'Our side will be a bit thin on the ground, with only Dad's family.' (Nick was always 'my father' to distinguish.) 'You'll be my only blood relation,' Jennetta pointed out.

'But there'll be heaps of friends, darling. Our pews won't be empty. You were my *only* relation when I married Daddy,' Beth smiled. 'And Penny's your blood relation too, don't forget.'

'Diluted blood, though. And scowling because she'll hate every minute. She'll wear her St Trinian's face all day and *kill* the photographs!' Jennetta wailed. 'She thinks I want her there just out of spite!'

'Don't you believe it,' Beth laughed – although it was touch and go, she knew. Penny hated the limelight. 'She's afraid she'll burst with pride before the day. She's been giving me more of her time recently and we've had some highly informative talks. She's amazed you asked her, you know.'

'How could she think I wouldn't?'

'Oh – Penny just doesn't see herself in a bridesmaidenly image and it's stunned her that anyone should. She's terrified of not matching up because she's – just

Penny.'

'She's just nuts! But anyway, *are* you? Going to invite them.'

Persistent was the word for Jennetta, but that was a valuable trait in its way. They were both survivors, Beth considered.

'Actually I've been trying to find where to get in touch with them. Apparently they've moved from Florida, but I've been given an address in Denver to try. Don't set your hopes too high, though, darling.'

'Oh, Mum! How like you to be beavering away without telling me! But – what does Dad think of it? I've only just realised. And you. Will you find it very awkward seeing them? I know you must've felt bad about them once.'

'Well, so did they feel bad about me marrying your father,' Beth said tranquilly. 'It's true that if he'd gone back to the States when he was supposed to, he wouldn't have been killed.'

'Even so, you'd think they might've shown just a flicker of interest in their grandchild.' That had always been the difficulty. 'Dammit, I was an orphan before I was even born.'

'Well, a *diluted* orphan. You still had me,' Beth murmured apologetically. Jennetta laughed.

'It's rotten of you to make me feel a pig and make me laugh at the same time. But – I don't really know *why* I want them here, Mum.'

'To be proud of you, darling, and to share your happiness. As we all are and do. I'd like them to come, since you've asked me, so they can see that in you at least they've nothing to regret.'

'Oh, and nor've I! Don't think I'm secretly glooming about it being Dad walking me up the aisle. I swear I haven't imagined any face but his.'

She'd be pushed to imagine her father's face, except mistakenly in her own image, Beth thought when Jennetta had gone. Not for the first time she wished she had even a snap of Nick to show his daughter; but he'd left Beth only his name, his flat – by default – and an uneasy preference for solitude. And Jennetta. That too Beth had always insisted upon, the use of Jennetta's full name. Whereas Penny, Duncan's choice, had always been 'Penny', and the older she grew the less appropriate Penelope seemed.

Beth herself could no longer recall Nick's features, although occasionally her memory was stirred by hints in the faces of strangers – the set of his eyes, the way his dark hair grew crisply back from his forehead. Ironically she'd never seen a sign of Nick in his daughter, although Jennetta had his colouring. She'd found no resemblance to herself either, however hard she'd looked for it as Jennetta was growing; a tiny narcissistic niggle she was ashamed of. Penny was more as she must have been at the same age, fair, freckled and nondescript.

But where Nick's black eyes had flashed with devilment, Jennetta's were mild and her disposition more reposeful than his, although she could be roused to the same sort of gaiety. Nick had wanted to try everything, have everything even fatherhood and marriage in the same careless, frenetic spirit. As if he'd known what little time he had. Beth had been drunk on his exuberance. It was a brief and fatal enchantment. Jennetta was less flamboyant and more discriminating. Possibly her

106

upbringing accounted for that, Beth brooded. God knew it hadn't encouraged flamboyance. But Jennetta got what she wanted even if she pushed for it more quietly, her grasp as soft and as inflexible as a baby's fist. It was a sort of greed, a selfishness, but Beth understood it.

This was a good match, in the old-fashioned phrase. Jennetta would be safe, with a 'proper' family of her own to come; children with matching parents and two sets of grandparents of clean reputation. To marry so young was maybe an unfashionable ambition, but it was Jennetta's and it made Beth happy. She had common sense as well as intelligence, perhaps more important than experience. And what sort of 'experience' would Alan have welcomed, anyway? He himself had never been 'young', Beth considered. Born middle-aged and fifty years out of date, she grinned to herself. She'd never mention it, but Alan had many of Duncan's qualities. It was hardly surprising that Jennetta had fallen for him.

'Jennetta said you were up to your ears.' Duncan gazed ruefully at the neat piles of invitation cards and envelopes on the dining-table. 'I think I married you for your tidiness,' he added inconsequentially.

'Because Jennetta picked you up, you mean.' Duncan grinned at this old joke between them, his teeth showing white in his tanned face.

'Why didn't you ask her to help?'

'Because,' Beth finished addressing an envelope, 'tidiness and Jennetta's help go together like – chips and trifle.' She leaned back in her chair and smiled up at him. It was almost a neurosis with her, she knew, keeping things tidy, tidying up, tucking away loose ends. It was a

107

habit learnt early in the restricted space allotted to her and was the only alternative, too, to chaos and panic in their cramped conditions during Jennetta's childhood.

It had been a delight to see how her daughter had spread herself after they'd come to live with Duncan, but a culture-shock for him. 'It denotes a generous nature,' she'd soothed when he mildly protested one evening. 'And it means she feels at home here.' That was important to him. But it wasn't until after Penny was born that Beth had set her own mark on Duncan's home, afraid even then that through ignorance or insensitivity she'd spoil its quiet magic.

'I'll take these out to the post for you.' Duncan picked up a pile of stamped envelopes and flicked through them. 'My dear, only sixty-four? So far. That's more than twelve pounds in postage alone. How paltry. When does the real spending start?'

'Would you begrudge a few coppers to make it the happiest day in a girl's life?' Beth whined, holding out an imaginary begging-bowl.

'The happiest day in a girl's *mother's* life,' Duncan corrected with a laugh and kissed the top of Beth's head. 'But I don't want to part with her, you know that.'

'"You're not losing a daughter" – dot, dot, dot,' Beth grinned.

'Tripe. What comfort's that to a man who doesn't want a son? Where's Penny?'

'With Sherry, naturally.'

Duncan went over to the window. 'We don't want her trying on dresses this afternoon smelling of horse, for heaven's sake! They'll all think it's me. I'll call her in.'

'No, let her be comfortable, Duncan. She'll get

showered and changed for lunch. And she may not try on anything, anyway. If Penny doesn't see what she likes I'll run her up something to her own design.'

'Something after Harry Hall with red rosettes, I suppose, God help us!' They laughed comfortably together.

'But do you mean you're intending to come with us?' Beth asked doubtfully. 'Most men would run a mile.'

'Would you rather I did too?'

Beth turned in her chair and considered Duncan thoughtfully. He was kind and self-sacrificing and he knew she found shopping in Town an ordeal, but she tried not to take advantage of him too often. That was her contribution to his generosity. If he'd already cancelled his usual Saturday golf, however –

'I'd like you to come, of course, but I'm not sure what Penny'll feel,' Beth warned. 'She may not want an audience. Ask her, but don't let it show.' But it was already decided, she could see from Duncan's face.

'Well, I *want* to go with you. I never had a proper wedding, remember. I want to see the nuts and bolts of this one. Beth – now that we're stuck into Jennetta's all-singing, all-dancing affair, have you still no regrets about insisting on a registry office for yourself?'

'Oh, get on with you, Duncan! *I* had no family to help foot the bills and I had a seven-year-old child to think of. You talk as though we've been living in sin all this time.'

Duncan sat down opposite Beth. Perhaps we'll get to the point at last, she thought, and capped her pen.

'Mister Masters' Mistress?' he grinned. 'You'll always be that. But – you never really explained at the time. Was it because after Nick – ?'

Beth coloured faintly. She hated discussing Nick with

109

Duncan.

'Duncan, Nick and I had a registry office wedding because he wanted us married before he took me back to his family,' Beth said patiently. 'I've told you all that. We stayed because Jennetta was on the way and Nick wanted her born in England. When I married you I still couldn't have afforded a posh knees-up and it wasn't – proper to leave the bills to you. I hadn't sold the flat then. If you're wondering whether I married you in a sort of second time around, second best attitude, you're being dozy. It simply made the best sense at the time. Work off your yearning for finery and beetle-coats on Jennetta.'

'*She* understands me. Er – she was wondering if I'd mind Nick's parents coming to the wedding. Of course I said I wouldn't, though it's really up to you. But do you think they will?' Duncan asked with a trace of anxiety. He was a rotten liar, Beth knew.

She ripped down a sheet of stamps and carefully folded the strip, concertina-wise, along the perforations. She tore off a stamp, licked it, stuck it on and thumped it with the edge of her fist. Rip, lick, stick, wallop. It was a satisfying sequence and she performed it deftly like everything else, while Duncan sat, half mesmerised, patiently waiting for an answer. After a dozen stamps Beth sat back in her chair and gazed apologetically at him.

'There *are* no Nicholls grandparents. At least, there may be, but Nick never mentioned his parents and I never met them – not even at his funeral as I've told Jennetta. I haven't a clue whether they even knew he'd married. It was all over so soon,' Beth explained soothingly at Duncan's incredulous expression. 'I invented his parents when Jennetta started asking questions. I

110

thought it was sad for her to have no one but me. And then, of course, I had to keep up the fantasy after *we* were married. I'm sorry about that – but that's how it was.'

Parents, family, simply hadn't figured. Memories of her own people had receded long before into the blur of continually changing faces. If she'd thought anything she'd assumed that Nick, his own master for the past ten years, wasn't tied to any apron-strings. Beth hadn't then very well understood families. It was only afterwards she'd even wondered about Nick's parents.

At the time Nick was all she'd wanted – everything she'd wanted. He was her family then, and her identity. Jennetta – she'd found the name in a book – had later authenticated this identity: Mrs Andrew Nicholls, widow and mother. Beth had filled in the supporting cast as the gaps appeared. She knew she was taking a risk now, tearing a hole in the backcloth, but she'd never realised before that Duncan felt diffident about Nick and his supposed family. Of course he'd hate the thought of Nick's parents watching a man who was not their son lead their son's daughter up the aisle. Duncan deserved to know the truth and Beth told it with no more than a shrug in her voice. Even so, she saw that he'd heard the embarrassment behind the words and would know how she'd hated the shifts and evasions. He was almost morbidly sensitive to her feelings – as well as being surprisingly easily hurt in his own.

'Poor little Sershy,' Duncan reached across for her hand. 'I wish you'd met your knight in shining armour earlier. He's done his best for you both since, though.' Typically he didn't ask why Beth hadn't told him before. Duncan only asked questions if the answers really mattered.

'But nobody's doubted that, Sershy said,' Beth smiled and leaned forward to touch his face.

'Ho-*ho*! Caught in the act,' Penny said dispassionately as she stumped through the french windows in socked feet, her riding hat pushed to the back of her head and her freckled face pink and perspiring. 'We're going shopping this afternoon, Daddy. Trying-on things.' She stood on one foot idly scratching the back of her leg with the other, as if she'd forgotten what she'd intended doing, her blue eyes fixed on some distant point.

'"May I go with you, my pretty maid?"' Duncan was inspired to ask.

'You'll miss the hoot of the year if you don't.' Penny trundled to the door. 'I've reserved seats. And less of the "pretty maid, sir, she said." 'I'm too old for that.'

'Your bottom's hanging out of those jeans!' Duncan called after her.

'I know,' she answered indifferently. 'Patch or pitch, Mummy?'

'Turn around. Heavens, darling, pitch! We'll get you a new pair this afternoon. Where're your boots?'

'Drying outside. I had to dunk them in the water-butt.' The room seemed to expand when she'd gone.

'You have your answer, I think,' Beth murmured, relieved.


London in August, and being wedged among the crowds of tourists while the heat hammered off walls and pavements, was Beth's idea of extreme hell. Even more than usual it was a relief to surrender and have tea at Dickins & Jones.

'Do you happen to know that chap?' Duncan muttered, frowning, as they were settling themselves at the table. 'The balding, middle-aged bloke with two women, a couple of tables behind me.' Beth glanced casually past Duncan and shook her head. 'He seems to know us,' he insisted. Beth poured out the tea and looked over again. The man was staring intently at Penny's profile beside her. Just then one of the women bit into her cake and nudged the other, who glanced up and then around at a discreet nod. For a moment both women seemed to look straight at Beth. The man's gaze too shifted from Penny, caught Beth's eye and turned aside. She examined the three of them a moment longer, fixing their appearance in her mind, and continued with her tea while a reel of remembered faces clicked busily behind her eyes.

The man wore a blazer and fawn trousers. His receding hair gave his forehead a domed effect over his sallow face and heavy eyebrows. When he turned away Beth saw that the dark hair at the back of his head was still thick and wavy. The younger woman, several years older than Jennetta, had shoulder-length mousy hair and there'd been nothing particularly noticeable about her features, the brief glimpse Beth had had of them. She wore a fussy summer dress with blue tights and light-coloured shoes like boats. Beth had a better view of the older woman, presumably her mother. She was slim and smart, with cold, light eyes, a well-shaped mouth and greying blonde hair smoothly framing her face. Rings flashed on her fingers and the skin at the edge of her right hand was palely dead-looking and puckered with scar tissue.

113

Beth had the vague feeling that she'd seen the woman before. Her eyes fell to the bag by the younger woman's chair. 'Bally', she read, and the sharp outline of a box showed through the plastic. All was explained. Jennetta had tried on shoes for her going-away outfit at the same shop in Regent Street only about an hour earlier. Beth must have noticed the woman then and had been recognised herself. The next time she glanced across the table was empty.

It was always a relief to be home and Beth's spirits lightened as usual as they walked to Duncan's Volvo left in the station park, the two girls going ahead. It had been only a moderately successful afternoon and they were all a little subdued on Penny's account. There'd been no problem buying her the replacement jeans, of course, and Jennetta had got the shoes she was looking for, but the weary trail after bridesmaids' dresses had been a disaster. Penny had grown more and more gloomy and self-conscious. Finally Duncan had announced, in a voice that turned heads, 'Come on, Penny. Let's find somewhere for tea. I don't know who they think would be seen dead in these things.' Beth could have hugged him.

But all the same, she knew that Penny felt they blamed her for causing unnecessary trouble, for being 'wrong' in some way. That was nonsense. There was nothing Beth would have seen her dead in. An unfussy, pastel-shaded – not pink – dress would suit her very well, but all they found were off-the-shoulders or puffed sleeves like bolsters and yards of ruching and frills. And the 'in' colours were electric emeralds or indigoes that made Penny's complexion look frost-bitten and drained the gold from her hair; all either too sophisticated or twee and at prices that outraged Duncan. Jennetta had been specially friendly and entertaining all through tea, but Beth could see that although Penny was grateful she wasn't convinced.

After tea they'd gone to Liberty's, that exotic bazaar of sumptuous materials in glorious colours, where it was impossible to feel pessimistic and where Beth's secretly flagging expectations revived. To Penny's relief she found a bolt of 'noiseless' blue in the exact shade Penny liked, and a pattern she could adapt to whatever Penny thought proper. They'd all cheered up a little then.

Beth had felt bound to give her the chance of at least looking for a dress she might like, because Jennetta's was to be bought – and therefore 'superior' – but now she wished she hadn't put the poor kid through so much torture. After all her gay courage, too, in bracing herself for something she dreaded. Apart from school uniform, dresses weren't Penny's natural gear. They didn't reflect her self-image. It was something Beth understood very well.

'That chap was waiting outside Dickins & Jones,' Duncan said quietly. 'Are you sure you don't know him from somewhere?'

'Who?' Beth surfaced from her thoughts.

'The one I pointed out to you at tea. Actually I'd seen him earlier, when we were buying Penny's jeans. He seemed interested in Jennetta. Apparently so interested as to follow us to Dickins & Jones and wait for us outside. She didn't give any sign of knowing him, though.' Beth glanced sharply at Duncan and checked her stride.

'They'd been shopping at Bally's too,' she said after a

moment. 'Just coincidence we overlapped a couple of times. The women had probably gone to the loo, or something, and he was waiting for them not us. I didn't recognise any of them, anyway.' Duncan's anxiously intent expression relaxed.

'Come on, Daddy! I promised Sherry!' Penny called, and the subject was dropped.

Beth couldn't, however, free herself from the rewakened memory of the balding man's interest in Penny. His expression had been – almost speculative, she thought. And when she caught his eye she'd had a fleeting sensation of physically interposing herself between him and her daughter. That feeling grew more disquieting as her thoughts unwillingly returned to the incident.

# Winter 1966-Summer 1968

# Seven

Sandra's amenable behaviour was directed solely at diddling Tom. Lucy did not count, and she made no particular efforts towards Beth after her early overtures were rebuffed. Sandra admired but could not like her, although she was willing to be friendly, in her careless, off-hand way. Her chief preoccupation was her solitary struggle for survival at Number 30 and nothing was allowed to interfere with that. Even Sandra's homesickness for the Meadows quickly faded, and in fact she never did write to her friends. More surprisingly, and more hurtfully for a time, she heard nothing from them either.

Beth herself was sometimes ashamed of her behaviour towards the younger girl. She knew Sandra was at first bewildered and unhappy, just as she had been, and she knew she could have done much more to make the first few months easier for her. But apart from that, Beth needed a friend, or even someone casually sympathetic to talk to, but her circumstances and her own timidity kept her aloof. Sandra was too reckless, too much inclined to rock the boat. Making a friend of Sandra would have put Beth in open defiance of Tom who plainly disliked her. Whereas he liked Beth. If she had ever hoped for advantages from Sandra's arrival, the only one she recognised was the furtive thrill of watching Tom trying to reduce her; for while he was locked in his antagonism with Sandra, Beth believed herself immune.

Tom did not always go to work on Saturdays and occasionally when he was at home Lucy visited her sister, a bus-ride away. Sometimes she took one of the girls with her, but usually she went alone. On one Saturday afternoon when Lucy was visiting and the girls sat silently over some simple mending she had looked out for them, Tom asked Beth to help him in the attic. There was jumble to be sorted for the chapel's Christmas Fair. Beth's unwillingness was obvious – surprisingly – and Sandra quickly offered to help instead. It was something different to do and the first time this novelty had presented itself.

'*When* you've learnt to be trustworthy,' Tom told her. 'It's up to you how soon that may be. Come along, Beth.'

Sandra shrugged. There was usually some sort of snide reproof if she spoke out of turn. She finished sewing on buttons and took the shirts into the kitchen for Lucy to iron later. The step-ladder was set up at the top of the stairs, outside the girls' room, but the loft trap-door was shut and there was nothing to see.

Sandra sat for a moment in the tall window at the bend of the stairs. Apart from the kitchen, bathroom and spare room it was the only sunny window, and even now the last of the autumn daylight filtered through it.

The design of the house gave an impression of spaciousness to the hall but at the expense of the staircase. This funnelled between two walls and was dark and so narrow as a result that even a handrail would have complicated the passage of anything bulky. The tall window had been inserted to light both the stairs and that end of the hall, but it was also pleasant to sit there in the sun with a book or some sewing; something Sandra often did in the holidays when Tom was at work. It would have been even pleasanter to sit on the bench just outside the window, but except for Sunday gardening or hanging out the washing the garden was out of bounds. It was vulgar to gossip with neighbours over the fence and so the temptation to do so was put out of reach.

Yet the Sinclairs' cat was out there, Sandra saw yearningly, and Tom was in the attic . . . Idly she picked at a soft patch in the ugly slatted barrier that protected the lowest eighteen inches of glass. It was a badly thought-out piece of home carpentry that prevented the window from being opened and was never made to remove for repainting. Condensation had gradually rotted the lower window-frame as well as the roots of the slats set in the sill, until parts were discoloured and spongy. Sandra cast one last look at the cat scraping in the vegetable beds and went back to some not too boring homework in the sitting-room.

She eventually heard Tom come carefully downstairs with the ladder and take it out through the kitchen to the garage where it was stored. Tom did not have a car – possibly he did not believe in them – and he had fitted up the garage as a workshop and garden store. Recalled to the present from *Emma* to find that she had read well beyond the allotted few chapters, Sandra ran upstairs to the bathroom.

Beth was standing in the bath soaping herself and Sandra checked her headlong gallop in surprise. Beth never permitted herself to be glimpsed undressed. She uttered a startled gasp now and flopped down into the water, crossing her arms over her chest.

'Can't wait!' Sandra sped on to the lavatory. 'Nobody

minded at the Meadows. Why're you having your bath now, anyway?'

'The attic's dusty,' Beth mumbled, her knees up to her chin.

'You're terribly skinny,' Sandra remarked, gazing at Beth's nodular spine. 'I bet you're lighter than me, even. You got worms or something?' She flushed the pan and ran some water into the basin. 'But you're growing bumpers, did you know? Anabelle at the Meadows – '

'It's none of your *business*!' Beth's voice rose and cracked. Her maturing form was hateful enough to her without hearing it casually compared with some unknown slag's. 'Get *out*, can't you!'

'Ho, pardon me breathing, I'm sure,' Sandra said haughtily. 'There's no need to squawk like a bear robbed of its whelks,' she added as she swept out.

Tom was reading his newspaper when she returned to the sitting-room and settled back with her book. (Nothing much happened in it but there was a character remarkably like Beth – like Beth usually was; cool and distant.)

'Where were you just now?' Tom asked absently.

'I went to the bathroom. Beth's having her bath already.' Sandra still seethed from their encounter.

'Do you enjoy reading?' Tom smiled at her round the paper.

'Sometimes,' Sandra admitted cautiously. Tom's interest was unexpected – and suspect therefore.

'You're obviously enjoying that book. But don't you think it's a little selfish of you to be enjoying yourself in here when there might be something more constructive for you to do?'

122

Homework was usually sacrosanct, but Tom was apparently intent on unsettling her and a straightforward explanation of why it had spilled over to the weekend might not shut him up.

'Oh, you mean I'm disturbing you in here? I'm sorry, Tom. I'll learn this in the dining-room, then. Will you hear me on it afterwards, please? It's for Monday's test and I want to get a really good mark,' Sandra added sanctimoniously.

'If you read it carefully and learn as you go, you shouldn't need anyone to hear you on it, Sandra,' Tom retorted predictably. 'Leave that here and bring me your homework record book.'

So, he didn't believe her, Sandra thought gleefully as she hurried to do as she was told. But there it was, recorded in black and white that a few chapters of *Emma* were set for Monday's test. *Poor* Tom, foiled again, Sandra hugged her tiny triumph. Now she was free to sit alone and undisturbed instead of being niggled into offering to clean the brass ornaments, or whatever Tom had in mind.

Tom made a point of checking the girls' homework, but what he liked to see were tidy pages of script and figures. He was no more able to judge their quality than Sandra herself, she had discovered to her surprise; as surprised as she had been to find that Beth was so much slower than herself. Tom made himself available to help with homework too, and was even prepared to hear a short poem set for learning, or verses from the Bible. Handing him a wodge of prose or French verbs, however, inspired the sort of lofty comment he had just made.

One evening when they were all in the sitting-room

after supper, Tom produced a letter from his pocket with a flourish.

'I met the postman this morning and intercepted this,' he unfolded the single sheet. 'It's from Exeter, Mother.'

'Oh! Well, there now, Dad!' Lucy focused myopically on the letter with something approaching a smile, while Sandra wondered dismally if Tom was in the habit of intercepting letters.

'I knew you'd be pleased,' he said unctuously. 'And Beth'll be pleased too to get a *personal* message from her Prince Charming,' he added with a sly grin in her direction. Beth did not look up from her sewing.

'Beth's Prince Charming, Dad? Whoever can that be?' Lucy wondered dimly.

'Our son, of course, Mother! Who else should be writing from Exeter? Oh, Beth will deny it, but I know she was developing quite a liking for him before he went away. Our little Beth's growing up, Mother.'

'Oh. Well, of course – '

'Ahah! She pretends not to know what I'm talking about!' Tom teased with elephantine playfulness. 'But we can all see her blushes!' Sandra was torn between cringeing embarrassment at the exhibition, and intrigue. Tom's manner was quite unprecedented.

'Anyway, he promises to be home for Christmas, Mother. He means to arrive on Christmas Eve and leave again on Boxing Day. It's a pity he can't spend more time with us, but apparently he's had a number of very pressing invitations and we mustn't be selfish.' Lucy went back to her sewing. 'But this is for your ears alone, Beth,' Tom returned to his arch manner. 'He writes, "Give Beth my love" – you see? – "and tell her I'm

124

looking forward to seeing her again".'

'He's always been very kind to Beth,' Lucy murmured.

'Indeed he has,' Tom agreed soberly. 'He does us credit, Mother, and so does Beth. But he may be surprised to see how thin our Beth has become. I thought she was picking up again, but now – Well, I know young ladies fret about their figures but dieting is vanity, Beth. I say this now in case Sandra should be tempted to follow your example. I don't like to see you starving yourself to suit some passing fashion. We are what *God* made us, not fashion. At this rate, Sandra will soon be as big as you and you may find you've a rival for the attentions of your Prince Charming.'

Sandra's growth-rate was not surprising. Lucy's meals were excellent, with none of the things Sandra loathed – sausages with varicose veins, tubular liver and slimy milk 'moulds' – and she ate like a starved wolf.

'I'm sorry, Tom. I didn't mean to be vain.' Beth bent lower over her sewing so that her hair swung silkily across her face. She'd turned as pale as she was scarlet before, Sandra noticed, and no wonder. For all his apparent amusement Tom's monologue had been a serious lecture, the first Sandra had heard directed at Beth. She wondered what on earth it had all been about – not dieting, knowing Tom.

'Christmas!' Sandra seized on the one thing that made sense to her. That letter had been the first reference to it at Number 30. She would not have been surprised to find that Christmas too was one of life's necessities that Tom found objectionable. 'Will you sew me something for a Christmas present, Beth? I'd love that!'

125

'I beg your pardon, Sandra?' asked Tom at his smoothest. 'Are you *begging* gifts from Beth? Gifts come out of gratitude and free choice from our *friends*, not on demand. Mother, I shall retain the money we would've spent on Sandra's presents and add it to our Charities Box instead. Is that clear, Sandra?' She was aghast.

'But – at the Meadows the Aunties used to *ask* us what we wanted,' she protested. 'I was only telling Beth in advance. I wasn't *begging*!'

'I'm sure they did what seemed best at the time, but you must learn that we expect better of you now in return for the undoubtedly greater advantages we provide.'

Even Beth was shocked enough to say afterwards, 'I'm sorry about Christmas.' Special occasions, even with their spurious gaiety, and presents were all that made life bearable at Number 30.

'Stuff him!' Sandra fought not to let her bitter disappointment show. 'Two can play at that. I shan't give them presents – ever – and they can keep their stinking money. And let's agree that *we* won't give each other presents either. It's less trouble.' (It was an attitude well known at the Home as 'Sandra cutting off her nose to spite her face', and she maintained it. With inward pain but no sign of embarrassment, at Christmas and birthdays Sandra would announce that her contribution had gone into the Charities Box and demand that the same should be done on her behalf. In fact she put in what she thought they were worth, a penny each.) 'But thanks, anyway,' she grinned at Beth. '*I'm* sorry he nagged on about Prince Charming. *Is* he?' Beth's earlier agitation revived.

'What – charming? Hasn't much competition, has he?' she pointed out sourly, again surprising Sandra with her openness. 'It's a stupid joke Tom cooked up when he went away to college. I'd even forgotten he might be home for Christmas.'

But if Sandra had any suspicion that college had interrupted a burgeoning romance between Beth and her Prince Charming – or PC as they referred to him after this – it was swept away almost as soon as he arrived and ran into Sandra in the hall.

'Hi, Beth!' he called carelessly over his shoulder as he started up the stairs.

'I'm *Sandra*!' she protested.

'Oh! I remember now – Sorry!' He hung on his heel for a moment. 'You're very alike.' Later at supper he added with a friendly grin, 'But you're smaller than Beth, now that I see you together. Sandra Little'un! And you've got more freckles.'

Sandra was as little pleased to hear her surname fiddled around with as her Christian name, but before she could protest Tom intervened with his soft laugh.

'It's not very gentlemanly to comment on Sandra's freckles! Never mind, Sandra, I'm sure they'll clear up in time.' Until which point she had never given them a thought and certainly had not considered them to be disfiguring. 'You see that Beth's freckles are fewer than they used to be,' Tom remarked to his son. 'Don't you think she's looking prettier than ever?' He grinned around like a mischievous goblin, reminding them of his teasing at Beth's expense. But the PC wasn't in on the joke, Sandra saw. He looked taken aback.

'I think Beth and Sandra are very alike,' he said stiffly.

127

He came home infrequently after that first Christmas, and then only for odd weekends when he barely exchanged a dozen words with the girls. Beth avoided him as much as possible and Sandra found him easily forgettable.

Tom's visits to the attic were not unusual but Sandra was thirteen before she was considered trustworthy enough to help him. One Saturday afternoon in late June, when Lucy had taken Beth with her to her sister's, Tom wanted to look out some pictures for the girls' room that Lucy supposed must be in the attic.

He went up the step-ladder first, laid back the trap-door and hoisted himself into the roof-space. He lit a torch and laid it beside him in the opening, waiting for Sandra. The ladder, an elderly wooden one, its legs splayed to the extent of a pair of knotted cords, stopped short of the trap by about three feet. It creaked and rocked as Sandra started up and she glanced nervously at the staircase that fell steeply away below.

Following Tom's instructions, she climbed on to the top step and found herself head and shoulders into the attic. She could easily have hoisted herself up as Tom had done, but she obediently shuffled around until she had her back to him. He caught her firmly under the arms and lifted her up to stand beside him.

'It's quite safe as long as you're sensible and do as you're told, you see.'

They had been on better terms for several months, but Sandra was not so affectionately disposed as to enjoy being touched by Tom. She disliked the way his hands had met across her breasts when he lifted her, and the

128

way he still held her to him. She squirmed free and picked up the torch, moving away from the opening. The attic was oppressively hot.

'Shine it here for a moment,' Tom asked, and he lowered the trap-door back into place. 'Just in case we drop something,' he explained a little breathlessly. 'There's nothing to stop it rolling down the stairs and damaging the paintwork.'

'I've never been in an attic before.' Sandra flashed the light around a maze of uprights and cross-beams that divided the space roughly into bays of varying heights. Everywhere was floored and neatly stowed. 'It's very tidy.' Disappointingly so.

'I like to know where everything is,' Tom came up beside her and held her arm. 'Even in the dark.' He took the torch from Sandra and switched it off. 'Does the dark give you dirty thoughts?' he asked softly, his voice unexpectedly close to her ear.

'I don't mind getting dusty,' Sandra said uneasily. She disliked dark, confined spaces, however. 'Let's find those pictures.' She tried to pull away from him but Tom tightened his grip on her arm.

'Don't you go into dark places with those boys – when you're practising for your plays?' Tom's voice sounded thick, as it sometimes did when he was angry but not showing it, and Sandra felt his breath unpleasantly moist on her cheek.

She thought she knew what he was about then. Tom occasionally teased her about her supposed boy-friends, in the same silly way he teased Beth about the PC, but she'd always sensed behind his archness a resentment at her involvement in something beyond his control. This

129

time it was the end of term play he was apparently angry about. He must know she didn't like the dark and this was his way of punishing her. She had yet to break the news to him of her part in the school's drama festival in the autumn, too.

'There aren't any boys this time, Tom,' Sandra explained patiently, 'and anyway, of course I don't go anywhere with them. I don't even like them.'

'Why not? What do they do? Do they touch you? Like this?' Tom released her arm and she felt his hand flutter over her breasts and slide away down her buttocks. She sprang away from him in revulsion and fetched up against one of the uprights. The torch beam sliced through the darkness and settled on her. 'They've frightened you, haven't they?' Tom's voice murmured from behind the beam. 'It's time you learned things for your own protection. You're old enough now, and it's what your parents would've explained to you. Now it's left to me. Come and see my secret den. There's a proper light there and we can talk.'

But whether he intended to instruct her in judo or the birds and bees, Sandra had no wish to remain alone with him in that musky atmosphere of enforced intimacy.

'I want to go downstairs,' she said shakily. 'I feel sick.' She was also bewildered, and horrified by a stealthy stirring of ancient memory.

'You'll feel better in my den. Come and see.' Tom put his arm around her shoulders and gripped. 'This is for your benefit, my dear. You'll see. You'll never be frightened again.'

She was a helpless child once more. The insufferable heat, the curiously crooning quality of Tom's persistent voice and the surprising strength of his arm were all part of a nightmare weakness as though she was drugged. Half suffocating and dizzy, she shuffled behind the cone of torch-light around and under beams until Tom stopped.

Through the humming in her head Sandra heard the sharp click of a light-switch and the corner in which they stood was suddenly flooded with brilliance.

'This is my den.' Tom was panting like a runner and his voice seemed to boom in her ears. His face was shiny with sweat. 'It's my secret place. I want to share it with you. It'll be our secret now. Can you keep a secret, Sandra? Little ladies who keep secrets get presents. Presents even you can't refuse, Sandra,' he nodded waggishly, a terrible parody of intimacy. 'I'll uncover the couch and you can lie down 'til you feel better. It's the heat. It gets very hot up here under the tiles. I'm hot myself. Clothes make you hot too. There – come and lie down,' he reached out a hand to her.

At Tom's touch Sandra felt as though a bucket of iced water had been emptied over her. The shock made her gasp, and the light dimmed as the buzzing grew louder in her ears. She clutched at a cross-beam for support, but the last thing she felt was the weight of her head dragging her down a black, unending hole in the floor.

Sandra woke with a galvanic threshing of her limbs to the sound of trickling water. She felt feverishly around the mattress on which she found herself lying, but it was quite dry. In a moment she had recovered from her disorientation, no longer the guiltstricken infant of long ago but no less terrified.

131

She lay still, trying to breathe evenly while she took stock. The light came from a table-lamp set on the bare boards. It was plugged into a socket screwed to an upright beam near which lay a roughly folded blanket. There was also an electric fire, its flex coiled round the beam but not plugged in. In view of the heat trapped in the roof-space it was a surprising thing to see there. The trickling sound came from the nearby water-tank because, of course, she was in the attic. In Tom's den. Thankfully Tom was nowhere to be seen.

She was lying on his 'couch', still hot but feeling strangely light-headed. There was a lump on the side of her head where she'd fallen, but she didn't think she'd been messed around. That had certainly been Tom's intention, Sandra knew instinctively, but although he must have lifted her on to the mattress she was still properly dressed. And she'd expect to feel something other than a headache if she'd been messed, she was certain.

At the same time, her situation was nothing at all like so humorous as the casual jokes she'd giggled over with her friends. What did he propose to do with her – keep her shut up there? It was obvious now how much he hated her. His recent friendliness had been as much of a blind as hers, but in the end he'd out-thought her.

Sandra had her own positive philosophy about pain. There were two kinds, unavoidable pain and that which you brought on yourself. The first, such as she'd suffered at the death of Smokey's predecessor at the Meadows or accidentally from skinning her knees in a fall, simply had to be borne and got over. But the pain that you brought on yourself often came through retribution. You had to take that into account if you planned doing something unlawful and decide beforehand if it was worth it. If you then were caught and suffered, again you had no option but to bear it without moaning. But this attic episode seemed to fit neither category; it was neither an accident nor retribution. For once Sandra was at a loss how to cope.

She was climbing shakily to her feet, intending at least to find the trap-door, when she heard the step-ladder creak. Hastily she lay down again and closed her eyes, her heart hammering. Steps hurried across the boards and a cold wet cloth was laid over her face. The unexpectedness of it threw her muscles into an uncontrollable fit of trembling.

'Sandra, please wake up!' It was Tom's voice, but concerned rather than vindictive or horridly insinuating. He wiped her face gently enough but Sandra was sickened by his touch. 'You're all right now, dear. Please wake up.' She obligingly opened her eyes and felt instantly less vulnerable. 'Have a drink of water. You'll feel better.' Tom's eyes no longer glittered and his hand holding the tooth-mug was shaking as much as her own. Looking into Tom's face as she drank, Sandra saw that he was frightened. The sight was wonderfully reviving. She surrendered to the first voluptuous waves of a deep, slow rage. She did not stop to think why he should be frightened; she merely accepted it as a reprieve.

'You tripped in the dark,' Tom gabbled urgently. 'Tripped and bumped your head, I'm afraid. Luckily this old mattress was stored up here. Are you feeling better now?'

'My head hurts,' Sandra told him in a small voice. It hurt inside and out. 'I don't know what happened.' She

133

certainly hadn't tripped and fallen. She must have just – blacked out. With funk?

'Don't you remember coming up to help me in the attic?' Tom asked eagerly. Too eagerly. He gave Sandra her cue. Her first priority was to get out of the attic as quickly as possible.

'Is that where we are?' She looked dazedly around.

'Don't you remember anything?' Sandra shook her head. A mistake. Something seemed to have come loose inside. She put up her hand in genuine distress.

'I think I'd like to lie on my bed for a while.'

'Of course. Yes, indeed. You'll soon feel better with an aspirin. And we won't need to worry Lucy – or Beth – with this, will we? Lucy will say it was my fault for not lighting your way properly. As indeed it was and I must make reparation. A present. But this'll be just our secret, won't it, Sandra?' He was almost pleading.

'I won't talk about it if you don't want me to, Tom,' she agreed submissively, and she could have laughed aloud at his look of relief.

The following week passed in a greater sense of ease and security for Sandra than it did for Tom, as she could see. And she had even more on him than he realised, she gloated. But she did not let anything show. Through long practice Sandra duplicated Beth's meek, eyes-down and virtually speechless manner, while she pondered on how best to make use of her knowledge in a way that would cause Tom maximum suffering.

As he pressed Sandra's pocket-money into her hand at the end of the week, Tom gave her a curious look which she interpreted as friendly. He'd taken to grimacing during the past few days. She examined her Savings book when she went up to bed, a private count of her funds being necessary ever since Tom once saw her at it and docked that week's pocket-money to teach her the difference between God and Mammon. What Sandra saw bewildered her, but not for long. A whole pound, of which she knew nothing, had been paid in the previous Tuesday but not at the usual post office, as the handstamp showed.

'I know who those extra pounds in your Savings book came from,' Sandra said quietly when Beth came to bed. There was no answer and she turned on the bedside light. Beth lay with the sheet wrapped tightly over her head. 'Don't try and hide, you stupid bitch!' Sandra leaned over and clumped her with one of the Bibles. 'Why the bloody hell didn't you warn me? Drooping about like the fucking Virgin Queen and all the time –'

'I didn't think he would, to you,' Beth whimpered. 'Honestly!' She wiped her eyes on the sheet and turned to face Sandra. 'Don't think I've been enjoying myself. I've *hated* it. And I hate *him*. Sometimes I'd like to *kill* him!'

'That's more like it,' Sandra grinned. 'But why didn't you pike off? Or tell Lucy, even?'

'What a joke!' Beth retorted bitterly. 'She only comes to life at feeding time. She wouldn't have believed me, anyway. Nobody'd believe us. We can't *prove* it and you know what a holy reputation he's got.' Sandra had not thought of that. One of her day-dreams was a public denunciation of Tom, but now she saw that such a showdown could well backfire. 'And anyway, he promised terrible things if I told anyone. And he – he seemed to like me, and I was already miserable enough without

135

putting him against me.'

' "Seemed to like you"!' Sandra jeered. 'He hates us! Do you think he had a go at me because he likes *me*? He won't again, though,' she said with satisfaction. 'I scared him shitless.'

'You did? How?' Beth was agog, but Sandra could hardly admit that she had been so frightened she fell into a dead faint.

'Told him where he got off,' she mumbled. 'How far's he gone with you?' she asked, hoping for positive ammunition. Sometimes there were photos, she'd heard.

'Almost as far as he can.' Beth lay back. 'Since not long before you came. Sometimes I know when it's going to happen. He sort of works himself up with that awful teasing – you know – about the PC. And it hurts so!' Beth lay crying softly and helplessly while Sandra fidgeted with impatience. There was so much to plan and decide, but she could not get another word out of Beth that night.

# Eight

Sandra hurried home from school the following day determined to pin Beth down to a proper discussion of strategy. They had to be allies now. Beth's CSE public exams were over and she was at home all day with only Lucy for company. She, too, seemed to be in the mood for discussion. They made their usual Monday trip to the post office and afterwards both retired to the dining-room, Beth on the pretext of hearing Sandra's lines for the end of term play. So they had an hour together before supper preparations and every reason to be talking quietly over the home-work table.

'All day I've felt so *different* now that you know everything,' Beth began impulsively. 'I feel I can face anything now because we're in this together. Aren't we, Sandra? Friends as well as sisters.' Her face was flushed with sincerity. 'I wanted to be friends with you before but I daren't in case he thought I was telling you things. He's always tried to set us against each other. I haven't dared to be friendly with *anyone*, Sandy.'

'What's this bloody "Sandy" business?' Sandra asked impatiently, roused from her wonderment at Beth's changed manner, her direct looks from eyes that sparkled, her flood of unprompted togetherness.

'Well, because we *are* friends now, aren't we?'

'Not for much longer if you call me Sandy.'

'Why are you so fussy about it?' Beth asked, intrigued.

137

'Because. If you must know, because it's the name I was given for *me*. It's the only thing that's really my own,' Sandra told her gruffly.

'That makes sense,' Beth was impressed. 'I don't mind being called Beth, though.'

'It doesn't mean anything but short for Elizabeth, does it?' Sandra pointed out. 'You'd like it less if it meant "tummybutton" or something. So I'm not "dirty", I'm Sandra.

'But anyway, what I've been thinking,' she went on briskly. 'Now's your chance to make a run for it, while that bastard doesn't know his arse from his elbow. If you don't think you've got enough dosh yet for whatever you've planned, you can have my savings too. It's not much, or I'd have run myself before now, but you're welcome to it. It's funny to think all that money he's been giving you's just been added to your absconding fund,' Sandra laughed; feebly, because the thought of giving away her carefully amassed wealth was painful.

'Absconding fund?' Beth stared in horror. Her assurance that she could face anything had been premature. 'But – where would I go? And who'd look after me? Of course I can't leave here alone – not before I get a proper job. If I've passed these CSEs this summer –'

'You mean you *aren't* planning to escape?' Sandra snapped out of her stupefaction. 'What the hell've you been saving up for, then? And there was me thinking you were so bloody clever! What a mug!'

She made a desperate attempt to inspire Beth with a belated lust for freedom. Even if she were caught after only a few days her flight would prompt an inquiry, surely, and *that* would expose Tom.

138

'Look, if you took your money out next Monday morning you'd be somewhere safe before anyone knew you'd gone. I'll even come with you, if you like. I was going to wait on and watch him bleed – But we could hitch to Wales or Scotland. Get work on a farm or skivvying in a hotel – '

'But they'd *find* us!' Beth wailed. '*I* don't want to end up in a remand Home! They wouldn't believe *why* and they'd punish us! He *said* so! You don't understand – grown-ups *always* win!'

That silenced Sandra. She'd been hopelessly mistaken in Beth. Beth was a complete wet-arse, a broken weed, but she was unwillingly convinced by her age and experience that their story wouldn't be believed.

'OK,' she shrugged, 'but you're only kidding yourself that he'll let you go, even if you get a job. Look how he won't let you do a Saturday job – "because of his position"! We know what *that* position is – on his fucking mattress. You'll be like a – a concubine. *And* you'll be alone again. I sure as hell aren't staying once I'm ready to go. Last night you talked as if you were ready to get even –'

'There's lots of ways you can hurt a man without putting yourself in the wrong,' Beth answered mysteriously. 'We're still under age and in care. How can he stop me getting a proper job, though? And when I do I'll move in with someone. A man. Get married, even. He'll have two of us to face then – '

'How can you ever bear to have anyone near you again?' Sandra asked in astonishment. 'That's not much of an escape.'

'Everyone gets married some day,' Beth pointed out.

139

'You'll love someone and want to live with them, you'll see.' Her patronising tone irritated Sandra.

'You weren't talking about *love*, you were talking about getting your own back – about just going on doing what *he* does but with someone else. Like cats and dogs,' Sandra said disgustedly. 'At least *they* don't pretend to be teaching each other the facts of life.'

'Is that what he told you?' Beth giggled. 'What did he do?' Sandra flushed and turned away from her eagerness. 'Oh, well, I suppose he felt you about a bit, did he? The next stage would be for you to touch *him*.' Sandra recoiled. 'True! One day he pulled this skinned turkey-neck out of his trousers –'

'In his *trousers*? A turkey-neck?' Sandra echoed in confused disbelief.

'It was his *thing*, silly!' Beth giggled again. 'But it looked all blotchy-purple and scraggy, like a turkey-neck. He liked me touching it. After that – well, I told you last night.'

There'd been boys at the Meadows – Sandra had often helped bath the littlest ones – and boys at her junior school, but none of them had displayed like poultry. She was nonplussed. The discussion wasn't going as she'd intended and she found the turn of subject distasteful and difficult to cope with. Now Beth's flippancy disconcerted her as well.

'Christ!' she muttered in horrified embarrassment. 'I mean – *Christ*! He – he was lucky not to give you a baby. You're so skinny it'd have shown straightaway, and then he'd have been in the shit.'

'*I'd* have been in the shit,' Beth corrected. 'He wouldn't have admitted anything. You know how he twists things. And skinny! People keep on about it. You don't have much appetite, I can tell you, when you're sitting at the same table as him with his godly talk and his mind on your cunt,' she startled Sandra by saying. 'You look so shocked, but you're such a baby still you don't know anything. *Buggering* doesn't give you babies. Did you think that was just a swear-word? It means being shafted up your backside and it hurts like hell. Who'd believe me if I told them *that* about him?'

Sandra had thrown up her hand as though to ward off Beth's anger, and perhaps also to ward off the ugly words so uncharacteristic of Beth's cool elegance. Their meaning was at once incomprehensible and so repulsive that their mere utterance was an abuse. Her freckles stood out against her pallor like tealeaves.

'But – But I don't understand,' Sandra floundered after a moment. 'That's disgusting! Didn't he know – ?'

'Of course he knew. You don't think Lucy whisked up the PC out of a recipe-book, do you? He knew that way wouldn't give me babies, *and* he knew that doctors can tell if you're still a virgin. *That's* why. Like I said, there's no proof. No one'd ever listen to people like us.'

'He's even *fouler* than I thought!' Sandra exploded. 'I – I'm – I'll *make* him stop – if I have to nail his balls to the floor!' She was trembling with furious loathing. To Beth, who was flattered by the savagery of what she assumed were Sandra's partisan feelings, she was also a comic little figure with her scowl and her freckles and her suddenly scarlet face. Like a baby in a tantrum. But when she giggled once more Sandra rounded on her. 'How can you still go on living here – and *laugh*! How could you even let him get that *far*?'

Beth sat still for a moment, the silky curtain of her hair hiding her face. It had been a mistake to show off her experience, she realised. This wasn't, after all, the sort of sniggering exchange she'd overheard at school between equals. Sandra was too young and childish not to be shocked and disgusted. But young though she was, her unlooked-for friendship was too important to be lost so soon. Beth tried to explain.

'It wasn't like you think,' she began slowly. 'He only wanted to touch me up a bit at first. That wasn't long after I came here. I didn't mind, because I thought he liked me and I knew that's the sort of thing people do when they like each other. He – he wasn't the first, you see.' Beth swung back her hair and gazed at Sandra, appealing for her understanding. 'Later I was afraid of what he'd do if I tried to stop him. I – I can't take rows. But then I found it – well, exciting that he could get so worked up about me. It made me feel – you know – not so helpless. In the end, of course, I hated what he was doing, but it was too late then. But it wasn't all hateful, you see. Some of the things he did – I liked.'

Sandra dropped her head on her arms.

'I can see what you think of me,' Beth said sadly. 'But when you're older and more – mature you'll understand. Your body wants things sometimes that your head wishes it didn't. It's a trap. I didn't understand at first what was happening to me, and there was no one I could talk to about it. Then I realised it was because I was growing up. You'll find the same thing. You think I haven't got the guts to break out of it. I haven't got the guts to do it your way, that's true. So I won't take your money, because I'm not going to run away, but I'll never

142

forget that you'd have done that for me. And one day I *will* get free and I'll rub his nose in it. And then I'll see he never has anyone again. People don't like dirty old men who get their rocks off with little girls. All the same, I've learnt a lot from him – and one of the things I've learnt is that people only listen to you if you're respectable. One day I'll be respectable and make him wish he'd never touched me.'

Sandra could not help being impressed by Beth's confidences and her adult calm. However, she had a deeply rooted sense of good, bad and ugly, and nothing Beth said disturbed that.

'You've only learnt the – mucky things from him,' she mumbled. 'You only have to read books or plays to see –'

'Books!' Beth read only what was strictly necessary. 'Fairystories for romantics like you. The same as people dressing-up for weddings – to hide the muckiness, as you call it. Real life isn't play-acting, and you have to learn that or get badly hurt.'

It never occurred to Beth that what she said that day would have such a traumatic effect on Sandra. It never crossed her mind that she herself played a major part in the tragedy that followed. Always the passive participant, it was Beth who released the demons.

Her plans for confounding Tom were too indirect and too far in the future for Sandra. She could see only more years of contained hatred ahead, but now punctuated with the sharper loathing of hearing Beth's summonses to the attic and knowing that she did not entirely dislike them. Sandra could not bear the prospect but she did not believe she could yet afford to escape alone. Not successfully. Her savings had yet to reach the target figure of £20. Her own account of the attic episode was negligible in comparison with Beth's, but if Beth refused to bear witness then her story alone would get her nowhere.

However, after Sandra's abortive visit Tom did not go up into the attic for several months. His attitude towards Sandra continued nervously placatory and life at Number 30 was at least quieter for that. Too quiet for Sandra who could never forgive him for his betrayal. She did not want a truce, she wanted victory. Her problem was how to win it decisively.

Sandra kept Tom on tenterhooks by drooping for a few weeks and she developed intermittent headaches. These were immediately followed by unremarked half-crowns paid into her post office Savings which caused her amusement but little satisfaction. Even at half a crown a throw, headaches were slow earners and she could not risk being too inventive. Tom was on the hop but not bleeding, not exposed as a dirty old man from whom it would be necessary to remove his foster-children. The thought never entered her head that he might actually be sent to prison. Between them, Sandra and Beth knew a great deal but they were not knowledgeable.

The situation between the girls changed even less noticeably than the small differences in atmosphere at Number 30. Having established their total incompatibility in outlook and intentions, they quickly drifted back into their separate enclosures. Their sisterly alliance was still-born.

Beth failed the four CSE exams she had sat that summer, two of them so comprehensively that they were not

144

worth sitting again at Christmas.

'Exam results aren't everything,' Tom reassured her. 'I know you did your best, and that's what matters. There's always a place in this world for your special talents, and you know you're safe here until such a place is ready for you. But if you can pass your shorthand and typing exams at Christmas, little lady, there might even be a job for you in our office!' he added as a final encouragement.

Sandra listened, grim-faced and stony. 'Safe here'! Images of dog-whips, cattle-goads, Lucy's hat-pins, even, judiciously applied, flitted through her daydreams as her plans for Tom's destruction were constantly recast and refuelled by his sanctimonious lies. It was cumulative poison that even obscured the half-term drama festival, and for the first time Sandra had difficulty learning her lines. But *Viceroy Sarah* never had such an evil adversary as Tom.

Just before the Autumn term started, Lucy had one of her fits of independent thinking. They struck at predictable intervals but the wonder was that they still came upon her. Lucy was sliding away into a greater passivity and silence, and she spent more time with her sister. It did not occur to either of the girls to wonder why, if they even noticed.

'We must soon take a ride out into the country, Dad, and see what the hedgerows have to offer this year,' Lucy uttered the standard September formula one supper-time. She did not appear to notice that she had cut across one of Tom's measured profundities.

'Is it time again already, Mother?' he asked with a wondering smile. '*Tempus fugaces, fugaces*! I'll get the jam jars down from the attic tomorrow!' Sandra kept her head lowered in case Beth tried to catch her eye, but the expected request for help in the attic did not come. 'That means our Harvest Festival can't be far off. I must urge on something suitable in my little plot,' Tom went on, oblivious of the fact that his foster-daughters imagined him urging on something quite other.

'That's right, Dad. I'll be at Olive's tomorrow,' Lucy murmured, and still there was no summons.

'Has the old bugg – pig *asked* you?' Sandra whispered in bed that night.

'No,' Beth replied. 'And he obviously hasn't asked you.'

'He won't,' Sandra was confident. '*Promise* you'll tell me as soon as he does,' she hissed fiercely. 'Just say' she paused to think of a suitable code-word; but the chances of Beth getting it right in her agitation, or rightly uttered in a context that didn't sound suspicious, were slim. 'Say anything, but call me Sandy, OK?'

'What're you going to do? You won't let on I've told you?' Beth asked in consternation.

''Course not,' Sandra promised, but she refused to explain any more.

In fact she had been hoping to provide a witness to the next scene in the den and had been racking her brains to think of possibles. Neither of the girls knew anyone well enough even to invite casually indoors, leave alone to keep them penned and then introduce them into the loft at the critical time. Nor did Sandra feel that she could haul a stranger in off the street to help with an unspecified emergency occurring shortly. Thumping footsteps and querulous demands for explanation would not make

146

for a subtle approach. She could not involve the police for the same reason, that she could not explain what she wanted witnessed, convinced now that she would not be believed. Even if Lucy weren't going to be away from home, she reflected, there was no possibility of inserting *her* silently into the attic. Not through that opening. The reason, perhaps, why Tom had made his den up there in the first place. It was the only part of the house where Lucy's mops and dusters didn't penetrate. Sandra fell asleep considering all the alternatives. Truly the dice were loaded in favour of the grown-ups, as Beth had said. What was required was the hand of God to give the dice a shake.

The spider still had not beckoned the fly by the time Lucy set out after lunch on the following day. Beth went to the piano in the sitting-room for her Saturday practice and Sandra took her part to learn out in the garden, occasionally declaiming aloud. Tom saw her there but did not reprove her. Those days were past. Mrs Sinclair of the partnering semi was adjusting her lines of washing. There was always washing draped about her garden; her three grammar school teenagers presumably led more active lives than Beth and Sandra. They certainly sounded more cheerful. Tom condemned Mrs Sinclair for hanging out washing sometimes even on a Sunday – and underclothes at that. Not very nice for other people. She was feckless.

The Sinclairs' cat, another instance of Sinclair fecklessness, came trilling along the top of the party fence for Sandra to tickle his ears.

'Don't let him be a nuisance, dear,' Mrs Sinclair called, mindful of Tom's physical objections to cats in his vegetable beds.

'It's all right. Skipper knows I'm his friend,' Sandra smiled back. Poor little bastard, thought Mrs Sinclair, vaguely wondering which of the girls she was.

Tom, meanwhile, busied himself in the garage, clearing and cleaning shelves ready for the pounds of jam Lucy intended to wring from the hedgerows, and bustling in and out of the kitchen for buckets of hot water. Every time he returned to the garage, Sandra ran in to ask Beth if he had summoned her to the attic and then ran outside again puzzled by her negative reply.

Eventually Tom went indoors carrying the step-ladder. Sandra watched through the staircase window as he set it up and ascended into the attic with a kick of his feet.

'He's in the attic!' She burst in on Beth once more. 'He must've asked you by now!'

'I tell you he *hasn't*! Whatever you said to him last time's obviously scared him off, so leave me alone, Sandra.'

Sandra hurried back to the staircase window, leaving the kitchen door wide open. She could hear Beth practising her inevitable hymn-tunes, and next door Mrs Sinclair huskily joined in as she trotted to and fro. Crouching on the bench with her head below the level of the party fence, Sandra kept a watch up the stairs through the mouldering window-bars; she didn't trust Beth. But the hymn-tunes thumped gently on like heartbeats.

Tom's legs suddenly reappeared, swinging for a moment above the ladder until his feet found the top step. Sandra watched him back slowly down with a large cardboard box in his arms which he put down on the landing. He went back up the ladder to disappear again

148

with that characteristic flip of his feet. Like a scaly lizard, thought Sandra. So, there was to be another box of jam-jars. And still no Beth. Sandra's bladder tightened warningly. She laid *Viceroy Sarah* under the bench and ran lightly upstairs.

Dully pom-pomming her way through Sankey and Moody, Beth was only vaguely conscious of a muffled thundering. The smash of splintering glass from the back of the house, however, froze her to the piano-keys. It was a stupefying sound. A shelf must have given way in the kitchen, she guessed, and after a moment she went uncertainly down the hall.

The step-ladder lay wedged across the bend of the stairs and the window above it was shattered, almost empty of glass but for a jagged frame of ugly spikes. Here was unforeseen excitement! Tom had dropped the ladder! Beth ran for the back door but stopped short as though she had slammed up against a wall. For Tom was not outside clearing up the broken glass but lying untidily among it.

Beth saw that Sandra was already there, kneeling by Tom's head. She was pale and intent, her hand hovering over Tom's face. For some reason a skein of scarlet embroidery silk hung from her fingers – and Tom's hands and bare arms were enmeshed in a net of crimson thread and cords. And his face – Beth's mouth fell open as she gasped in realisation. Sandra glanced up and shouted something. She moved her hand, and the scarlet skein stood on its own above Tom's eye. Beth gagged painfully and the sound like a whistling kettle cut off at once.

'Don't stand there screaming get *help*!' Sandra

149

shouted again, and her voice was high-pitched and wild. Mrs Sinclair's disembodied face suddenly bobbed over the fence, its eyes wide and staring, and she too shouted at Beth.

'Whatever's happened?' gabbled the talking head. 'That *noise*! Oh, my God!' The head wobbled and then rolled off on the far side of the fence. It was the final straw in Beth's confusion. She turned and blundered back through the house, wanting only to get away from that bloodied mess in the garden. She ran into Mrs Sinclair, fully assembled now, at the front door and nearly screamed again. 'Ring 999 for an ambulance!' Mrs Sinclair gasped as she bundled Beth back into the hall and thrust past her. 'I must get that child away from there!'

Beth remembered the rest of that terrible afternoon only in snatches, as if she had closed her eyes for long periods between glimpses of the events. The neighbours first, crowding the usually silent house with a mutter of voices and tramp of feet. Broken, bloody glass crackling underfoot outside and blood in the kitchen as well from Sandra's cut hand. They did not hover long round the dead man but gathered in the kitchen, just far enough still to display their respect but not so far as to miss anything. Somebody ran Sandra's hand under the tap and wrapped it in a tea-towel as white as her face. Somebody else called the ambulance, for Beth was too shaken to think properly. She only just about managed to tell them Olive's address where Lucy could be found, and someone drove away to break the news to her and take her to the hospital – 'She'd better stay with me 'til her boy gets back.'

The others looked doubtfully at the two girls, wondering whose responsibility they were now. No one offered to take them in while that question was resolved. One of the neighbours privately intended to phone the local Welfare office and tell them what had happened. He did not announce this in case he found himself committed to taking charge of the girls while the wheels turned God knew how slowly.

It was to everyone's relief that a policeman arrived just as the corpse was stretchered out to the ambulance. They told him what they knew and quietly faded away – to prepare themselves, perhaps, for the task of comforting the widow. Without her grief to sustain them, few felt inclined to mourn a man whose righteousness had set him so apart.

PC Mason handled the girls tenderly when he finally came to them in the sitting-room. He had uncovered the dead face as the stretcher went past and he knew what they had been through. They were shooed from the kitchen when the ambulance-men arrived and now they numbly waited to be organised, too shocked and preoccupied to speak or even glance at each other.

While Sandra sat bowed over her hand, Beth, recovering a little from her horror and reassured by PC Mason's fatherly manner, once again explained what must have happened: how Tom had been fetching things down from the attic and had lost his balance on the stepladder. PC Mason had seen the ladder lying on the stairs and noted the dangerous siting of the trap in the landing ceiling. Below it lay a large cardboard box full of empty jam-jars, and another lay on the stairs but filled now with smashed glass.

'But I didn't actually see what happened because I was practising in here,' Beth went on in her soft voice. 'I heard the noise, though, and ran out to look.' A fat book of hymn-tunes was still propped on the piano-rest and the lady next door had heard the piano, so the complete picture was clear enough to PC Mason without eye-witnesses.

The man had been climbing down the ladder carrying the heavy, unwieldy box. He'd lost his balance, and without a free hand to recover himself he'd fallen straight down the stairs and gone through the window at the bend. There was no handrail, the bars protecting the glass were rotten and the window-sill was below knee-height. Asking for trouble, really. On his way the poor devil had been cut and pierced by fixed and flying glass and was unlucky enough to catch a piece through his eye. That might not even have been the actual cause of death. It was a hell of a fall.

The other girl, PC Mason had been told, was in the garden, learning her part for some play – understandably well away from the hymn-tunes – when her foster-father had come crashing through the window. She'd tried to revive him, he'd been told too, and got herself cut. Plucky little kid, thought PC Mason, but she was paying for it now. Shock, he diagnosed.

'How bad's your hand?' he asked Sandra gently. 'Let's have a look.' He should have checked earlier that she didn't need hospital treatment. The blood still oozed sluggishly from parallel slits across her palm and fingers; stingingly painful, certainly, but clean and not deep, he saw with relief. Puzzling, though. 'How did you manage to cut yourself like that?' he asked, carefully wrapping up her hand again. To his horror she rolled up her eyes and he thought she was going to faint. Cursed himself for his thoughtlessness.

'There was some – glass – in Tom's eye,' Sandra mumbled thickly. 'I – tried to – to pull it out. It made a noise – like a jelly.' She was suddenly sick over his feet.

That just about made his day, thought PC Mason glumly, wishing he'd had the wit to summon a police-woman earlier – though he hadn't dreamt that the girls had been left unattended. He squelched to the phone and rang the local Children's Department. He explained the situation forcefully and wrung out a promise to get things moving straight away, the foster-mother being unavailable and unlikely to want to cope for a few days at least. This was not an eventuality that took account of the days of the week, he grimly overrode a demur.

'And tell them to have a medic handy,' he warned. Then he rang his base to say that he would be sitting with the girls until somewhere was found for them.

'Better pack a few things,' PC Mason told Beth and Sandra. 'Just for a couple of days.' Before going upstairs to supervise them he sponged his boots in the kitchen and put the kettle on. They sat silently drinking tea together until the car arrived and PC Mason could lock up and go.

# Summer-Autumn 1989

# Nine

On the night of their shopping trip for Penny's brides-maid's dress Beth locked herself in for the bath she always took when the family was in bed. Showers were all very well and useful – especially in times of drought, she thought guiltily – but there was nothing like the tranquil luxury of an unhurried bath when the house was quiet and there were no demands for her attention. Apart from which it was the only real privacy she could expect during the school holidays and she'd been aching for it since their return from Town. For once her homecoming had been overcast. Duncan's insistence that the balding man had followed them about had startled her, although she'd suggested a reasonable explanation at the time. Beth's old fear of Nick's friends had surfaced and sunk all evening, and now it was waving not drowning as she tried to relax in the scented water.

She hadn't cared for any of Nick's friends, partly through fastidiousness and partly because she'd felt somehow not accepted by them – and that was throwing roses at it, Beth reflected sourly. They hadn't wanted her there. Given that she was nearly always the only woman in the party, it had seemed a surprising reaction at the time and she'd been hurt by it. After a couple of occa-sions when she was frozen out early to bed, Nick took to meeting them away from the flat and Beth felt she'd let him down. She hadn't expected him to give up the friends of his bachelor days but his apparent insensitivity to her feelings had puzzled her. Afterwards, of course, she'd realised that he probably owed more than friendship to those people while she was merely the outsider.

After his death she'd dreaded their visits of condolence or offers of help, and to that extent she was relieved that there were none, and was fearful of even meeting them in the street. Beth dreaded being in any way involved with anyone on Nick's account. When Jennetta was born her fear of his friends had so intensified that she hardly left the shelter of the flat except to dart to the nearby shops and back. Beth never had fully thrown off her habit of unease at stepping out across her own doorstep. Jennetta's airings, until she grew too active and the fear was forced to recede to manageable proportions, were taken on the sitting-room balcony.

Now Beth drove herself again to remember faces she'd successfully forgotten, faces that anyway hadn't fixed themselves on her attention more than eighteen years before. She couldn't place the balding man among them, even allowing for his ageing, but she knew that didn't mean anything. He might have recognised *her*.

Beth suspected that Nick's friends had more reason for interesting themselves in her, for all their aloofness, than she in them. The flat could have been watched for long after Nick's death without her being aware of any surveillance. Any of the lodgers she'd taken in while Jennetta was tiny could have been planted to keep an eye on Nick's widow. That was a new idea and even at that distance it made Beth shiver. She turned on the hot tap again.

The man that afternoon had seemed interested in

Penny and herself, although Duncan had imagined Jennetta to be the reason for his pursuit. Beth doubted if anyone would recognise Jennetta as Nick's daughter unless she'd been watched as she grew up, and that was surely improbable. But in this age of casual violence, was it so improbable that a chance recognition of herself – something she'd always been afraid of – had given one of Nick's old associates the idea, say, of kidnapping one of the girls?

Suddenly the blood seemed to drain from Beth's body and the bath-water felt unbearably hot. She stepped quickly out, her head swimming, roughly dried off and sat on the bathmat with her back to the cool tiled wall. That night her relaxing bath was not working its usual magic. Sense and sensitivity clamoured at each other across the years instead.

Penny was a sitting target for someone with abduction in mind. She was out on Sherry, often alone, every day of the holidays. She was a child. Jennetta would be more of a handful, and anyway she wasn't often out on her own. No one, seeing her with Alan, would take on the pair of them, surely. But Penny – Nick hadn't died worth a pile, as far as she'd discovered at the time, but his interests, known only among themselves, might lead his old friends to wonder if Beth still had something, or knew something, that could be exchanged for Penny.

Then why hadn't they accosted her long ago, when she'd been on her own? And had they found her now by chance, coincidentally visiting the same shops in Town, or had they followed her family actually from the house? Were those three in Dickins & Jones, ostensibly a family outing, part of a surveillance team? Beth was on the point of running in to Duncan, naked as she was, to ask whether he'd seen any of them again on the train back to Epsom.

The thought of explaining such uncharacteristic impetuosity brought her up short. Duncan didn't know about Nick's friends, and they weren't something Beth felt she could tell him about now. They should have been notified, like Colorado Beetle or smallpox, before she agreed to marry him; but a line had to be drawn somewhere. And anyway, she'd believed herself to be free of them then and herself out of quarantine.

Duncan would surely have mentioned if he'd seen the balding man or any of his party again. She was being hysterical. She was under pressure. Jennetta's wedding, a triumph though it was, had its wearying aspects. The planning and even the peripheral arrangements filled Beth's head all her waking hours. It was merely because of an old habit that her mind had flown back to Nick's blasted friends. And because of all that talk before lunch, first with Jennetta and then with Duncan, about Nick and his imaginary parents. And someone else had been talking about Nick, not so long ago. Jane Mallinson, of all people, Beth frowned, remembering. Because of her insufferable aunt. There'd been altogether too much unhealthy recollection of absent friends.

With an effort Beth imposed her habitual self-control. She drained the bath, cleaned it and slid into her dressing-gown, its silk folds comforting in their sensual touch.

'Mm-mm. You smell nice,' Duncan murmured as he always did when Beth came to bed. Sleepily he took her in his arms. 'You've been a long time – and you're cold.

What've you been doing?'

'Fell asleep in the bath,' she mumbled against his shoulder. 'The water got cold.'

'I'll soon warm you. Did I hear you go in to Penny?'

'Just – checking.'

'Enough to give any healthy kid nightmares, those snooty baggages in those ghastly wedding departments. And the kids' fathers as well.'

Beth couldn't sleep. The reverberations of the shock she'd imaginatively wished on herself resounded through her head, while dim images of black-haired figures materialised like reflections in a dark mirror and beckoned for attention. Not from the Nick era, for she'd already talked herself out of that possibility.

However, Duncan's mention of childhood nightmares had, in her current state of mind, struck another chord; an older can of worms buried deep in the darkness from where they'd once crawled. For there were dark-haired members of her own family, Beth remembered unwillingly; or two much older boys she vaguely recalled had been dark and, because they'd lived in the same house, were presumably related to her.

She'd been very young then and remembered them at all, as in ancient nightmares, only because they'd terrified her. Long after she'd been moved from there she'd wake in the night, sweating and fearful at some sound made, she'd imagine, by one of them creeping in to where she slept.

By chance she'd spent her life almost within pip-spit of that same area: might those boys, middle-aged men now, recognise her? Not because they'd remember her from so long ago, but because her features *now* reminded them of whose child she'd been. Was the balding man possibly a relative? And if so, what was his interest now; casual, curious, remorseful, or vicious?

Except for a sickening interval, Beth had smothered the horror of that place until the close confinement of Jennetta's babyhood – washing drying over the fire, the sharp reek of the nappy bucket – had brought her own childhood memories crowding back. Now once more they stumbled out of control across her mind's vision as she stared into the dark.

Beth shifted uncomfortably and moved away from Duncan. Not all the scented baths in a lifetime would clean her of scenes from which even Duncan was powerless to protect her. They were a part of her she could never share nor completely exorcise. And if Penny had been the target that afternoon of *such* fantasies – Penny wasn't automatically immune because she was Duncan's daughter and not a poor bloody little runt for whom attention had more usually meant pain.

The thought nauseated Beth as much as the flood of bile into her mouth. She sprang hastily out of bed, snatching up her dressing-gown on the way to the bathroom.

She awoke the next morning feeling as though she was gripped in the toils of a heavy hangover. Her head seemed to ring with pain and she was sick. The light-hearted prattle over breakfast jangled her nerves. When Penny dropped a spoon its clatter was like a physical assault. Beth rounded on the child with an anguished cry that shocked them all into silence.

'Sorry,' she muttered after a deathly moment, her

head in her hands. 'Made me jump. Headache.' She was still shaking, Penny's expression of dismay frozen on her mind.

'You overdid it in Town yesterday,' Duncan sympathised with a reassuring glance at the girls. 'You were restless all night. Take it easy today, darling. We can hold the fort. Jennetta, are you seeing Alan today?' She shook her head.

'Ironing and packing for Weymouth tomorrow.'

'Then you'll have a chance to practise your culinary arts on us,' Duncan grinned. 'I'll do the veges. What's to come out of the garden for lunch, darling?' he turned back to Beth. 'Or may we burgle the freezer?'

Beth was grateful for his efforts to distract the girls' attention but she was too close to tears to answer.

'Freezer it is, then,' Duncan went on unperturbed. 'So much for my magnanimous offer to do the veges, Jennetta. I'll just be your skivvy. What're you going to do today, Penny?'

'I'm riding Sherry over to Debbie's before lunch,' Penny answered in a small voice. 'Then she's coming here after lunch.'

'You didn't warn me of this,' Beth accused, dropping her hands from her face. 'Debbie who?' Jonquil was still away, of course.

'Debbie Lyon. But Mummy, I'm not missing any meals,' Penny said defensively, 'so you don't usually *need* to know.'

'These *aren't* usual days. There's far too much to be done for any of us to take time off without reference – without asking first if it'll be convenient. If Jennetta likes to get on with the lunch – fine. But don't forget

163

you've got thank-you letters to write for those early presents, Jennetta. You're keeping a list, I hope. Remember you'll be away next week and I can't be expected to do everything for you.' The words and tone of voice leaked on unstoppably from some overflowing slough in Beth's memory, and with them drained away her headache. 'But Penny, I want you here today. I want to make a start on that dress.'

'But Mummy, I *promised* Debbie!' Penny protested, aghast.

'Then you'll simply have to phone and cancel. And Daddy'll go with you, now, to help with whatever has to be done in the paddock for today. I want you *quickly* in the sewing-room.'

It sounded almost as though Beth suspected Penny of planning to sneak off with Sherry, but she couldn't help that. The thought of Penny riding alone to and from the Lyons', or even being alone in the paddock, aroused all Beth's horrors of her sleepless night. She stared unmoved at Penny's look of shocked disbelief before she turned and went without another word. She ignored the bewildered glance Duncan directed at her before he followed Penny out. Jennetta, eyes downcast, cleared the table and loaded the dish-washer, then she too left the room.

Having reduced her family to the level of idiot two-year-olds, Beth went heavily up to the sewing-room feeling alone in the world but curiously refreshed. It was a long time since she'd let herself go like that, she mused, but they said it did you good sometimes.

Beth couldn't expect to interest Penny in the mechanics of dress-making, nor hope to distract her mind from her natural preference to be with Sherry – with Debbie – with anyone and anywhere but in the sewing-room. But none of that mattered as long as she had Penny safe. Term was due to begin on Monday week, but the evenings would still be light enough for her to ride when she came home, and there were the weekends – Beth racked her brains to think of ways by which she might keep Penny indoors then.

Meanwhile Penny's resentment at spending her days with paper patterns and meaningless pieces of material or, for a change, chasing dropped pins on the carpet, turned to bitter misery as it dawned on her that dressmaking was merely an excuse to keep her from Sherry. To punish her. For what, Penny couldn't imagine, and she was too over awed by Beth's air of stern preoccupation to ask.

Beth herself found the situation restricting. It was irritating to have to drag Penny with her when she needed to go out, and it wasn't always convenient to leave the gardening until Penny was in bed. And her daughter's silent distress tore at Beth's heartstrings too, but she steeled herself to continue her private guardianship. It was all up to her. Meanwhile the sewing-room offered fine views to front and rear; if anyone was watching the house, Beth would know.

Penny's slumped shoulders and listlessness finally warned Duncan that his daughter was finding life unusually irksome.

'Penny isn't making her dress herself, is she?' he asked. 'She looks as though she's all the cares of the world on her shoulders.'

'Of course she isn't sewing her own dress!' Beth

165

laughed. 'I wish she *could* help. It's taking longer than I'd anticipated.'

'Well, she hasn't ridden since Saturday. I gather she spends her time with you in the sewing-room, when you aren't out somewhere together. What's stopping her riding in the evenings?'

'I don't want to risk the material smelling of Sherry while she's still being fitted,' Beth explained patiently.

'Why? Has she complained?'

'No. I asked her, that's all. How much longer will it take?'

'That depends on Penny herself,' Beth felt her irritation mounting. 'She isn't the easiest of children, with all her fads and fancies. Sherry will just have to wait.' Duncan stared at hearing such discordant heresies.

'She isn't happy,' he said at last. 'And *I'm* not happy about this, darling. I don't want you put to such trouble when you've so much else to do. Farm out the dress if you can't be finished, say, by tomorrow.'

'I can't promise anything,' Beth told him brusquely. 'If other people pulled their weight I'd have more time to concentrate on Penny's dress – '

'Beth, that's not fair,' Duncan protested. 'At least let Penny out when you don't need her. Can't you arrange the fittings for early in the day, before she rides? Darling, I've never known you so apparently unreasonable! You've been jumpy and quite unlike yourself since Sunday. You're behaving as though you're *afraid* to allow Penny out. What's bothering you?'

'Oh, for heaven's *sake*!' Beth leapt to her feet. 'Haven't I enough on my mind without you inventing things for me to worry about?' She went, leaving

166

Duncan quite as hurt and bewildered as Penny.

The following afternoon, Wednesday, while Beth was painstakingly hand-stitching a seam, the sewing-room door opened and Jennetta stood there, happy and smiling.

'*Here* you both are!'

Penny gaped in surprise, then flew to her and wrapped her arms around Jennetta's waist. 'And I'm pleased to see you too!' Jennetta laughed, ruffling Penny's hair. Her sister wasn't usually so demonstrative.

'What on earth are you doing here?' Beth was momentarily nonplussed.

'Surely I told you I'd be home today? Gran and Pops send their love, and Alan was a smash-hit, is my news. How's the dress going? I thought you'd be finished by now – you're usually so quick. I looked for you in the paddock, Penny.'

'She's been a great help to me in here the past few days,' Beth murmured.

'Has she?' Jennetta gazed down into Penny's tight little face. 'I could murder a cup of tea, Penny. Will you make us some?' Penny scurried out. The sense of having walked into the same thunderstorm that had broken on Sunday grew on Jennetta.

'Isn't Penny well?' she asked, glancing around the room.

'Bored. Fittings aren't her favourite pastime,' Beth smiled meaningly.

'Poor Penny! And the machine's broken down too.' Jennetta moved away from the door.

'Machine?' Beth looked up vaguely. 'No?'

'Then why're you sewing that seam by hand? And this,' Jennetta picked over pieces of Penny's dress.

'You've done it all by hand so far. No wonder Penny looks as though the stuffing's been knocked out of her.' Jennetta sank into the old basketchair. 'Have you set yourself a penance or something, Mum?' After a moment Beth put down her work with a sigh.

'I can't think of another way to keep Penny from riding,' she admitted. 'I'm terrified she'll have an accident on the roads, or that *some*thing'll go wrong just before the wedding. You don't want it spoiled or put off at the last moment.'

'Good God, I don't want it at all, if this is what it means to Penny!' Jennetta burst out. Whilst she couldn't share Duncan's vision of her mother as a fragile petal, Jennetta knew Beth had her odd doubts and hang-ups and could also be obsessive. There had been times in her childhood when it had puzzled Jennetta to follow her mother's reasoning. 'Over-conscientious', she'd grown to think of her. This Penny business appeared to be an extreme example.

'What I mean is,' Jennetta said firmly, 'that I'd rather have a registry office wedding than have my last weeks with Penny spoiled. She likes the idea of my marriage little enough and this is torturing her.' She swept aside Beth's protest. 'I'm amazed you haven't noticed. We'll sort out something about the riding, but unless you finish that thing quickly I'll tell Alan the big wedding's off. He'll agree when he understands why – that it's putting too much strain on you. It was selfish of me not to've thought of that at the beginning.'

Beth had a fleeting sense of being defeated by her own heredity. This was a rerun of Jennetta's confrontation with Duncan when, half amused, she'd recognised herself in her daughter's determination – blackmail, virtually. Jennetta meant what she said. Beth's annoyance at her ultimatum suddenly dissolved into resignation. She even felt relief that Penny's burden had been eased from her lone shoulders. The past few days had been a fearful strain, Beth realised.

'I've set my heart on your wedding,' she said shakily. 'What should we do about Penny?'

'Compromise,' Jennetta replied quickly. 'Penny can practise her jumping in the paddock – she's far too competent to come to any harm there – and she can have her friends over. But she's not to ride out alone, OK?'

'It's time you were home,' Beth smiled. 'I just got everything out of proportion. Give Penny a hand-up with the tea-tray, will you, darling, and I'll get out the machine. And on Saturday we'll have a hunt for your dress,' she added gaily, struck by a sudden idea. 'I'm really looking forward to that.'

'Wouldn't a weekday be better?' Jennetta hesitated in the doorway. 'Marginally less of a crush?'

'Eh? Oh – but Daddy'll be here for Penny on Saturday,' Beth reminded.

That page was turned but the chapter wasn't closed. The nightmare interlude of the sewing-room was permanently registered in Penny's mind as an example of the inexplicable misbehaviour grown-ups can get away with. She accepted her partial release gratefully, as the necessary first step back to her old freedom, and the completion of her dress – she couldn't care less now how she looked in it – confirmed the end of her worst agony. Penny clamped on her hat, stepped into her boots and got on with her own life.

Duncan couldn't regard the episode with the same rugged insouciance. The memory of how Beth's normally gentle voice had modulated to strident, how her aquamarine eyes had sharpened to colourless ice when he'd tried to intervene on Penny's behalf, caused him an emotional shudder. He decided, however, that he'd been wrong to leave so much to Beth and then step in merely to criticise. Her momentary and uncharacteristic exasperation was understandable. Duncan searched anxiously for ways to save Beth over-burdening herself.

From what she'd seen, Beth's behaviour hadn't seemed so out of character to Jennetta but it never crossed her mind to compare notes with Duncan. They had their own ways of protecting Beth. But the 'Penny business' bothered Jennetta for she had suffered from her mother's fiercely protective instinct. She could still remember her sense of freedom, somehow illicit, at making her first uncensored friendships when she started at school. Now it looked very much as though, with her elder daughter away, Beth might revert to that stifling kind of love for her younger. Jennetta considered ways of making their approaching separation less of a strain for Beth and therefore easier for Penny.

For Beth herself all was now quite straightforward. Satisfied that Penny would hardly ever be alone, at least as long as she did as she'd promised, and that the house wasn't being watched, there remained only to discover from where the perceived threat had come. She needed to identify, or eliminate from her suspicions, the balding man and his family. Only then could she plan what action to take. Jennetta's wedding, maybe her whole future, was at stake.

# Ten

In the hopes of breaking the back of their shopping before the day grew unbearably hot, Beth and Jennetta caught an early train to Town on Saturday. Duncan wanted to accompany them, to carry bags and generally minister, but Beth refused his offer firmly. Then, in case he should think of playing a round of golf instead,

'I want you to keep an eye on Penny,' she explained quietly so that Jennetta shouldn't hear. 'Meg Lyon says there're some unsavoury characters hanging about. You know what Penny is. She'll talk to anyone who admires Sherry.' The paddock was hedged with hawthorn and a line of poplars on the downland side, but it could be vulnerable to a determined infiltrator from that open land. Duncan looked serious. 'Unsavoury characters' weren't unprecedented even in Connaught Drive, although they usually coincided with race meetings.

'So this is what's been worrying you. Why on earth didn't you – '

'And anyway,' Jennetta broke in archly, 'no one's to see the dress until The Day. Then I'll burst upon you in all my glory.'

'As far as I'm concerned,' Duncan grinned, 'you'd do well enough just as you are in that shift thing.'

'Shift!' Jennetta and Beth squealed in unison. They giggled their way out to the car squeaking 'Camisole!' and 'Liberty bodice!' at each other between gasps for breath.

171

I'll miss this heavenly silliness, thought Beth dully as they crossed the car park to the station a few minutes later. Duncan was right, though, she noticed. Jennetta's simple white cotton dress set off her tan and figure to perfection. She might have stepped straight out of a seductive health advertisement on her way from a top-class fashion house.

'Have you a particular style in mind?' Beth asked as they dived for the Underground at Victoria.

'I noticed a few possibilities last Saturday but I'm open to suggestion. I think I'll know it when I see it – and fit it – but it could be a long hike, I'm afraid, Mum.' But for once Beth, who was hunting on her own account, was prepared to dawdle through all the necessary shops in and around Regent Street and Oxford Street until Jennetta had found exactly what she wanted. She had no worries about her daughter's taste.

'Do you get the feeling you've been here before?' Jennetta grinned as they took their bearings at Oxford Circus.

'Better success this time, I hope,' Beth returned. 'This way –' She darted over a crossing and Jennetta skipped hurriedly after. From then on, however, it was Jennetta who led while Beth followed, alert and noticing. Her usual progress in Town was a scurry from shop to shop as if they were just closing, her head down and eyes to herself.

Beth left it to Jennetta to choose for herself what she wanted to try on – as far as was possible in the face of high-pressure salesmanship – while she perched on velvet-seated gilt chairs, watching the other customers and waiting to be regaled. And Jennetta punctually

172

swept in and out of curtained cubicles – like an up-market Swiss toy, Beth smiled to herself – saying 'No', or 'Maybe. What do you think, Mum?' in front of long mirrors; while assistants cooed encouragingly and swore they'd never seen the dress look so well.

They probably hadn't; and nor had Jennetta looked so well, Beth considered. She was tall and well shaped, easy to fit and with a natural dignity, while the sparkle in her eyes wouldn't be dimmed if she dressed in a sack. As it was, satin, silk, lace, brocade – she enhanced them all. Jennetta was loving every minute. And Beth, like a sly procuress, watched those who watched Jennetta.

In the end she was satisfied she'd found the very dress and Beth, who hadn't bothered all morning to look at prices, wrote out the cheque with less thought than if she'd been composing a shopping-list. Her daughter's engaging preening was, after all, little more than a sideshow to the real business of the day.

'Crikey, Mum! A mere bagatelle?' Jennetta was awed. 'You rolled off those noughts as if they were nothing! But – are you sure? That third one'd suit me almost as well.'

'Almost isn't quite,' Beth murmured absently. 'Now then, your accessories.'

Jennetta tried on and chose for herself the precisely suitable accessories she needed while Beth wrote out cheques when prompted.

'You'll stun them, darling,' she said simply when at last she surveyed her daughter in the complete outfit. She wished it could have been a day of undivided delight for both of them; for after all, there was nothing personal or intimate in the semiautomatic signing of cheques.

Beth was suddenly conscious of having missed out even on the naughty thrill of a lavish splurge. All she'd get from that, she thought wryly, would be a nasty turn when she totted up at the end of the day. She'd just have to remind herself that the cheque-stubs were at least in part fulfilment of her long-standing ambition for Jennetta.

'What a marvellous day it's been!' Jennetta enthused happily when everything was packed up. 'We've got everything – *look* at all those parcels! – and I'm in raptures over everything we've got. *Thank* you and Dad! I *wish* he didn't have to wait to see all this. And Penny. I'm *dying* to show it off!'

'Save your powder,' Beth smiled. 'Tea, now, I think. Back to Dickins & Jones. Come on.'

'With all this lot?' Jennetta asked in astonishment. 'I thought you'd want to get straight back home.'

'Faint-heart never won fair tea-cake,' Beth said briskly, threading her fingers through various carrier handles. 'I'll leave the dress-box to you, darling,' she added with a sidelong grin. It looked heavy and unwieldy.

'Forward, then,' Jennetta laughed. 'And the tea's on me.'

The restaurant was more crowded than on the previous Saturday, but Beth found two seats at a table for four against the wall. When the occupied chairs became free they piled their parcels on to them.

'Too easy to overlook one on the floor. That's why I didn't want a table for two,' Beth explained.

'And effective also in repelling boarders,' Jennetta, who wanted to talk, added gleefully as she mounded pyramids of parcels. 'Now, you may have whatever you

174

like for being such a patient little Mum. Actually, I didn't want to try on *half* those things but they *push* stuff at you so. And everything's so marvellous on – to listen to them. I mean, I know they can't say, "Modom, that makes you look like the back end of a pantomime horse", but why *force* things on you that're obviously unsuitable or not what you want? You didn't see that taffeta underskirt – it was *deafening*.'

'Mm. Like estate agents,' Beth murmured vaguely, momentarily surfacing.

'Yerwot?'

'They push things. You ask about a two-bedroom flat and for the next eighteen months they send you details of anything but. Laura was telling me.'

'Yes – well,' Jennetta mentally felt around for lost threads. 'And *did* you see that poor kid in a sort of segmented frilly tube? She was as broad as she was long and it made her look like a rubber Michelin Man. In drag. But her mother was ecstatic! Honestly, I wanted to –'

Jennetta's happiness and excitement bubbled over in a torrent while Beth quietly detached herself. The restaurant was her last hope. In widening sweeps she scanned the crowds for a face she knew; then started again, working from their table outwards. Once or twice she failed to hear what Jennetta said and had to be prompted. But when her daughter suggested,

'Shall we go, Mum? I've already been to pay,' and Beth didn't answer, Jennetta too lapsed into silence, puzzled and watchful.

It wasn't like Beth to prolong a day in Town and risk catching the early evening crush when the shops shut. Her mother was knackered after all their tramping about, Jennetta decided, and didn't want to make a fuss, typically. She waited for Beth to recover, but she soon realised to her amazement that her mother was expecting someone. That seemed to explain her choice of a table for four more convincingly. Thoroughly intrigued by now, Jennetta waited to see what would transpire.

'Move the parcels off the chairs, darling.' Beth was suddenly animated and waving to someone across the room. Jennetta craned to see who'd been invited to join them. Her mother's friends were local; the neighbours, parents of her daughters' friends, mothers running school lifts – and intimate only as far as her reserve outside the family permitted. But it was a complete stranger to Jennetta who walked towards their table with a hesitant smile: a smartly dressed blonde woman, a little older than her mother. Jennetta was even more surprised to find that the woman was a stranger to her mother as well, and yet she'd seemed expected.

'You were waving to me, I hope?'

'I hadn't realised how crowded the place had become until I saw you looking for a table. I'm afraid we've been hogging more chairs than we need. Wedding-clothes – for my daughter, Jennetta,' Beth explained, introducing her. Jennetta's amazement increased. She'd never seen her mother so relaxed with a stranger. 'I remember you here last Saturday. Are you alone today?' So, just a chance encounter after all, Jennetta decided.

'Oof! You've saved my life!' The woman sat down with relief. 'Congratulations!' she smiled at Jennetta. 'Or should it be felicitations? When's the great day?'

After a polite exchange the woman ordered her tea and turned back to Beth.

176

'I went through this a couple of years ago – lovely but *exhausting*! I'm Anna, by the way.'

'Yes, you were here for tea last Saturday,' Beth found herself impatiently rattling on. 'With your family.'

'Mm, my daughter – off the hook for a long weekend. This is my weekly treat, window-shopping and tea here. Saturdays are such a *drag* when you're on your own. Sundays I laze and recover.'

'Oh – I thought that was *your* husband with you last Saturday.'

'Did you?' Anna murmured vaguely. 'No, nor my daughter's.'

It was on the tip of Beth's tongue to ask, 'Are you sure?' she felt so disoriented. And more suspicious.

'What a – a silly mistake. There was a man with you and I thought –' Beth trailed off, suddenly aware of Jennetta's embarrassment and the woman's distant expression.

'Oh, but so there was!' Anna brightened. 'I remember now. He was only someone who asked to share the table, though. And now I remember noticing you then, too. Was that your husband – big, blond and hunky?' Jennetta sputtered with laughter and Anna gave her a friendly grin. 'And there was a fair-haired girl with you too, wasn't there? Your younger daughter? She's very like you.'

Anna laughed suddenly and tapped Beth's arm in an intimate gesture that startled her.

'You'll think it ridiculous, but when that man came to sit with us I wondered if he had, well, designs! No, really, I've had some. They say London's a lonely place for a single woman, but I can't say I've found that – the

177

brutes!' She made an unconscious preening movement of her shoulders. 'But the laugh was on me in the end, because he was more interested in your table than ours. There's an unmistakable radiance about a bride-to-be, isn't there? Even my plain Jane was transformed – as who wouldn't be. Frank was quite a catch. What does your lucky young man do, my dear?'

That prompted enough chat between them to leave Beth to herself for a while to consider what Anna had said. The balding man had been alone, then, or Anna wouldn't have mentioned his interest in Beth's family. So why was he waiting outside the store, but for them? Beth's eyes flitted about the room again, but there was no sign of him and there hadn't been all day.

Anna's explanation for the man's presence at her table sounded genuine, Beth brooded, studying her covertly. She couldn't help noticing again the ugly, fish-belly scars on her hand. In spite of her rings and her stylish clothes, Anna's speech – never mind her manner – echoed what Beth had learnt to recognise as 'common' overtones; so perhaps the scars were the result of some industrial accident. She was probably a factory girl, Beth imagined hazily, who'd married well.

The sense of recognition when she'd noticed Anna the previous Saturday had now grown to one of familiarity, partly fostered by the woman's casually friendly conversation. But the positive voice, the (controlled) local accent, the sod-you confidence – Beth had known women like Anna. Hard as nails. Survivors. That's what was so familiar, Beth realised.

'Well, I must get back to my cat,' Anna said at last. 'One of the advantages of a mews cottage over a flat.

178

You're terribly lucky not to have to be house-hunting at today's lunatic prices,' she told Jennetta as she stood up to go. 'Goodbye and good luck. It's been lovely talking to you both. Perhaps we'll meet again?' Anna smiled at Beth. No one spoke to her and no one followed her out, Beth saw.

'I can believe she's never lonely, the vulgar way she gossips with strangers,' she commented.

'Mum, how acid!' Jennetta grinned. 'But you did call her over and make her feel wanted. I think she gossips because she's lonely, actually. I liked her.' But Beth wasn't listening.

'A taxi, I think. It'll be hell on the tube with all this stuff. Let's go.' Suddenly she couldn't bear the faceless crowds; full of eyes, she sensed, assessing her. *Planning*.

Beth was withdrawn and silent at first on the journey home. She realised that Jennetta felt the anticlimax badly – the glow had faded from her face – but she couldn't keep her mind off her worries. It could be to Jennetta's advantage, lumbered with the Nicholls name as she was, to have the worries resolved, Beth excused herself. Any sniff of a blackmail attempt – not that Nick's friends or her own family, whoever they might be, had anything to blackmail Beth with. Quite the contrary. But the last thing she wanted was someone out of Nick's life or from her own childhood to get in touch, for whatever reason and however friendly the intention. With the wedding announced in two major dailies and banns published in the church, the Masterses were no longer private people. Even if some form of blackmail wasn't intended, the effect would be the same just before

179

Jennetta's wedding.

Beth was shocked suddenly to realise that her fear of a planned abduction had somehow reduced through attempted blackmail to mere contact, in spite of her recent dread at hearing that the balding man hadn't been one of an innocent family party. How illogical can you get, she wondered disgustedly, trying to unravel the course of her paranoia during the past week. Fear for a good reason was understandable but her panic had hopped about like a spring bunny, unable to decide on which unlikely reason. And that was unreasonable. She'd spoiled the shopping expedition for herself and now she was upsetting Jennetta – and all for nothing. Beth felt ashamed of herself and especially horrified when she remembered the way she'd bullied Penny.

Perhaps her return to sanity had been inspired by Anna's supremely commonplace natter over the teacups. There's nothing like normality in others for pointing up your own silliness, Beth decided. She could see now what was at the bottom of her over-reaction to what Duncan had said about the balding man; she was simply afraid that anything would happen to mar Jennetta's wedding, from a cold to a kidnapping. Jennetta's marriage into secure respectability was, for Beth, the culmination of her own development since – well, certainly since Nick's death.

Beth remembered with a private smile Jennetta's earliest, unprompted, steps along this path at her first school 'do', a production of *Toad of Toad Hall*. She'd latched on to the man sitting next to her in the audience and was inclined to cling grimly through the interval. Somebody's father, Beth had assumed. She'd apolo-

180

gised for her daughter's importunity, intending to yank her off for some pop and a bun. But Jennetta had already conducted her own interview and learned that Duncan was nobody's father but merely a guest. He'd been good-humouredly ready to oblige a little girl with a surrogate for the evening; for everyone had a visible father, Jennetta had discovered by then. So 'Jennetta's pick-up' Duncan had become, and remained; flattered to pieces by her calm appropriation of him and increasingly fascinated by her courageous mother.

Jennetta could certainly pick them, Beth reflected, amused. Duncan's house was the old family home on the outskirts of Epsom, double-fronted, roomy and spaciously set; a paradise after the flat. Where others had sold off land for bungalows to crouch in the shadow of their stately Victorian forebears, Duncan's family had not only cannily held on to what it had but increased it when immediate neighbours were tempted to sell their too-large gardens for building plots. There was enough for a decent paddock when Penny started nagging for a pony. So far had Beth come, who not so many days before was miserably remembering her childhood lack of dry clothing. She had so much more to lose.

And now there was Alan, about to become something – and no doubt in time Someone – in the Consular Service. Beth wasn't certain how minor his status or precisely what his function was, but neither mattered. It was enough that her daughter would be out of reach of anyone who might pull her down. And out of Beth's reach too, while they were abroad, but that would be borne. And meanwhile they were nearly home, she saw. Her heart lifted again.

'Darling, I'm so happy for you!' Beth turned impulsively to Jennetta.

'I know, Mum. Don't worry. Today's shopping's finally brought it home to you, hasn't it?' She'd been trying to find a reasonable explanation for her mother's moody behaviour, Beth realised, cringeing. 'I've been wanting to ask – can Penny stay up for dinner when Alan and his family come on Wednesday week? It is a family affair and I'd like her to be there. So what if she's tired the next day. I'm sure she'll want to if you suggest it.' Oh, God. Say it with nails!

'I was going to talk to Daddy about it,' Beth said smoothly, accepting Jennetta's cue to make up to Penny for her beastliness over that bloody dress.

Satisfied, Jennetta changed the subject.

'Did you notice the scars on Anna's hand? From where I was sitting I could see more scarring under her hair, by her ear. A car-smash, maybe? She was lucky not to lose a finger or be disfigured. I nearly died when she said she had to get back to her cat in her mews cottage!' Jennetta laughed. 'Are you going to tell His Hunkyness what a hit he made with her?' She was the best kind of daughter, Beth thought warmly. Jennetta always accepted olive branches and made them take root.

'I wonder what she does for a living?' Beth was anxious to show a friendly interest now.

'But she told us, Mum.' Jennetta glanced at her curiously. 'She runs a private business school for women, a sort of young executives' Lucy Clayton. Motto: Don't Get Mad, Get On. She must be pretty high-powered. But weren't you listening? I thought that's why you found her a bit – strong.'

'Gossipy and inquisitive, certainly. Why "strong"?'

'Well, she said,' Jennetta grinned, ' "I make sure they end up with diplomas and balls if I have to staple them on"!'

'Jennetta!' Beth recoiled.

'You did ask, Mum!'

But Beth had heard the echo of a tight little voice say furiously,

'I'll make him stop – if I have to nail his balls to the floor!' It was an unpleasant, not even very appropriate memory, and made more shocking by Jennetta's laughter. Beth wiped it away like a film of filth on a window pane.

# Eleven

Duncan was looking out for them when Beth and Jennetta returned home.

'Oh, Dad! We've got the most heavenly things!' Jennetta swooped at him as he came down the steps to meet them. 'Thank you!'

'Thank your proud Mama,' Duncan grinned, hugging her. 'Success, then?' He glanced at Beth.

'Every ball a coconut,' she told him happily, opening the Polo's tail-gate with a flourish.

'Gawd!'

'Well, some of it's for Penny,' Jennetta murmured as she hauled out packages and hung them around Duncan.

'But I thought her outfit was finished?'

'By no means,' said Beth, tenderly laying the dress-box across Jennetta's arms. 'She must have gloves. Where is she?'

'Clearing up. We called it a day just before you arrived. We've clipped the hedge,' Duncan cast up his eyes as they went indoors, 'and thank God for electric clippers. We've drained, degreened and refilled the trough. We've swept out the stable, cleaned the tack and polished and trimmed Sherry 'til I'm dead on my feet and weak from hunger. You two've had it easy.' And glancing at him, Beth thought he did look tired.

'Supper in half an hour,' she soothed. 'Just help Jennetta up to her room with that lot first – but no peeping, mind!'

Beth heard them meet Penny on the stairs.

'Do I blind you with my bride-to-be radiance, little sister?'

'I can see you're terribly hot in that engagement ring, if that's what you mean. Did you get your Carmen heated tiara?'

'*And* a super *rustly*, hooped, looped and drooped underskirt for *you*, Penny!'

'Wow, thanks,' came Penny's dispassionate reply, and Beth laughed quietly to herself as she went into the kitchen.

After the girls had gone to bed the light-hearted mood of the evening collapsed in a way that Beth had failed to anticipate.

'I phoned Meg Lyon when you'd left for Town,' Duncan began casually.

'M? What about?' Beth sat relaxed, her shoes off and her feet on a stool.

'Well, after what you told me, I naturally wanted to know more. Meg, however, has heard nothing at all of any shady characters hanging around.' Beth swung her feet down and sat straight. 'Look, I know something's been worrying you all week,' Duncan went on gently. 'Won't you tell me what it is, darling? Haven't I a right to know?' Beth wrung out an apologetic smile.

'It's nothing, Duncan, really. I let myself get in a tizz about – oh, about silly things. Like not being ready for the wedding, or the wedding having to be put off if Penny had a bad fall. But now that Jennetta's clothes are all bought I'm feeling much more optimistic. Fine, in fact. I'm sorry I let it worry you.' Beth held out a hand to him but Duncan didn't take it. Instead he stared hard at

186

her for a moment.

'Beth, if that were all you'd have told me – spelled it out as you just have. You'd have explained to Penny, instead of issuing unlikely fiats and confusing her. You wouldn't then have had to invent those shady characters.' Beth dropped her eyes. 'But actually, they're not pure invention, are they?' Duncan startled her by asking. 'I've been thinking it out all afternoon. Ever since our shopping trip last Saturday you've been behaving as though you knew of some – threat.' Beth shook her head numbly. 'That's how it's seemed to me. *Did* you, in fact, see someone in Town you recognised? Or perhaps you realised you'd been seen by someone you knew. That chap I pointed out to you? Isn't it the fear of just *that*, and not the crowds, that makes you so anxious in Town?'

Duncan waited for Beth to answer, and when she didn't he continued with the air of a man jumping without a parachute.

'You've never kept in touch with anyone from the days before we were married, even your foster-parents. Or so I've believed. I've always supposed that for some reason you *wanted* to cut yourself off.' Beth drew her feet up under her, curling up in self-defence, and watched Duncan like a rabbit with a stoat. He left his chair for the footstool and gripped Beth's clasped hands between his own.

'Darling, I've never questioned you about your early life and your first marriage. Maybe you've thought I wasn't interested, but you've told me what you've seen fit and that's been enough for me to know it wasn't an easy life. In fact a tragic one. I don't want to – to *pry* now, but if there's something in the past that makes you so

187

uneasy then I must know. Because you *are* bothered, darling, and unhappy.' Duncan gave Beth's hands a little shake. She saw that it was at least as much to steady himself as to reassure her.

'Here you are, working so hard for Jennetta's wedding,' he went on gently. 'I've wondered if you're preoccupied with thoughts of Nick? Of *course* that would be understandable. And perhaps Jennetta wishes that her own father could be at her wedding. That would be understandable too. It should be *Nick* giving her away next month. Perhaps you share her regrets. At a time like this your memories must be full of regrets.'

Beth knew she should stop him. Duncan looked so earnestly sympathetic and felt so hurt, but she couldn't find the words or the necessary physical response. She just crouched in her chair, fascinated and appalled.

'I can see from your face that I'm somewhere near the mark,' Duncan said humbly. 'But none of this explains why you've been so – distracted,' he added after a moment. 'So I'm even wondering–even thought of something that *could* cause embarrassment, whatever your feelings. You see, I can't be certain now just how much of what Jennetta and I have accepted about Nick is true. Not since you explained about his invented parents. So - I've even wondered if Nick himself has been in touch with you.'

'Nick?' Beth uncoiled like a spring so that Duncan sat hastily back. '*Nick* in touch with me?'

For a moment she stared, unable to believe that Duncan could talk so wildly.

'Are you mad? Nick was smashed up in his car three months before Jennetta was born. I've told you. He was so dead it wasn't easy to identify him. *I* identified him. But I didn't recognise the woman who died with him – and nor did I ever learn who she was. Nick had irons in the fire I knew nothing about until after he was dead.' Beth clasped her head and rocked in a brief anguish. 'I've never told you how the accident happened.' She dropped her hands. 'They found his flies open when they cut him free, and – and other evidence that his mind hadn't been on his driving,' Beth moderated her description at the sight of Duncan's shocked expression.

But it hadn't been merely Nick's infidelity that had nearly destroyed her; it was the ugly manner of his betrayal and death that had left her hating him. He'd deprived her of any pretence of romance in her life. The realisation that all these years Duncan had actually sentimentalised her feelings for Nick made Beth feel physically unwell.

'No, I don't hanker to have Nick at Jennetta's wedding,' she said steadily. 'Spare yourself that thought. But do you wonder that I invented a father for Jennetta who would never disgust her, his parents at a safe distance she wouldn't constantly expect to meet? English parents, by the way, so there's no question of her nationality. And do you wonder that I never poured all this out to you? As for Jennetta wanting her father at the wedding – she said only the other day that she's no regrets that it'll be you walking her up the aisle. *That's* true.'

Duncan had never realised that Beth could be so angry. She hardly raised her voice but he felt her fury – not directed at him, thank God – and it shocked him to see her so emotional. He wanted to believe that her outburst would be cathartic for both of them and he started towards her with words of sympathy and tenderness, ready to close the subject. Beth hadn't finished, however.

'Look in my writing-case in the desk. You've never asked to see it but now you must. A copy of Nick's death certificate is in there.' Impatiently Beth went to the desk herself. 'And you'd better know the rest now.' She handed Duncan the certificate and dropped back in her chair. 'When Nick died I quite thought I'd be out on the street. I thought the flat was rented and there was no way I could've continued paying rent. But the flat was his. It wasn't even mortgaged. I found the legal details of that, at least, among his things. But there was no will, so the flat became mine. And something else I found, a valid passport with ten £20 notes inside. I assumed it was Nick's from the photo, but it wasn't in his name. If he had other personal papers he didn't keep them at the flat.

'So I've never known for certain if the man I married really was Andrew Nicholls, as stated on my marriage certificate, or why he needed two names. Or whether he really was a quantity surveyor, as he told me and as I put on Jennetta's birth certificate. I didn't even know which firm to notify of his death. No one ever contacted me about him. I knew nothing about him before we were married and even less after he was dead. I didn't try to find out anything, either, because how would it have helped to know, perhaps, that my marriage wasn't legal. Nor my possession of the flat.' A possession she was always terrified might be challenged.

'But Jennetta was too old when we married ever to forget her own surname or the stories I'd fed her about her father's family, stories that gave her a coherent background if anyone needed to know. Alan, for instance. I've regretted it since that she didn't take your name, but I didn't want her to feel that anything had been camouflaged. I wanted her never to feel ashamed of her birth or of her family – and I don't want her to feel it now, of all times.' Beth steadied her voice and spoke more composedly.

'When you said that man last Saturday apparently followed us about, I was suddenly afraid that one of Nick's friends had recognised me and – and would resurrect all that old nausea and spoil the wedding. Duncan, I was even afraid that they might – use Penny in some way. Underworld stuff,' she smiled self-deprecatingly. 'Nick was obviously involved in something illegal, you see. *Now* it seems a ridiculous panic, but you're right – I have always been afraid of running into any of that crowd. I wish I'd explained, but I didn't want to tell you all this about Nick unnecessarily. You can understand that.'

Beth had destroyed the passport, but the £200 and the last of her own savings tided her over until Jennetta was a few weeks old. What there was in Nick's bank account covered the funeral and legal expenses with very little over. But at least she had the flat, and although she'd have preferred to sell it and move right away it was more than she had the energy for at the time. Later she came to appreciate its bland suburban location; a virtue that covered a multitude of sins, as she already knew, and might even have prompted Nick to settle there in the first place.

Beth had thought it surprising that Nick should have had anything so permanent in his life as the flat, bought outright. But it was actually more in character that he hadn't landed himself with the regular drain of rent or

191

mortgage repayments – and both required proof of a steady job anyway. Nick's bank statements showed past bursts of solvency but no evidence of a regular income.

Beth had moved her and the baby's things into the sitting-room and let the two bedrooms to single women. She stayed carefully aloof, trying to keep her child as placid as possible and using the kitchen and bathroom when the others were out. Her arrangements had worked, but only at a cost to herself and with a fortunately less permanent effect on Jennetta. She'd grown up shy and clinging, a solemn-eyed child who was too quiet. School had sorted that, however, as well as freeing Beth for a part-time job.

The elderly manageress of the craft-shop that Beth had kept intermittently supplied with exhibition knitting and needlework, a widow, had long before offered her a regular job as an assistant. When Jennetta started at school Beth gratefully accepted the offer and considered herself fortunate. The rate of pay wasn't high, but it enabled her to dispense with one of her lodgers and claw back more living-space in the flat. The hours permitted her to escort Jennetta to and from school, and the widow's generosity allowed Beth to bring her child with her during school holidays. Jennetta would sit out of the way in the tiny back room, where there were a couple of chairs and a one-bar fire, with her felt-pens and books. They'd meet like conspirators over their sandwiches at lunch. They used to make a game of it.

But as well as these advantages, the shop put Beth back in touch with humanity. She might have been the part-time employee, but Beth was also the consultant expert; a dual role through which she gradually won back the confidence and sense of being accepted that Nick's death had shocked out of her. As educating was her quiet study of the subtle social nuances that less obviously distinguished her customers. It was from the widow, an archetypal 'gentlewoman', that Beth first learnt the difference between genteel and gentility.

No other job would have suited Beth's circumstances so well; certainly none for which she had recognised qualifications – fairly basic shorthand and typing. She was a newly appointed office-clerk in a car-hire firm when she first met Nick. They all called him Nick. Someone brought him to the office Christmas party and he'd done the rounds like a bee in a meadow. He'd singled Beth out in the end. She'd fallen for him so hard that it had hurt to breathe. Nothing had prepared her for such an intensity of feeling, such a wholesale abandonment of preconceived notions. Nick was a man ten years older than herself who seemed to move in a nimbus of glamour and sophistication against which she'd learnt no defence. Actually a cheap, brash showman, but how would she know? She'd been conned.

At the time she'd have done anything for him, and he must have known it. She certainly lied to him about her family – Mummy a former model, Daddy a solicitor. She'd got her own act together enough by then to be convincing; but he'd never mentioned her parents again, even in connection with their wedding – which should have given her pause for thought. But then, she didn't harp on about them herself.

Four months after that office party Beth knew she was pregnant.

'What'll you do?' he'd asked, casually plunging a

knife into her heart. She was too proud to let him see how stunned and hurt she was, how mistaken in her assumptions. Despair had swamped that pain a split second later as she recognised the steps of the familiar treadmill from which she'd not long freed herself.

'Go home to Mummy and Daddy, I suppose,' she shrugged, hardly able to speak.

'Why not get rid of it?'

'Because I love you!' She might as passionately have cried out, 'Because it's mine!' but probably without the same result.

'Best get you married, then,' Nick had grinned.

Beth had wondered since if he'd married her for the new experience or to prevent an inconvenient visit from her solicitor father. Or perhaps a wife and child actually provided him with some sort of cover in a more dubious ploy than the adultery he had in mind.

Life hadn't taught Beth optimism or brought her much happiness until she met Nick. That's what had made him so special. His defection, leaving her with possible hassle from his associates and even from the Law, was deadly. It had taken all Beth's courage to survive it and prevent it from tainting Jennetta. She hadn't looked for someone like Duncan, wanting no one herself now and trusting no one, but Duncan had unwittingly offered himself as the perfect antidote to Nick.

Even so, it took her more than two years to step off her private life-raft and accept him and his background of people so different from her own. She'd grown wiser since Nick's death – she'd had to – and by dint of waiting for her cues with her mouth shut and her eyes open, Beth managed to pass and then to be accepted herself.

194

Her worst test was in meeting Duncan's parents. Beth didn't know it then, but they were prejudiced in her favour before ever seeing her, since they'd pretty well given up hope for their stodgy only child. His late blossoming was Beth's chief recommendation. And since Jennetta was entirely lovable and loving, Duncan's parents were glad to welcome them both. The home front had been conquered and was safely held.

After the wedding Beth sold the flat. Some of the money she put aside for emergencies. Her second marriage might survive no better than her first. Some she spent on Jennetta and herself, on clothes and possessions that befitted Duncan's wife and child, unwilling that he should meet all the expenses incurred by his second-hand family and perhaps come to resent it. In Beth's experience favours were like scorpions: they trailed stings. And some she'd reserved towards Jennetta's wedding. A proper wedding.

That was now at hand. In spite of her past misfortunes, Beth might justifiably claim that she'd led a charmed life complete with story-book ending. She didn't however, care to be reminded of her earlier troubles. But in recent weeks their memory had repeatedly materialised, like something out of Elsinore, in a way that disconcerted Beth. While Duncan believed that her confidences had cleared the air, Beth could only regret the release of so many poisons from the Pandora's box of her past. The effect on her was the reverse of therapeutic, as Duncan imagined it must be; instead she felt soiled and dishonoured by their publication. Beth was oppressed too by the feeling that the past was being revived – nourished – with words, a corpse transfused with living blood. That image didn't make for pleasant dreams.

And she had one other worry. For the present Duncan was relieved and even grateful that in the end Beth had confided in him, and he'd exerted all his tenderness to make her comfortable again. The fact remained that she'd been forced to resurrect that old story because Duncan had caught her out in a stupid, hasty lie. Whatever her unwillingness, she would have retained at least her dignity by explaining her fears to him from the start, but as it was she'd risked her credibility and his trust. Beth's deception of Jennetta all those years might be understandable, but being caught lying by Duncan didn't suit her image and did nothing for her confidence. For if Duncan were ever to think less of her, then where was the spring-board for her self-esteem?

Beth turned to her usual supports in times of self-doubt: routine, gardening and Jane Mallinson, who was a reliable barometer.

The Mallinsons were home again that weekend in time for the start of the Autumn term on Monday. Beth rang Jane on Sunday night to check the school lifts rota and invited her for coffee on Tuesday.

'It'll only be the two of us,' she added apologetically. 'The house is a tip just now.' It was the sort of disguised compliment that amused Jane.

'My dear, don't tell me! I felt as though I was going down for the third time – and occasionally wished I was,' Jane reassured with a laugh. So on Tuesday there was only Beth to listen appreciatively to Jane's account of their enjoyable boating holiday while she finished hemming Penny's dress.

'I'm sorry we had to pull Penny out at the last

moment,' Beth said easily, 'but I felt that I had to get her dress done before term started. There was simply nothing suitable for her in the shops.' Jane's reaction was gratifying.

'But Beth, it's lovely! *Far* better than any ready-made. She'll look sweet in it – she's got such a dear little face. What're you wearing?'

'I felt strangely drawn to a particular shade of pastel mintgreen I saw in Liberty's when I got Penny's material, but there isn't really time to get it made up. I'll have to wander out and hope to find something suitable off the peg. Care to come with me and give me the benefit of your Mother-of-the-Bride experience?'

'I'd love to, Beth! You must have a ferociously smart hat for a start.' Jane was enthusiastic. 'So, you're not superstitious about green at weddings, then?' Beth glanced up quickly.

'What supersitition?'

'My dear, it's supposed to bring bad luck – like emeralds. Though I should be so lucky,' Jane laughed. 'How's the organisation going?'

'Pretty well. It's now more or less only a question of pulling everything together at the right moment. Jennetta's stuff's all ready, thank heaven.'

'No cold feet on her part?'

'Lord, no!' Beth smiled at the idea. 'It's Duncan who's suffering from stage-fright. Jennetta's the life and soul of the household.'

'You're going to miss her, my dear,' Jane said quietly. Beth came to the end of her hemming and snipped off the thread.

'I hope she'll be as fortunate in her own daughters,'

she murmured, satisfied that her credibility still survived and reassured of Jane's friendship when she needed it.

By the time Colonel and Mrs Buckingham came to dinner with Alan and their younger son, Christopher, harmony had been so fully restored at home that Beth looked forward to the evening with unclouded pleasure. Penny's reaction to the suggestion that she should make one of the party had been satisfactory: she'd flushed beetroot and been struck dumb. 'Going out' was one thing, and plenty of her friends did that; but staying up for an adult dinner-party was something else. Beth and Duncan had already met Christopher, who was to be Alan's best man and was as exuberant as Alan was serious. It was going to be the sort of gathering Beth most enjoyed, small, cheerful and friendly, and where she knew everyone. As if in sympathy with her happy anticipation, the temperature had dropped during the past week but the days remained bright.

At Jennetta's suggestion Beth sat Penny next to Alan and, briefly listening in to their quiet conversation, was relieved to hear that Penny wasn't overawed by the occasion.

'Well, we *sort* of learn cookery. We've got a new teacher who calls it "Home Craft". She was expelled from Lucy Clayton's, you know, and of course nobody'd have her but Greenbanks – ' As well as putting Penny at her ease, Alan could be relied on to keep a straight face and not embarrass the child. Beth liked him more and more.

Her complacent mood began to disintegrate, however, when Alan had to cry off an outing with Jennetta.

'Sorry, I can't. I've got the Board that day. What about the day after?'

'What boring old Board?' Jennetta asked.

'For my security clearance. What about the day after?' Alan tried again.

'You'll have to be vetted too, Jennetta,' Christopher teased. 'I hope you've got a clean provisional driving-licence?'

'Is this something to do with your passport, Alan?' Beth asked vaguely as she started to clear away the main course. Alan had been born in Germany and she knew his birth had had to be registered at the British Consulate to confirm his nationality, or he might have been liable for German military service.

'No, just a character approval for the job,' Alan smiled at her.

By the time Beth had served the dessert and sat down again the subject had changed but not her interest.

'Tell me more about this Board, Alan.' She interrupted his discussion with Penny. 'What sort of details will they want to know about you?'

'Oh – I suppose that there's nothing in the background that might give someone a handle for blackmail – or for bribes, like a pile of debts. That sort of thing,' Alan replied casually.

'They'd hardly expect you to *admit* anything like that, though,' Jennetta laughed.

'Ah, but they use secret informers,' Christopher told her darkly. 'What'll *you* give me for the low-down on Alan?' he muttered behind his hand.

'Hear what Chris has to offer first,' Alan advised with

199

a grin and turned back to Penny. 'Yes, some of these imported saddles *are* cheaper but the trees can break too easily. Much better to go for a good second-hand English or German one, tell your friend.'

Beth had caught the look on Penny's face when she'd interrupted earlier, too full of her thoughts. Now she hid her impatience and waited for Alan to finish speaking.

'But seriously, Alan, they must actually investigate your private life, mustn't they? To find out about debts and things, I mean.'

'Oh – the Board.' His face cleared. 'Yes, I suppose so, but it doesn't worry me.'

'And I suppose they must check up on your friends too, as well as your family background?'

'Er – I imagine so.' Alan looked uncomfortable. 'But I don't really know what this interview involves. I believe it's standard practice, though, in the higher branches of the Civil Service. In the Forces too, isn't it, Dad?' The others had fallen silent, listening to the conversation between Beth and Alan.

'Certainly if you're serving abroad,' the Colonel agreed. 'They grew a little excited over your mother's Irish connections, I remember. I doubt if we'd have got away with it so easily now, my love,' he smiled at his wife. 'Laura's first husband came from County Cork,' he explained to Beth.

'So they investigated you, too, Laura,' Beth persisted. 'How interesting.'

'Well, pretty superficially, as Chaz says –' Laura began.

'And they must've looked into your first husband's history as well?'

200

'If they did, he wasn't inconvenienced,' Laura told her placidly.

Beth became aware at the same time of her own clumsiness and Duncan's efforts to turn the subject.

'Darling, I've been wondering if we wouldn't be more comfortable in the other room, now that we've all finished. Let's have our coffee in there.'

'Of course.' Beth flushed. 'Go on through, everyone, and I'll bring it in.' They moved out fast enough to convince her of their relief in getting away. She was dismally conscious that her interest in Alan's security check had grown tedious and finally embarrassing. For once she'd been guilty of social ineptitude.

# Twelve

Beth insisted on clearing up alone after the Buckinghams had gone and her family went to bed.

'I can't bear the kitchen left as it is, and you've all got a full day tomorrow.' She washed and dried the silver and glasses, put the rest through the dish-washer and cleared the table. Then she manically tidied the sitting-room. Soon she'd come to the end of what she might reasonably do at that time of night and then her mind would slip its collar and run wild. Beth knew she wouldn't sleep, tired though she was. Worse, she felt shaky and ill, as though she was going down with flu. For the last hour of her carefully planned dinner-party it had been a strain to present her usual social calm.

Beth put out the lights and opened the curtains over the patio doors. Far out into the night the windbreak of poplars that sheltered Sherry's paddock stood ranked against the spangled sky, the sentinels as well of her material achievements. Beth slumped into a chair and surrendered to the darkness.

How far would Alan's people vet Jennetta? And would they investigate Jennetta's family as well? Had the investigation already begun – the balding man? Would Alan or Jennetta be told about what was discovered in her family background? Suppose they found out something that made her 'unsuitable' – they'd have to tell Alan then. And that would kibosh the wedding. Men had missed out on promotion because their wives were 'unsuitable' for one reason or another; Alan couldn't ignore such a warning. Beth wouldn't expect him to – and Jennetta would never forgive her. But what, exactly, might be considered 'unsuitable'?

Jennetta's birth was as legitimate as Beth's first marriage, as far as Beth knew and on paper at least. Her daughter's life since had been as blameless as the day she was born. Her speech and manners had been carefully schooled by Beth herself, and Duncan's family background had given her all the protection and social cachet that anyone could ask. For a bonus, she was educated and intelligent. Surely they wouldn't bother to look up Nick who'd died even before Jennetta was born? Damn her misplaced concern, Beth cursed herself, for insisting that Jennetta kept her father's name.

She'd told her daughter that her own parents had died young in a boating accident before she could remember them; that she, their only child, had been brought up by aunts who'd died before Jennetta was born. Death, it seemed, was endemic in the poor kid's family, Beth thought grimly. Because one day her private papers would come into Jennetta's possession, Beth had kept to the details on her birth certificate. Gone were the model mother and solicitor father with whom she'd hoped to impress Nick. The birth certificate showed that Elizabeth Carole was the daughter of Brian and Elaine Ramsay; her father a merchant seaman, her mother a 'housewife'. Beth had fleshed out that skeleton with a few details supposedly supplied by the aunts, but her parents were too dead to interest Jennetta; unlike Nick's, whom she still hoped to meet.

But Beth had felt that she owed more of the truth to

Duncan before she married him. He had a greater experience of family togetherness than Nick, who'd asked and volunteered nothing. Duncan expected surviving family to have crammed the orphan Beth with information about her parents, little personal details that would have brought them alive for her. Anything but the truth would have been too much of a strain on Beth's imagination and her memory. Good liars needed good memories. So, quite early in their relationship, Duncan knew that Beth had been cared for by foster-parents and that all she knew of Brian and Elaine Ramsay could be read on her birth certificate. That confidence had made her even more dear to him.

In fact Beth remembered more than she cared to of her early childhood and the memories appalled her. Apart from that, she had no idea whether either of the Ramsays could be produced to wreck her family as they'd mangled their own. Their deaths had been merely wishful thinking on her part.

Beth had doubts about her legitimacy too, although there was no question of it on that all-important birth certificate. The fact had no bearing on Alan's security check but it was another personal detail that undermined her self-assurance. For if those dark-haired adolescents she'd remembered with such loathing were indeed her brothers, then her own pale colouring was at least surprising. She'd seen the same thought strike those who didn't realise that Jennetta was Duncan's adopted daughter – evil-minded sods. Light-haired, blue-eyed parents, Beth knew, produced offspring like Penny. Those black-eyed boys must have had at least one similar parent, as Jennetta had, and the other had to have been fair if Beth was legitimate. It was too long ago and too deeply buried, however, to remember details.

For a while Beth racked her memory to picture the loudmouthed crone who'd fed her and slapped her, and whose only means of communication was a bellow that turned Beth's guts to water. She could only visualise a vague, threatening bulk the boys called 'Mum'. She couldn't otherwise remember names being used at all. 'You.' 'You dirty little bleeder, you're more trouble than a puppy.' 'Shut up, you, or I'll fetch you such a welt . . .' It was a mistake, painfully learned, ever to cry or even to be noticed.

Beth couldn't recall ever seeing 'Dad', although his frightening authority seemed to bulge the walls. 'Dad' was the ultimate threat used against the boys, even more final than a crack on the head with anything handy. 'Wait 'til Dad hears about this.' 'I'll tell your Dad.' And 'Dad' in turn was the threat the boys used against Beth. 'Belt up, or I'll tell Dad.' 'Come here, or I'll tell Dad.' Of course she always did, and suffered at least the Devil she knew.

Some sort of accident had befallen Dad but Beth never knew what it was or how terminal. Somebody came to tell them about it, and after they'd gone there'd been raucous recriminations and a lashing-out all round. Then the boys had vanished, but whether or not of their own volition Beth was too relieved to care. After that someone had come and wrapped her in a blanket and taken her away.

That was a change for the better, but she was too wary and too – antisocial to appreciate it at first; too suspicious of the others and terrified of the adults who called themselves 'Aunties'. But she herself was addressed by her own name and they gave her presents and parties for her birthday. She had things of her own. Beth couldn't tell how long she was there, that first stretch; until after she'd started at school, anyway. She was undersized but older than the other beginners; because she hadn't been 'ready', they'd told her.

In time she was 'ready' to be fostered too. A betrayal. They'd wanted her to call them Mum and Dad, but she wouldn't. *Couldn't*. She'd moped and regressed, feeling too much noticed without the protective shield of the other children. They'd found her unresponsive. 'Surly', they said. 'We want to make you happy. Won't you try to please us?' But they couldn't *make* her happy, and she didn't understand what they wanted of her. In the end she stopped eating, an unexpectedly powerful weapon.

Beth had returned to the Home – or *a* Home – and that was a conscious experience of happiness she could still remember. She'd settled comfortably back into the secure routine. School was a blot, but housemothers, 'Aunts', her own friends and the younger children – they'd been her family then and all she wanted. Others left, and she pitied them. They went back to their own parents or were fostered, but she felt she was especially favoured.

But then they'd betrayed her again; prattled about their fear of her becoming 'institutionalised' – where once they'd pestered her to conform – and packed her off 'for her own good', the lying swine, to another foster-home. She could never forgive them.

There'd been two of them fostered there. They had a son of their own, but he was away most of the time and

207

he didn't give her any trouble. She'd stayed there for several years, but now she couldn't even remember their names. When she and her foster-sister left they'd made a pact never to speak of them again but put them right out of their minds. Beth had succeeded in doing so, at least up to a point. They'd been betrayers too. The worst of the lot – until Nick.

Duncan came downstairs looking for Beth.

'I only sat down for a moment,' she excused herself guiltily, blinking in the sudden light. She glanced at her watch; it was after two o'clock. 'I must've dropped off. Heavens, I'm thirsty!' Duncan went into the kitchen without commenting and after a moment Beth heard the percolator guggling. She was still trying to pull herself together when Duncan reappeared.

'Strong and sweet, just as you are,' he smiled as he handed Beth a mug of coffee and sat down. 'It'll probably keep you awake, but then – you weren't expecting to sleep tonight, I think. And you weren't asleep just now when I came in, so less of the wool-pulling.' For the life of her, Beth could think of nothing to say. 'I wish you wouldn't take things on single-handed these days. You don't need to and it makes me feel inadequate. I saw what bothered you tonight – probably we all did. All that hoo-ha about Alan's security clearance. You behaved as though you were a paid-up member of the Mafia. What's the problem, Beth?'

'I – wondered if that man you pointed out in Dickins & Jones was one of their security people, that's all. Don't make too much of this, Duncan.'

'No, Beth, *you're* making too much of it, and that's not like you. You understate, play down, smooth over –

208

that's your form. But nowadays you seem to've lost your marbles. Why couldn't you utter that single sentence earlier, instead of brooding over it for nearly three hours and giving the impression of a galloping persecution complex? No, really, ducky! Why should *we* interest Alan's security gorillas?' Beth eyed Duncan over her mug, trying to gauge his mood. The coffee helped both to revive and calm her.

'You heard what was said – about Jennetta being vetted.'

'They're not going to snoop around like cock-eyed cloak and dagger merchants, though, are they?' Duncan demanded impatiently. He needed his sleep. 'What – follow us up to Town and all? Alan's right at the bottom of the pile. It'll be a formality only. They'll trust him at least to choose a wife who doesn't eat with her mouth open and won't screw his friends or gamble away his salary.'

'Why demand my confidence if you won't treat it seriously?' Beth asked coldly.

'Look,' Duncan began with controlled patience. 'Jennetta hasn't a record, she's British and she's mine – to all intents. Sorry – I don't mean to be offensive, but they won't look further than that. Are you afraid they'll back-track to Nasty Nick? Forget it. Now, then,' Duncan came to stand over Beth, 'come to bed, woman, or do you want me to haul you off by your hair? Said he, hopefully.'

'Wait 'til I've finished my coffee, Attila. And you're forgetting Jennetta's mother. *I'm* still around to be investigated. How much do these people tell of what they've discovered, do you know?'

'But they're not remotely likely to delve into your past, and anyway – why should that bother you?' Duncan resignedly sat down again.

'What if – Duncan, what if my marriage to Nick wasn't legal? Jennetta –'

' – is legally adopted,' Duncan interrupted, 'and we're *certainly* legally married. All else is cancelled. Next question.'

'Well, if they do make a full investigation – the foster-home. "Aunts", you see, gave Jennetta a sense of family when she needed it. If she were to learn about the foster-home it'd take that away – as well as showing that I'd lied to her. She'd wonder how much she believes of herself is true, don't you see? You said something like that on your own account not so long ago.'

Beth had never told Duncan about the local authority children's Homes, nor told him that, being 'in need of care and protection', she'd been taken into care as the result of a court order. They were all terms too readily associated in the minds of the fortunate with being remanded, as she'd discovered from reactions at school. Certainly there'd been some pretty tough nuts at her last Home. Dover House had had an unfortunate reputation. What would an investigator make of Beth's history which had included more than a year there?

'You don't credit your daughter with much common gumption, do you?' Duncan was saying. 'Jennetta won't now feel so much in need of a family as she did then. And she'd certainly appreciate why you fudged the truth. But no one's going to inform against you, good God, any more than they'd think that being fostered was a security risk.'

210

'No, you're wrong about Jennetta.' Beth was instantly sidetracked. '*More* than ever now she needs a sense of family behind her. She's afraid of being swamped in Alan's, all those cousins by the dozens. Afraid she'll – get taken over. She's fretting that even if every single one of your relations comes to the wedding, her family's going to be thin on the ground by comparison with Alan's. *I* can't produce any. That's why she's hoping Nick's supposed parents will come over – *no* reflection on you, Duncan. You know – exotic American connections in lieu of numbers. A crowned head or two wouldn't come amiss,' Beth smiled suddenly.

Duncan was thoughtful for a moment.

'In other words, what Jennetta said rang a bell you were ready to hear. You want to give her a great send-off – you'd like to give her everything she wants, especially now because it's your last chance. After this it's Alan's responsibility. But you can't turn fantasy relations into flesh and blood for her, so you feel you're letting her down just when it matters most. And because you're helpless there, you feel you've shattered the protection you've built round her. Because it was built on a false-hood. *That's* why you've got so jittery about Nick's dead past and his shady friends – and about your own lack of family. I'm right, aren't I?'

'Oh, but only partly, Duncan – '

'You don't have to tell me the rest, darling.' Duncan laid a comforting hand on Beth's knee. 'It's a terribly emotional time for you, I know. Jennetta hinted at it the other day, but I'm not so blind I can't see to the end of my nose. We neither of us want to lose her, but that's an emotive, negative way of looking at it. Of course she has her

211

secret worries too, she's hardly more than a child. She knows things can't be the same again but she doesn't know *how* they'll be. So it's up to us to show they can be better than ever. Agreed?' Beth nodded absently, still puzzling over what 'emotional' thing about her mother Jennetta had 'hinted' to Duncan. Whatever it was, it seemed to have satisfied him.

'Well, then,' Duncan went on. 'You just have to accept that Alan will be looking after her and will keep her safe, but that she'll always be your daughter. You know what they say – "A son is your son 'til he gets him a wife, but a daughter's your daughter the whole of her life".'

'They also say that a daughter doesn't grow up until her mother's *dead*,' Beth snapped, suddenly remembering screeched admonitions to 'Shaddap!' How closely was she still tied to her own loathsome heredity? 'Too bad I can't be around to learn the truth of either useless saying.' She drained her mug and clacked it down on the table.

There was a startled silence before Duncan said quietly.

'Penny's your daughter too. She'll miss Jennetta perhaps more than we realise. She'll need you, Beth.' She took this as an indirect criticism. Duncan was being unusually insensitive, Beth decided.

'Penny's always been *safe*,' she observed coldly, forgetting her recent panic on her younger daughter's account. It was true, though. Turn back Penny's antecedents through the Masterses, Beth reflected, and it was roses, roses all the way. Trace Jennetta's through her Nicholls connection and find maggots – and God alone knew what might be uncovered through the Ramsays.

But Duncan's expression was warning Beth that again she'd been too sharp for one whose worries had supposedly been soothed away not many minutes earlier.

'Penny doesn't need the protection I've owed Jennetta,' she explained. 'I won't overlook Penny. I never have. But surely it's not too much for me to ask a *little* privacy for – for a grateful tear that Jennetta's marrying so well in spite of my lack of family.' Beth's voice shook and Duncan went quickly to her.

'Let's privately weep together, then, darling, because I'll miss her too. And so will she miss us. In fact, I wonder if the wedding's such a good idea after all. Shall I tell Alan I've revoked my blessing?'

'Idiot!' Beth blurted an unsteady laugh.

'What you need is a good sleep and a lie-in tomorrow. It's not your morning for school lifts, is it? Right, then. I'll get the girls up and see Penny off. You take it easy for once.'

Beth was grateful for Duncan's cold-shower reasoning and his understanding, within the limits of the little she'd told him. *He'd* never write off her ditheriness with some casual gynaecological cliché. And he was right, he must be right. It wasn't after all as if Alan was being recruited by MI5.

'I must do this more often. I don't usually get the chance to see you in bed,' Duncan grinned when he woke Beth the following morning. 'Coffee, toast and madam's home-made marmalade. And it's another lovely day,' he added as he opened the curtains. Beth slewed round to look at the clock on the bedside table and struggled upright.

'Hell!'

'It's all right. Penny's been safely yawning at school for the last couple of hours and I've given Jennetta an extra driving lesson, so don't think I've been kicking my heels waiting for your shining morning face. She's gone off now for a Greek lesson with Alan. I've brought up a cup for myself as well but I'll have to get off soon. Take your time, though. The toast'll keep warm for a bit.' There was a napkin-wrapped mound of it on the tray, enough for the whole family. Beth smiled at the sight. 'You're looking rested. Feeling better?' Duncan asked solicitously. Beth supposed she was. It seemed a long haul back to full consciousness, however.

Duncan transferred the coffee things from the tray to the bedside table and sat patiently on the bed watching her. There was something almost knowing in his look, Beth thought. As if he realised exactly how exposed and confused she felt. Vulnerable. All her recent confessions, all that raking over the midden of her past, seemed to have left her entirely stripped. Peeled, layer by layer like an onion, until only the phantom tears remained. What, she wondered as at last she arranged herself for the tray, is the difference between an understanding and a knowing look?

'There're a couple of letters for you. More invitation replies, I imagine. Shall I open them while you start your breakfast?' Duncan asked as he poured the coffee and put Beth's cup within easy reach.

'No – I'll look at them now,' she said, glad of a neutral topic of conversation while Duncan drank his coffee.

'Heavens, what luxury!' she added, buttering toast and spreading marmalade. She opened the first envelope, a typewritten one; a business letter.

Dear Mrs Masters,
I hope I am correct in the belief that you are the same Elizabeth Masters who was formerly married to Mr Andrew Nicholls and whose maiden name was Ramsay -

Beth read no further. '*Christ*!'
Duncan looked up, startled by an expletive he'd never heard on her lips. Beth was chalk-white and staring, sitting bolt upright with one hand at her throat and the other clenched around the letter. He thought she was choking and quickly moved the tray from her lap. Beth fought him away savagely when he tried to thump her back.

'Get *off*! You *knew* about this, damn you! Waiting to watch me read it – ' She wrenched furiously at the bedclothes, flung herself out of bed and nearly fell. There was no strength in her legs. Duncan caught and held her, felt her whole body trembling.

'Beth! For God's sake! What's all this about?' Beth turned within the circle of his arms, her face tilted to his. Duncan released her, horrified by her transformation; lips strained back over her teeth, eyes wide and unfocused. As if she was having a fit. Beth fell back on the bed.

'This!' she screamed, shaking the letter at him. 'I *knew* they were looking for me! I told you and *you've* led them to me! You – ' Beth collapsed suddenly and curled up into a foetal ball, her arms wrapped tightly round her

215

head.

For a moment Duncan was too stunned to do more than stare down at her; then he mechanically drew the duvet over her and picked up the letter. He smoothed out the paper, noticing the business heading, and read on.

Dear Mrs Masters,

I hope I am correct in the belief that you are the same Elizabeth Masters who was formerly married to Mr Andrew Nicholls and whose maiden name was Ramsay. If I am wrong please accept my apologies for troubling you with this letter.

I am trying to trace Sandra Littlejohn in the matter of a legacy. Sandra was Elizabeth Ramsay's friend when, in or about 1966, they shared the same foster-home at 30, Churchill Avenue, Fulham. Later they were together at High Bank Hostel.

The Warden at High Bank, now retired, was able to help me up to a point since she has kept the letters Elizabeth and others wrote after they had left. She told me that Elizabeth – Beth – had occasionally written to Sandra at the Hostel but that Sandra had already moved on. The Warden never had an address to forward the letters, and she has no knowledge now of Sandra's whereabouts.

I hoped that if Sandra ever contacted you, you might know at least whether she is married and would supply me with her married name. I would be grateful for any other information.
David Morgan.

Duncan gently pulled the duvet away from Beth's face.

'Darling, you can't have read far enough. This letter's nothing to do with Nick. Beth, listen to me. It's a simple request for news of an old friend of yours. Are you listening? Do you remember anyone called Sandra Littlejohn? Apparently you were together at your foster-home in Fulham. Do you remember that? She's been left a legacy and they're trying to find her, that's all. Really, that's all.' But Beth wasn't so easily revived and after a while Duncan left the room. She lay still, feeling her entire body rebound on the mattress from the thumping of her heart.

When Beth eventually stirred the house was silent. She read and reread the letter Duncan had left on the table. The business heading was 'Fleetwood & Partners' with an address in Bromley. How the hell had they tracked her to Epsom, she wondered.

Beth's memory never lingered over it, but she couldn't forget that foster-home. It wasn't possible to blank everything out. She'd always given Duncan to understand that she'd gone straight from there to her first job, but she hadn't. There'd been the spell back in close care at Dover House, a Home for older girls. 'Scabies, babies and rabies', Sandra had dismissed their antisocial problems with a grin, but that was a window on to a world far different from Duncan's and Beth preferred it unknown that she'd looked through it. Some of them were 'beyond parental control' and some were so far beyond that they were on assessment with a view to enforcing a more meaningful control behind bars. Others were on place-of-safety orders. There'd been no

217

'Aunts' play-acting at happy families.

Sandra had made a fair mess of her enforced transition from the foster-home to Dover House. Beth could hardly forget Sandra, unnerving though the memories were – and the Beth of those days hadn't much to congratulate herself upon, either, she reflected. She still had an old snap of the two girls tucked away in her handkerchief-case. Beth padded across the room to find it. On the back was written, 'When you look at this remember Anne'. She'd certainly forgotten Anne, but the snap must have been taken during the year after they'd left the foster-home. Their foster-parents weren't the snap-happy kind.

This was a head-and-shoulders shot of two teenage girls, alike in colouring and hair-styles, their unformed, immature faces giving them the look of sisters that Sandra had cultivated. Or perhaps it had been Beth who so sincerely flattered by imitation. Not everything could be remembered without confusion after so long, although the worst of the past seemed to survive somehow. Sod's Law. And after a while the girls had even exchanged personalities in a sense. Beth had grown more dominant, even domineering, in her understated way.

Beth didn't want to remember or be reminded of that time. She'd hoped that Dover House and the Hostel at least might have been lost in the mists of the past. But now it seemed that, like a roulette ball finally settling into its slot – will it, won't it – the preliminary rattle of warning had tipped over at last into probability.

# Summer 1968 –
# Winter 1970

# Thirteen

Beth was glad to be getting away without seeing Lucy. The further they went from Churchill Avenue the more she revived, like a flower turning to the sun. It was an adventure, after all. A new beginning. There'd be no pursuit now, and she'd be looked after.

'I've told them all about you,' the woman in the driving-seat broke brightly in on Beth's thoughts. She had introduced herself as Miss Roberts, but Beth had no idea whether she was from the Children's Department or some Home. 'You'll still be together, which is marvellous news, isn't it? You'll find them all very understanding and friendly.' Well, sometimes they were, she added a mental rider. Surprisingly so. And these two looked shattered enough to be harmless.

Beth wondered what Sandra was thinking, but Sandra sat huddled next to her on the back seat with her head turned away. She spoke only once, as they pulled up outside a square brick building set back from the road.

'Here we are!' Miss Roberts chirped.

'*This* isn't the Meadows!' Sandra said accusingly. She'd apparently overlooked the fact that at thirteen and fifteen she and Beth were well over the Meadows age-limit of eleven.

'No, dear.' Miss Roberts slewed round in her seat, hearing trouble in Sandra's tone. 'It's Dover House.'

For the rest of that evening Sandra either sat staring without response at the television in the common-room,

221

or sleep-walking her way to supper and bed via the surgery for treatment to her hand. For the present at least they had a room to themselves.

'Traumatised,' one of the girls muttered knowledgeably to Beth, glancing significantly at Sandra. Beth, who had stayed close all evening, nodded.

'Traumatised,' she agreed, seizing on the word. 'She actually saw it happen, you see. I came on the scene just after.'

'What actually *did* happen?' The willing new friend sat beside her and Beth turned to her, whispering. Her openness, she realised instinctively, not Sandra's dumb indifference, was their passport to acceptance in that place.

Nothing was said about their returning to Lucy, but when the rest of their clothes arrived after a day or so Beth knew with relief that she would not be leaving her new friends. It was a heady time for her, to be sought after and know herself to be well thought of by the staff too for her patience with Sandra. Sandra repulsed all advances and for a while she was watched anxiously for signs of a serious breakdown. Beth was credited with the fact that it did not occur.

Dover House was partly an assessment centre, partly a Home for unfortunates like Beth and Sandra whose lives had been dislocated through no fault of their own. There was some attempt to segregate the delinquents, for whose benefit it was a 'secure' Home, in that they had a separate common-room and slept in a different wing. Bolts and bars were not conspicuous in the main building, although close supervision was, and delinquents and unfortunates met together only for meals or in the 'garden'. This was a quadrangle behind the main building enclosed on its other three sides by the newer school and kitchen blocks and the more positively secure medical and assessment wings, all added as the nature of the original Home had changed.

The Superintendent was a married man who, together with his wife, controlled the daily running and discipline of Dover House, and the place was comfortably full of adults. Residential staff, working in day and night shifts, administrative and kitchen staff, cleaners – in the main building at least; the delinquents did the cleaning in their wing – and visiting Welfare assistants, all helped to make Beth feel secure. She understood adults.

The girls never saw Lucy again but their foster-brother visited them a week or so after their admission, and they were tactfully left alone with him. He wanted to hear their account of his father's death in return for a description of the funeral, rather than to enquire after their welfare, however.

'We sent a wreath from you both. But why didn't Dad ask one of you to give him a hand?' he asked despairingly. Beth wondered if he'd been into the attic since, and what he made of Tom's love-nest if so. She was surprised at the feeling he showed, having assumed that his visits home were infrequent because he disliked his father. It flashed through her mind that there might have been some truth in Tom's teasing: that her own dangerous presence at Number 30 had kept the PC away. Perhaps he'd been warned off, even. She saved that interesting idea to examine later. Beth was quickly developing a new sense of her own worth.

'You know what Tom was like,' she answered uncomfortably. 'He'd never interrupt our homework or practising. At supper the night before Lucy said it was time for jam-making, and Tom just went up for the jars the next day.' He cried a little at that. Everyone in Churchill Avenue now knew the fatal consequences of Lucy's suggestion. And Beth, who was worried by his visit, cried too. Sandra, her hand still bandaged, merely went on staring out of the window and left all the talking to Beth. She seemed to have resigned every initiative since Tom's death.

He'd brought a few things left behind at the house: Beth's framed sampler, their Savings books, school reports and personal papers for the Superintendent and, incredibly, a pot each of home-made damson jam from Lucy. She had not been deterred from her forage along the hedgerows, there being a time to mourn and a time to make jam. Beth was so affected she could hardly sob out her thanks, a marked contrast to Sandra's stony-faced silence.

'*You're* not bothered, are you?' Her foster-brother rounded on her. 'Don't you feel *anything* for him? He wanted to *adopt* you both!' Their narrow escape from that irretrievable disaster shocked Sandra into blurting.

'He wanted to *screw* us both, you mean.' That silenced Beth's placatory attempt to explain Sandra's traumatisation. He lost his temper then and slapped Sandra so hard across the face that her head jerked back.

'You lying, foul-mouthed little – *bitch*!' Then he went. It was as well that Sandra's hand was still painful or she'd have run at him. Beth saw it in her face. Then they'd all have had to explain themselves.

She pointed this out afterwards.

'We don't want anyone knowing about what happened in that bloody attic. Just forget there ever was such a place,' Beth ended. She was reconstructing her own defences, of course. The situation at Number 30, were it generally known, would undermine her revised image of a grieving but pure innocence. It would also knock a hole in the kudos she earned from her care for Sandra and her friendly but modest manner – no longer the aloof ice-maiden. Respect might be withdrawn altogether if it should ever seem that she had been the willing victim in a far from innocent foster-relationship. Sandra's reactions to her admissions had taught Beth what others might think. She was quick in her learning of human nature. But Sandra was so angry and so careless lately she seemed scarcely to think before she spoke – if she spoke. Beth stayed close to her.

'Beth, will you look after Linda?' the supervisor asked one evening in the common-room. She brought over a new girl and retired to the back of the room with her knitting, unobtrusive but watchful. Beth could be relied on for surrogate mothering.

Beth looked up with a smile and made room for Linda beside her. She had reverted to her needlework in the evenings – and her skill was much admired – but Sandra was as usual glued to the television.

'This is Sandra,' Beth indicated her unwelcoming back. 'We're foster-sisters. Are you here for long?' Confidences in return for kindness were the acceptable bricks in a wall to keep out loneliness.

'Only for tonight. My little sister's in hospital but tomorrow they're going to take us both to Gran's.'

Their talk penetrated Sandra's indiscriminate concen-

225

tration on the television screen only in snatches at first, Linda doing most of the talking.

'. . . early from school with the gripes . . . Didn't ask why he was home already. We don't talk . . . Joanie . . . upstairs crying . . . bruises . . . He used to roger me, see, but Jesus! she isn't yet five! . . . took her out the back way . . . Told 'em about myself too . . . sent a car for him so he's in the nick tonight, the bastard. Joanie's being kept overnight for observation.' An avid group had gathered and Sandra was jostled into greater awareness.

'But what about your Mum? Didn't she – ?' one of them began.

'Her! Anything for a quiet life, her! She blames me for shit-stirring. If it wasn't for Gran we'd both be in care tonight and separated for years, maybe. I'm leaving school next summer but they wouldn't be letting me have Joanie.'

'But – prison!' said a younger girl in horror.

'Yep. Remanded without bail now, then a good long term inside, with luck,' Linda told her with relish. 'Why not? He'd get prison anyway for stuffing girls under fifteen but we're his daughters as well. That's rape and incest. You just dropped out of Heaven or something?'

'Did your Dad admit it all, then?'

'Don't make me laugh! 'Course he didn't! But it didn't matter – there was the proof, never mind the bruises and everything. The police doctor found the stuff still inside Joanie – and I told 'em where to look for it. When they tested him they could tell he'd not long – you know. They can, you see. It was when I heard you could get proof like that – if you're quick – that I threatened the old sod with it a couple of years ago and made him lay off

226

me. But I never thought he'd have a go at poor little Joanie instead. God, I'd like a couple of minutes alone with him! I'd crack his nuts!'

Linda's home-life had similarities with their own at Number 30 and Beth was not surprised when Sandra suddenly got up and walked out, looking grim.

'Our foster-father's just died,' she explained to Linda, 'and Sandra's still very upset. Had I better go after her, Miss Burrows?' she asked the supervisor who was preparing to follow Sandra.

'Yes, will you, Beth. Let her put herself to bed if she doesn't want to come back.' Linda's story anyway had not been one for weak stomachs.

'It's always the wrong people who die,' Linda muttered sympathetically as Beth went.

Sandra was lying on the bed, her hands tucked behind her head.

'You nearly dropped us both in it, stamping off like that,' Beth warned her. 'I had to think up something fast to cover for you.'

'Shouldn't have found that difficult, you lying cow,' Sandra replied in her tight voice. 'Don't come near me or I'll bloody crack you one. *You* told me we wouldn't be believed. *You* told me there was no proof. *You* told me there was no way of stopping him. But now we know the truth, don't we. You could've stopped him any time but you just didn't *want* to. He could be in prison now. You're as disgusting as he was. Christ, if I'd *known* –'

Sandra turned on to her face – to Beth's relief. Until then she had not even connected Linda's remedies with her own situation at Number 30 and Sandra's renewed accusations stunned her. There was also something

227

unnerving about Sandra's coldly furious contempt. In this mood she could do irreparable damage to Beth's peace of mind. The gentle reproof she had intended died on her lips. After a moment she moved cautiously closer to the bed.

'If you'd known – what then? You wouldn't have killed him?' she whispered, and recoiled hastily as Sandra whipped around. 'I saw you,' Beth added quickly. 'I saw you – push that glass in his eye.'

'You're *mad*!' Sandra croaked after a moment's shocked silence. 'I was trying to get it out!'

Beth smiled her small smile and edged towards the door.

'That's your story, and I've gone along with it. It's all turned out for the best and I'll keep quiet. But that's what I mean. It's turned out too well to have it spoiled now. I don't want people to know what he got up to. I don't want that hung round my neck for the rest of my life. But if you don't control yourself people'll start wondering and it'll all come out. If it does, because of you, *I'll* say you killed him. That'll make more trouble for you than me in the end.' Sandra did not respond immediately. She stared at Beth, fascinated by her latest transformation. Once again she had misjudged Beth.

'But honestly, I *didn't* know of any way I could prove what he did,' Beth insisted as the silence lengthened. 'You didn't know either, come to that. What Linda said was news to both of us. You're wrong about me wanting it to go on but you're not the only one who'll think that. So, you see.'

'Yes, I see,' Sandra murmured, suddenly relaxing with a sigh. 'And you're wrong about me too. *I* wanted him – you know – disgraced somehow and have to live with it. He had it too easy in the end and that's been niggling me. I reckon he cheated us, going like that. So OK, then. We've got something on each other – *if* we can ever find someone twisted enough to listen.' Sandra grinned and swung her legs off the bed. 'It'll be bloody difficult, but we'll agree to put Number 30 out of our minds. And I'll try and behave as if we've lost a beloved foster-father– '

' – but are being brave about it,' Beth warned. 'You don't want to go too far the other way.'

'And we're friends still?' Sandra asked anxiously.

'And foster-sisters,' Beth insisted. Relief made her generous. 'We're in this together. I can't ever forget that.'

Beth was accustomed to manipulation as a form of self-defence; now her new popularity permitted manipulation for simple vanity. Both versions required effort and adjustments of her own behaviour, and Beth found that popularity was as tiring to maintain at Dover House as it had been at Number 30 but more unpredictable. Her first real taste of power, however, was exhilarating and virtually effortless. How easily Sandra had surrendered! Admirers might come and go but Sandra was shackled for ever. It was not difficult for Beth to convince herself that she'd actually done Sandra a good turn. But for her, Sandra might easily sulk her way into trouble. Beth was Sandra's guardian angel, and you don't lightly shuck off guardian angels.

It was not at first possible for Beth to resist tweaking Sandra's halter occasionally, partly to feel her control and partly for seeing Sandra's reactions. Inappropriate

229

ones were corrected by subtle references to jam-jars and broken windows, and they soon became fewer. She never entirely ran out of sources of amusement, however. The others had quickly slipped into the habit of calling Sandra 'Sandy'. Beth waited for her to weary of fighting that issue – a self-defeating exercise anyway – and then sometimes called her Sandy too.

'You even asked me to call you Sandy once,' she reminded when Sandra raved at her for it. It was almost the last reference between them to their lives at Number 30.

There was some truth in Beth's vision of herself as Sandra's guardian angel and Sandra seemed to recognise it herself. In spite of minor resentments at first their relationship grew closer. Sandra deferred to Beth but Beth lent her clothes, a sure sign of the highest favour at Dover House. Sandra's behaviour grew generally more friendly and she made a determined effort at school, actually with greater success than Beth. Beth resat her shorthand and typing exams at the end of their first term at Dover House, but failed them again to no one's surprise after the events of the previous few months.

Impressed by her earnest plea to try once more in the hopes of leaving with at least some qualifications, the authorities agreed to let Beth stay on for a final attempt in the summer. With the school-leaving age then at fifteen, Beth would normally have been moved to the Hostel but for this extension. This was a debriefing station where suitably trustworthy unfortunates and reformed delinquents still in care at fifteen learned to look after themselves in greater independence. They helped with the housework, worked at a paid but simple job in the outside world, and gradually threw off the grip of their institutionalised past until they had proved themselves ready for full independence.

High Bank Hostel was the immediate goal of all Beth's older friends but she was secretly relieved not to be leaving Dover House before the summer. Beth was happier there than she could ever remember being and was disinclined to believe that any change could be for the better. 'Independence' had never held any lure for her anyway; but neither was she ready yet to be separated from Sandra, whose company was necessary for her sense of security as well as for the more perverted strength it gave her. And after all, they were foster-sisters, the nearest family relationship either could lay claim to. That point at least was appreciated by the staff, who viewed Beth's continued stay with relief; there was still the possibility that Sandra would revert to her anti-social manners in Beth's absence.

By the end of the summer, however, Beth was quite ready to move on. She had passed her two exams at last and her success gave her added confidence. She looked forward to greater freedom to experience the all but compulsory delights that others boasted about. A more mature attitude, too, carefully fostered by the staff, had weaned her from her emotional dependence on Sandra, whose close friendship Beth now found too limiting. Sandra was a child still, after all.

Beth's departure for the Hostel seemed to rouse Sandra's dormant sense of responsibility and confounded the pessimists. Beth's absence might have left Sandra vulnerable but her newly revealed quickness of wit and sense of humour, in abeyance while she had played second fiddle to Beth, gave her protection. Her gift for mimicry, sometimes unkind and therefore all the more appealing, amused even the staff. But Sandra could be relied on now not to make waves, and this as well as her continued improvement at school was known to be motivated by her wish to rejoin her foster-sister. How much time they would have together at the Hostel, if any, depended on how quickly Beth was considered fit for complete independence as a useful member of Society; but there were some who believed that Sandra would do herself a favour if she kept away from Beth's suffocating over-protection.

The girls wrote to each other regularly and Beth visited Dover House – quite often at first since the Hostel was only a few rail-stops away. In both their interests effort would be made to find Sandra a job within reach of Beth when it came to her turn to leave the Hostel; but meanwhile she had another year to go at school and at least as long to maintain her improved record at Dover House.

In the event, her qualifying age, grim determination and half a dozen CSE passes wafted Sandra to the Hostel – with a warning of demotion for unsatisfactory behaviour – just a couple of months before Beth left it. If, in hindsight, points were overstretched in Sandra's favour at that transition, it was out of compassion not carelessness.

Their reunion at the Hostel much moved the well-meaning, sentimental but essentially foolish woman who was the Warden and with whom Beth had always been a favourite. Her genuine commitment to her work was handicapped by an unfortunate capacity for being personally wounded by the ingratitude of her charges, and by her ability to inspire her assistants with a sometimes passionate contempt.

'Thank God on your knees for the friendship between you two girls,' she told Beth and Sandra. 'I'm blest in my family but even so I know there's nothing more sacred than true friendship.'

'We're foster-sisters, not just friends,' Beth displayed her old talisman fondly, for she was touched by Sandra's unexpectedly demonstrative greeting: 'At last! Together again at last!'

'A double bond indeed!' the Warden beamed dewily. 'I'm delighted to welcome you, Sandra, for both your sakes.'

Her delight was modified within a few days. Slightly misguided by Beth's account of herself as rescuing Sandra, the brand, as it were, from the burning, the Warden had imagined the younger girl to be an impressionable duplicate of Beth. She anticipated cherishing Sandra in the same soothing aura of mutual flattery when Beth had gone. It was not the first time such a misjudgement had been made about her.

Tied at first to 'Home Duties' in the Hostel, Sandra's cleaning and housework were meticulous. She could not be faulted there. In fact it was difficult positively to spell out Sandra's faults anywhere, yet the Warden could sense them. Sandra tended to laugh unexpectedly, to question when she might more properly have listened, and even her requests for advice sometimes left the Warden uncomfortably feeling that she was being made fun of. Sandra showed none of Beth's reverential willingness to succumb to the Warden's favour – an acquiescence that had left Beth isolated. Sandra was more likely to be the centre of a noisy group providing entertainment that the Warden instinctively felt was subversive.

She mentioned her disappointment to Beth one evening.

'I'm afraid Sandra's nothing like as ready to settle as you were, dear. In fact she's not at all what I expected. You mustn't mind me saying this, dear,' she added, twisting the ring she wore on her middle finger. It was a habit when she became agitated. Beth knew it had been her mother's wedding ring, and her mother the Warden's truest friend as she never tired of telling them all. Perhaps a little insensitively, given their family circumstances.

She had other true friends, particularly her sister in whose family she took an absorbing interest. Her accounts of her sister's intellect and her niece's tribulations as a teacher unfortunately inspired nothing but boredom in her captive listeners.

'Of course, I'd never expect her to visit me here,' she'd once said unguardedly, and Sandra had flashed,

'Why not? I believe you can visit even prisons these days without catching anything,' which had flustered the Warden and made her even more uneasy about Sandra.

'Oh – Sandra's always been a bit lively,' Beth reassured absently, 'but she doesn't want to lose my respect so she never goes too far. She'll do anything for me. I've always looked after her, you see.'

'Yes, I know, dear, and I admire you for it, but you'll be leaving us soon and she does seem to've learnt some rather *forward* manners since you were together at Dover House.' That equated with being pert, Beth knew.

Humble, grateful girls attracted the Warden's compassion and her best efforts to encourage their self-respect and confidence, but 'forwardness' excluded one from her inner circle. 'I'm thinking of her influence on some of our weaker characters after you've gone. She seems to've made herself very popular.' It was another damning with faint praise. Popularity was certainly a suspect attribute and probably dishonestly acquired.

'I'll speak to Sandra about her manners if you like,' Beth promised, bored.

'I wish you would, dear. For her own sake.'

But Beth was less concerned these days with Sandra's sake. Sandra was something of a blight difficult to explain away in the outside world. The last thing Beth wanted carried over into her new life, so soon to be entered upon, was an insistent connection with the Hostel or any part of her past, and Sandra was a ticking bomb. Boy-friends, menfriends, aftershave-scented bosses – they had not swarmed around her in the numbers she had expected. Beth attributed the lack to her connection with the Hostel and looked forward to greater success in her life thereafter. As far as she was concerned, it was a great pity she hadn't managed to get away before Sandra had arrived at the Hostel.

To Beth's dismay, it seemed that Sandra was becoming aware of her indifference and self-preoccupation. A job was found for Beth, a real job as an office-clerk with a car-hire firm in Surrey. It was near enough for her to keep in touch with her old friends if she chose, yet not on the very doorstep of places she might in future prefer to avoid. That was the usual principle. Sandra had been pleased for her and was ready enough to hear about the job and Beth's prospects, but with an air of sad reserve that was not characteristic. As if she knew, thought Beth uneasily, that their imminent separation was going to be final and absolute. She'd rather Sandra was miserable more conveniently out of sight and when it was all over.

Respectable lodgings too had been found for Beth conveniently near her new job, and she was taken to view her new address and meet her landlady the weekend before she left the Hostel for good. Sandra watched her get ready and saw her off in the Warden's car.

'I'd better take my birth certificate – in case I have to sign a lease or something,' Beth murmured self-importantly, folding the document into her new shoulder-bag.

'What's that for? To prove you're born?' Sandra grinned, lounging on the bed.

'It proves who I am and who my parents were,' Beth said solemnly, amazed that Sandra could be so ignorant. She was still such a child.

'Here, let's have a see. "Elizabeth Carole Ramsay",' Sandra read. 'I didn't know you had this!'

'We've all got one, silly! They gave me my documents when they knew I'd got the job. This too.' Beth held up her post office Savings book. A whiff of Number 30 hung in the air but neither girl commented.

'Do you remember your parents?' Sandra asked, turning her attention back to the certificate. Families had never been discussed between them.

'No.' Beth settled her scarf in the mirror. First impressions were so important. To be really comfortable in her new digs she needed to be liked by the woman who owned the house. A safe house in the best sense. 'I used to dream about them sometimes. Bad dreams. But I

don't remember them. Come on, it's time I was ready.'
She held out her hand for the birth certificate and
replaced it in her bag.

'You aren't at all worried about being out on your own
next weekend, are you?' Sandra observed wonderingly.
'Just the thought frightens the pants off me.'

'Frightens you?' Beth smiled as she closed her room
door behind them. 'I thought nothing frightened you.'

'Being alone does,' Sandra admitted in a small voice.
'We've always been looked after – and for me, at least,
there's always been you. Or it seems like it. Even being
without you frightens me. I never got used to being without you at Dover House, you know. That's why I worked
so hard to get to the Hostel – but you're already going.
We'll both be alone again.' Beth was flattered into an
irritating sense of guilt at the sight of Sandra's woebe-
gone face as the Warden drove her away.

Beth's new room, the house, its location, her landlady
– all seemed to be exactly what Beth might have wished
if she had known what to wish for, but on the journey to
Banstead and back Sandra's unexpected admissions
kept repeating themselves in her head. 'We've always
been looked after.' Sandra, Beth decided impatiently,
really was institutionalised. The Warden was right;
Sandra wasn't ready to settle into independence.

Yet it was strange that Sandra the adventurous
shouldn't be envying Beth her freedom, she reflected.
Of course it was bound to feel odd at first, to be on one's
own – not that she'd be entirely alone. To be completely
responsible for one's own life, anyway. But a relief as
well to be out of the female environment of the Hostel
and that chattering typing-pool. The anticipated relief

237

was suddenly difficult to conjure up, however. Beth's old timidity reared out of her past instead and was beaten back only with an effort.

During the following week Sandra grew more and more morose, ate little and spent hours by herself. Beth occasionally found her even in tears, a condition she never associated with Sandra. She wondered uneasily about suicidal tendencies and terrified the Warden with her hints.

'We've always been so close, you see, and she's worked so hard to reach me but only to be left again. Ours is such a very special relationship.'

'Don't take it so hard. After all, you managed at Dover House without me,' Beth tried to brace Sandra.

'Because I knew you'd still be looked after properly here. But you'll be much further away this time. Suppose you're ill or in some kind of trouble? You'll be miles from your friends and with no one to look after you but your landlady. If she will.' Beth hoped to have moved in on an accommodating male before such an eventuality but she did not mention this contentious fire-exit now. 'If only I could see where you're going to live we wouldn't seem so far apart, but I've had this awful feeling that you won't want me visiting once you've settled in. I think you're quite glad to be leaving me behind, yet it was you who said we were in this together. We're foster-sisters, after all. I'm sorry, Beth. I know I'm being a bore.' Sandra turned away despairingly.

She was quite right, Beth thought grimly; she certainly didn't want Sandra visiting in Banstead. And Sandra was mischievous enough to do just that if she thought she was being shut out, just to spite Beth. Yet

Sandra's loyalty was sneakingly gratifying, though at the same time her words nibbled insidiously at Beth's confidence. The final break seemed daily less desirable.

'Sandra!' Beth was suddenly inspired. 'I'll ask Nosy if you can come with me on Saturday – just to say good-bye. I'm sure she'd allow it – for me.'

The Warden's nickname seemed appropriate to the Hostel inmates not only because of her surname but because of her eager curiosity in the girls' intimate lives. Beth herself had found it hard to resist confiding the secrets of Tom's den, so rude did it seem not to reward the Warden's pastoral interest. The general opinion was that, disadvantaged by her blameless life – which in other contexts offered material for hilariously slander-ous guesswork – the Warden was forced to get her kicks vicariously. Beth's use of her nickname now indicated her realignment with Sandra.

For Sandra to accompany Beth to Banstead and spend the day with her there was the last thing the Warden would have wished on herself. She had planned to spend the rest of her own free day with her sister, and it would be an inconvenient detour to collect Sandra on her way back. But she did not want to deny Beth a last innocent favour, once she had heard her explanation, and she did not want to risk Sandra turning moody when Beth was out of sight. She hoped too that her generosity would win Sandra over, and agreed to her outing. Certainly Sandra brightened up after that, and Beth herself felt less as if she was being pitched in at the deep end. So their old alliance was restored; but despite that, on the Friday night both girls viewed the next day with a certain amount of apprehension.

# Fourteen

Saturday was a bright, brisk November day, however, and Beth was able to shrug off her doubts and ignore Sandra's loaded silence. Fortune was obviously smiling. And in the end even Sandra roused herself to gaze out of the window with a show of interest as they drove into Surrey in the Warden's Morris Minor. None of them was talkative, however, each busy with her own plans for the day and aware, too, of the inevitable embarrassment of farewells at the end of it.

'What's this place?' Sandra asked suddenly as a stretch of open country unfurled on their right. It seemed to roll on ahead for ever.

'It's Banstead Downs. We're nearly there now,' the Warden spoke over her shoulder. 'Can you remember the way, Beth?'

'Don't we turn off to the left near here?' Beth leaned forward to stare through the windscreen.

'So, is this country, then?' Sandra persisted, still gazing out at shrubby clumps spiked with near-leafless trees and with intermittent flashes of green between.

'It's a bit of heathland turned into a public golf-course. Here's the turning you remembered, Beth.' They dived down to the left; a few houses, some shops, a turn to the right. 'Here we are!' Another car-ride, another destination: always the same optimistic words.

The Warden braked outside a house that looked to Sandra pretty much the same as others in the road.

Something dead trailed over the front of this one and narrow, empty beds framed a square of lawn behind a low white fence.

'Here's my phone-number for today – just in case.' The Warden scribbled on a page from her diary and passed it back to Beth, who perfectly understood. In case Sandra turned moody and was best retrieved early.

'You see it's a detached house,' Beth pointed out proudly to her friend, slipping the Warden's note into her shoulder-bag. 'My landlady says it looks ever so pretty in the summer when that creeper flowers. I've forgotten its name, but it's blue.'

'It looks ever so pretty manky now,' Sandra observed sourly. Beth wished she would at least *try* to be cheerful, for her sake, instead of criticising. She went round to the boot for her case, wondering if after all it had been such a good idea to have Sandra tagging along and spoiling her big day. She'd wanted everything to go right and to be envied – for maximum confidence-boosting – not to be gloomed at.

The Warden led the girls up the path and rang the door-bell.

'Here's Beth, with her foster-sister to keep her company for the day,' she told the big woman who filled the doorway.

'Built like a brick shit-house with a face like a cat's twat,' Sandra muttered, standing behind Beth. 'She'll flatten you if you step out of line,' she added with unpleasant relish. Beth's special smile wavered. She wished Sandra would grow out of making childish personal comments on fatness, the Warden's moustache, that sort of thing. She'd wanted her landlady to be

242

admired as well as the house, and she was anyway bothered when Sandra's language turned blue in one of her 'don't care' moods. She wasn't much of an advertisement for Beth altogether.

'I'll be back for Sandra about six,' the Warden went on. 'They'll keep themselves occupied until then.'

Beth was anxious to show off the virtues of her room, which was large but slightly dimmed by the oversized furniture pushed into the corners – 'It's all *family* stuff, you know'; the mirrored wardrobe that Beth intended to fill with new clothes, the chest of drawers as dark and solid, the gas-ring for making hot drinks and snacks as soon as she'd bought herself a kettle and pan. Breakfast and the evening meal were included in the rent.

'There're some tanners in my purse, Sandra. Put one in the meter and light the fire,' Beth invited expansively. 'We don't need to be cold.' But even then she saw Sandra wasn't interested, dawdling through the contents of Beth's bag and slouching over to the fire. After a cursory glance around she wanted to go out and explore. Beth should have suspected something then.

'What's her name – that old screw downstairs?' Sandra interrupted a proprietorial eulogy on the wallpaper and curtains.

'Mrs Peabody. And she's very nice,' Beth answered repressively.

'*Pea*body? *That* size?' Sandra burst out laughing. It was a relief to see her snap out of her resentful mood and Beth joined in the laughter, suddenly lighter-hearted. They egged each other on to the verge of giggling hysteria. 'Mrs Marrowfat Peabody!' 'Mrs Marrow Fatbody!' 'Mrs Fatpea Marrowbody!'

243

'You'll have to watch yourself with her,' Sandra advised with a grin. 'Or did our dear Warden give you a taste for that sort of thing?' she added when Beth looked blank. 'Oh, come on! It's the talk of the Hostel – you and old Nosy! I did you a favour by insisting you're a red-blooded hetero, but Fatty may find that a turn-on. They do, you know. And you've never been bothered by *how* or *where*. Lend me your comb and I'll go and ask her the way to that golf-course bit we came past. It's not far.' Sandra helped herself from Beth's bag and combed out her pony-tail tidily while Beth stood dumb with shock. If rumours like *that* had flitted round the typing-pool then no wonder –

'It's absolutely untrue!' she protested at last. 'About Nosy and me –'

'Oh, I know *that*,' Sandra grinned into the mirror. 'But I didn't tell them *how* I know, don't worry – Shit! You got a rubber-band? Mine's just bust.' But Beth still wore her shoulder-length hair loose with an Alice band and Sandra had to make do with one of her spares. 'You finish unpacking – I won't be long,' Sandra assured breezily. Beth stared at the closed door, wondering just how free was the first element of freedom and trying not to feel sick. She had not missed one of Sandra's thrusts – or rather, Sandra had got home with every one.

Sandra found Mrs Peabody busy in the kitchen. She seemed glad to get them out of the house.

'You'll pass some shops on the way – why not get yourselves something for a picnic? But make sure your friend's back for six. It'll be dark by then anyway, and that main road's not safe to cross when it's dark. Wait – you must have your own key now.' She wiped her hands

244

and went out to the hall for a spare key from the hallstand drawer. 'Keep it safe – and be careful crossing that road.'

'Permission to go out,' Sandra told Beth. 'I've got some dosh – we'll get something to eat. She isn't much of a watch-dog, your Podbod. All she said was to be back before six and here's a key,' Sandra handed it over. 'She even thought I was you, so she's blind as well as fat.' Beth had recovered her calm, her last defence.

'It's a home, not a *Home*,' she smiled, a little superior, tucking the key into her shoulder-bag. 'She isn't supposed to be a watch-dog. It's worth the effort to get this far, honestly, Sandra.'

'Yeah, yeah,' Sandra agreed equably. 'You're not coming out like that, are you?'

Beth had dressed carefully that morning in a skirt with a jumper of her own knitting. Sandra, who was never much concerned with first impressions – although she might have made an effort today of all days, Beth considered – was wearing her inevitable jeans. Trousers were suitable for a picnic, however, and Beth changed into a pair of crimplene slacks and more comfortable shoes. She wore jeans only for housework. Beth had standards, thought Sandra, like other people had dandruff: obvious and unattractive. She intended to enjoy herself that afternoon, whatever Beth's po-faced attitude. But she need not have worried; Beth seemed intent on throwing off the unflattering image she had inadvertently slipped into at the Hostel and was as carefree as Sandra could have wished.

In spite of Beth's advice on gaining independence through honest effort and Mrs Peabody's digs, only one of the girls returned; at about five o'clock, when it was

245

already dark and beginning to rain. Sandra had taken a quicker way to freedom.

Mrs Peabody answered a knock at her sitting-room door to find a scrap of paper agitatedly waved in her face.

'It's Beth, Mrs Peabody. May I borrow your phone to ring this number? Sandra's decided not to wait for Miss Parker and I ought to warn her.'

'You mean she's *absconded*?' Yes, she'd been in the business, all right. 'And what's happened to your face?' She eyed the damp, dishevelled girl. 'You've been fighting!'

'Oh, no! That is – Sandra hasn't run away, but we had a – a bit of an argument and she decided to hitch into London. It's all right – she's got money enough for bus and tube fares when she gets there, but I ought to save Miss Parker a journey for nothing. Sandra's broken up, you see, because I'm leaving her. I've always looked after her.'

'Then it's great pity you didn't stop her doing such a foolish thing! I can see you tried, however,' Mrs Peabody added more gently. '*I'd* better speak to Miss Parker. Oh, *really*!' She took the slip of paper and tramped into the hall for the phone.

But Mrs Peabody was too late. Sandra had already rung, she was told, and Miss Parker had left for the Hostel about half an hour earlier. Mrs Peabody's shoulders heaved in exasperation and she dialled again; this time the Hostel's number noted on a scratch-pad beside the phone. The Warden had not long arrived back and was herself about to phone Banstead. Mrs Peabody was terse and self-exculpatory at first, but she gradually relaxed as the clucking sounded down the line almost as

246

clearly to each of the apprehensive listeners in the hall.

Yes, the Warden had already heard from Sandra – poor background – unpredictable – no great surprise she'd abused their trust and spoiled a treat for her friend. Only too sorry Mrs Peabody should have been worried. At least Sandra had had the decency to think of her friend and warn that she wouldn't be coming back – the police had been notified, of course . . . No, not coming back. She'd met someone who'd offered her a job.

The Warden asked to speak to Beth. The girl was almost incoherent with distress.

'You know what's happened?' the Warden's voice crackled with consternation.

'Yes, I could hear a little, but *truly* I'm not to blame, Miss Parker. Sandra turned really nasty, like she can sometimes – but only because she hated us being separated again. She wanted me to come back to the Hostel, but when I said I *couldn't* go back she didn't want to wait for you. I *believed* her when she said she was going straight back to the Hostel. I did all I could to make her wait – honestly – but when she wouldn't I made sure she hitched someone respectable. A Mrs Hawthorn. Yes, a lady-driver.'

'Well, that's a relief, anyway. Can you describe her, dear?'

'She was, well, about your age, I suppose, and she had a grey or fawn-coloured car. I'm no good at makes – and I'm sorry but I didn't think to write down the number. It was getting dark then – about four-thirty – and I was too miserable to think straight. Then I got terribly lost trying to find my way back to Mrs Peabody's to phone you – '

'You should've used a call-box straight away. How

did Sandra know where to find me? Surely that should've warned you – '

'But she didn't ask me! She must've read your number when she looked in my bag for a sixpence for the meter before we went out.'

'You're lucky if she didn't take your money as well as leaving you to take the blame for her inconsiderate behaviour. She's on her way to Norfolk now, to a job on a farm.'

'But she *promised* she was going back to the Hostel –'

'Well, never mind that. Did she have friends in Norfolk, dear?'

'Not that I know – but I don't know what friends she made after I left Dover House. But *honestly* I couldn't have stopped her, Miss Parker. I did all I could!' She burst into tears and Mrs Peabody, tutting, took the receiver from her hand. She muttered briefly down the phone and led her away to soothe the scratches across her face with antiseptic ointment.

They never caught up with Sandra that Beth ever heard. She wrote to her at the Hostel once or twice, hoping Sandra had returned there of her own accord or that at least they'd know where to forward her letters; neatly but cheekily typed on the firm's headed paper because it looked important and would amuse Sandra. She'd urged her to keep her head down and concentrate on getting a properly authorised job – 'You've got so much to offer, Sandra.'

But the only reply had been from the Warden, so Beth demonstrated her typing to her too a few times, although not on the firm's paper; just to say how kind Mrs Peabody was, how well the clerking job was going, and that she'd made some nice friends. She assumed that reports of her were being sent back and for a while wondered if the Warden might visit her, but she never did.

Beth wrote one last time, when she married. There'd been no one else but Mrs Peabody to impress with her success she was bursting to broadcast. You can't crow in the same way among your equals. But after that she'd been too preoccupied and the Warden's letters were left unanswered.

A policeman called on her after that Saturday in November and Beth made up her mind to mention a suspicion sparked off by the Warden's phone conversation. She had already discussed it with Mrs Peabody.

'It was when Miss Parker asked me about Sandra's friends. I don't know any of her recent friends but something bothered me that day and I was too upset at the time to make sense of it. I've been thinking about it ever since,' Beth began hesitantly. 'You see, the car came out of Banstead and crossed the main road to where Sandra was thumbing. I thought the driver stopped just because she – Mrs Hawthorn – didn't happen to be tearing past like the others. But I remembered later that there was a light-coloured car parked for a while at that junction – as it if was having difficulty getting out on to the main road. I think now it was the same one that stopped for Sandra.' The policeman made conscientious notes but no encouraging noises.

'So, I've been wondering if this was a prearranged meeting,' Beth went on drearily. 'Sandra was terribly keen to come with me that day. That didn't surprise me. We're foster-sisters, you see. But when we got here she wanted to go straight out again, up to that bit of open heath, and then she told me she was going to hitch back to London. When I wouldn't leave her at the roadside she – beat me up.'

'Beth was quite badly knocked about,' said Mrs Peabody gruffly. She'd insisted on being present. The policeman folded back a fresh page in his notebook.

'Tell me all you can remember of this Mrs Hawthorn.' He suppressed a sigh.

'I didn't get much of a look at her, I'm afraid,' Beth said apologetically. 'It was getting dark and Sandra had already hopped in, so I was seeing across her. But she was middle-agedish, because her dark hair had grey in it. It was cut like Mrs Peabody's.' Beth didn't like to describe it as a pudding-basin cut, but he could see for himself. 'She was wearing a sheepskin jacket and dark slacks. She had a deep sort of voice – quite a nice voice. I only had time to ask her name before Sandra wound up the window and they drove off. No "goodbye" or anything,' Beth ended miserably, but he'd obviously heard too much and seen too much in the line of duty to be overset by her small tragedy. Beth would have been surprised if she could have read his notes: 'Query, *female* driver? Obvious only one of the girls thumbing – Chance pick-up?' But he only asked,

'What was your friend wearing?'

'Jeans and a patterned jumper with a dark-blue anorak – Like this one.' Beth went quickly out into the hall for hers. It was shiny nylon with a thin layer of quilting, shower-proof but not frost-proof. 'It's not much if she's stranded somewhere,' she added worriedly. The policeman made no comment but merely asked Beth to let them know at the local station if she heard from Sandra.

The visit had been only a formality. Kids of all ages absconded daily. Generally they were looked for around their old haunts but otherwise they were recovered almost by chance or if they got into some fresh trouble. Sandra had no old haunts and she obviously hadn't attracted attention wherever she had gone to ground. Beth was not surprised that she never heard from her. Mrs Peabody would have been on the look-out for letters and phone-calls and that alone would have discouraged contact.

# Autumn 1989

# Fifteen

Beth puzzled over David Morgan's letter for a while but she had nothing new to add to what she'd reported twenty years before. She wondered briefly about the legacy he mentioned and what would happen to it if it was never claimed, but she was more concerned to know how she'd been traced. Who in Purley would still remember Nick's widow, for God's sake? Except perhaps one of Nick's friends. The old fear fluttered again in Beth's heart. And who'd have dreamt that Nosy Parker might keep her letters? That thought was not much less nerve-tingling.

All this rigmarole would have to be explained to Duncan, Beth supposed wearily. Even if he didn't refer to the letter, it would appear singular if she ignored it herself. What a fool she'd made of herself – as if she didn't have enough on her mind already. Duncan would be justified in believing that she had some sort of neurotic 'thing' about Nick's reach from beyond the grave. Neurotic – she'd wondered uneasily in the last day or so at how quickly she went over the top. It was uncharacteristic and worrying. As though some natural resilience had run out of elastic. If Duncan weren't so caring – But anyway, he needn't know all the details about her foster-father, dear God! Nor about Sandra's broken-window episode. He'd never understand why Beth had kept quiet about that, even if he knew all the circumstances. Beth shuddered at the memory, pressing her hands to her eyes

255

in an instinctive gesture to blot out the scene.

Sandra had been like a wild animal then, out of her mind with hate and fury. Perhaps with fear and panic too in case he was still alive. She hadn't much in her life to be grateful for, but she'd always been grateful to Beth for keeping her mouth shut. After all, Sandra had done it at least partly for her, Beth reflected. As she'd said, they were in it together. Their destinies were interweaved like daisy-roots in the grass – or so it had seemed then.

Beth was dressed and downstairs, tidily engaged in replying to David Morgan's letter, when Duncan came home at lunch-time. He didn't usually come home at midday but Beth knew he'd be worried about her and she was half expecting him. Duncan was the only reason she'd bothered to answer the letter. She saw his relief at finding her composed and peacefully occupied.

Duncan crossed the room and took Beth in his arms without a word.

'Everything's all right,' he said after a moment, but it was a question not a statement.

'I'm answering that letter.' Beth didn't need to specify. 'I've been trying to remember all I can of Sandra Littlejohn, but I don't think I can help Mr Morgan much.' She gave Duncan an expurgated account of their old association. 'I've never heard from her since,' she ended. 'She'd been in a funny mood all day, almost as if she was – spoiling for a row. But I'd betrayed her, you see. Deserted her. Poor Sandy.' Beth's hand flew to her mouth. 'I've just remembered,' she smiled unsteadily. 'She loathed being called Sandy.'

'You *mustn't* think of it as desertion or betrayal,' Duncan glanced sharply at her. 'Good God, what were you then – seventeen? No one could expect you to sacrifice your future for a hysterical girl who wasn't even family! What a bolt from the past for you, though, poor darling. But how on earth did this chap know where to find you?' It had been a question much exercising Beth's mind but she'd found an answer. 'Have you kept in touch with this Warden he mentioned?'

'Lord, no! But she'd have told him where she last heard from me – in Purley, when I wrote that I'd married Nick. On the offchance that there were children he must then've enquired round the local schools. They keep their records for ever and I'd left them this address and my change of name at Jennetta's school. Of course I left a forwarding address when I sold the flat too, but that wouldn't have been available after ten years, I don't suppose. Have you eaten?'

'Mm. Grabbed a sandwich,' Duncan murmured abstractedly.

He was obviously wanting to change to a more interesting subject than forwarding-addresses but was uncertain how to go about it. He glanced at Beth and away, brushing his hands up the back of his head so that a little drake's-tail curl of agitation formed at the crown. It was inevitable that Duncan would make some reference to the scene in the bedroom and Beth wished she could think of a dignified way of mentioning it first, but it was beyond casual apology.

It transpired – hesitantly – that Duncan had called on their GP for advice. He was embarrassed about admitting to this unilateral step and worried how Beth might react, but after a stunned moment Beth heard him out with resignation. Her behaviour couldn't be ignored and

257

she'd better make the best of it.

'I can't just watch you crack up without trying to do something about it,' Duncan explained. 'You frightened me this morning.' She found it a relief after all to talk about it, and with Duncan, not herself, on the defensive.

'But I've been frightened too, and not being able to understand *why* this is happening is doubly frightening. My fears can easily be explained away, you see, but they still persist – and that can't be right. And to see the effect it's having on you all – Duncan, if I'd behaved like that intentionally this morning, or even with good reason, I'd be ashamed of myself. I apologise, of course, but I just couldn't *help* myself. It terrified me. I seemed to lose all control, even physically. I just dread to think how I might've gone on if you hadn't been there.' Duncan had wondered that himself.

'Well, Patterson has a few ideas,' he told Beth, moving close to her, 'but he'd really like to see you, of course. Apparently he's always felt that you ask too much of yourself. When the children fell ill, for instance, he thought you too calm and collected for your own good because you didn't want *them* upset. But a quick panic would've been quite natural and a relief for you. And because that's how we saw you, unflappable, that's what we've demanded of you. It's been an increasing strain for you because it's an increasing load. Patterson says you've carried us – emotionally – and have left yourself with no one to share your worries. It's too easy to become selfish. Now, all that makes sense to me, darling, but there's more,' Duncan warned, pleased to see that Beth was receptive. 'In fact we had a long talk because I convinced him I needed to know of any way I could help. I couldn't guarantee you'd see him your-self,' he explained.

'The *timing's* so significant, Beth. Patterson suspects that the wedding's causing you real distress. However much you want it for Jennetta, you don't want it for your-self. You don't want to lose her.' Sudden tears prickled her eyelids and Beth froze into a monument of self-con-trol. Duncan saw her stiffen but he had to go on. 'That makes you feel guilty, so you can't talk about it. Patterson wonders whether subconsciously, this is all an expression of your *hope*,' Duncan took Beth's hands, 'not fear, that something will stop the wedding.'

Beth snatched her hands away and her mouth opened in protest but Duncan forestalled her.

'I know – I *know* what you're going to say. I've already said it all to Patterson. But when I told him that even Penny'd had a rough time, and that this morning you accused *me* of being in the conspiracy against you, he wasn't surprised. He explained that your fear for Penny was an expression of your dread of losing Jennetta, and as for me – well, I'm your "transferred guilt object",' Duncan smiled bleakly. 'Your whipping-boy. When I said your behaviour seemed more to me like a persecution complex, he said, "Self-persecution. She's looking for sticks to beat herself with".'

'Mother-love's a funny thing,' Patterson had added, and Duncan had no intention of mentioning it to Beth. 'We think of it as a virtue, but in its perverted form it's the most destructive poison a woman has access to. It cripples far more than the object of her mother-love.'

Beth sat thoughtfully, trying to apply Duncan's half-familiar phrases to herself and feel comfortable in them;

259

but in one essential respect they simply didn't fit.

'So no wonder your control's slipping,' he went on, encouraged by Beth's silence. 'You've had a terrible life – by my standards, anyway – and it's amazing that you've emerged unscathed. I realise now that's the result of conscious effort as well as your strength of character. I've abused that strength.

'I didn't realise at first that you were actually fearful of meeting anyone from your past – and no wonder that you were – but even Nick's crooks are "transferred guilt objects" now. You thought you had good reason then, no doubt, but it's a mistake to cut off all your roots. If you do, you have to be very certain of your support, and I'm afraid your support wasn't as strong as it might've been. It even leaned on you. It must've helped, marrying me – I hope it did – but I never knew how much *I* needed to help. I should've encouraged you to screech like a fishwife,' Duncan smiled fleetingly at an image that once would have been unthinkable, 'and throw things. Instead of which I've sat around admiring your courage or being impatient now because the strain *I've* helped to impose on you is finally beginning to tell. Believe me, Patterson told me a few home-truths!

'Well, there you are,' Duncan raised his hands and let them fall as he sat back in his chair. 'You've been very patient and civilised, but so you usually are. I can't tell whether you've accepted any of this. I hope some of it's made sense and you feel better for understanding yourself. But anyway I wish you'd see Patterson. It's the – involuntary aspect that's so upsetting, isn't it? But it won't be any less involuntary merely for understanding the cause. You need his help to cope, darling.'

Duncan looked so worried and so loving that impulsively Beth reached towards him.

'I won't have you blaming yourself for any of this! It's shameful of Patterson to put such an idea into your head, Duncan. I couldn't have married a more unselfish, understanding man – and if I haven't said that before,' Beth added with a wry smile, 'then I should be beaten soundly. But some of what you've said *sounds* logical enough to provoke thought – though of course I deny that I'm hoping Jennetta's wedding falls through. Good heavens, I can't begin to tell you how much I want it. Even subconsciously that suggestion's horrible!'

'Quite. And that's Patterson's point,' Duncan was ready. 'Because you find it horrible you're flaying yourself. But it's understandable, darling. Your whole life and behaviour were geared to Jennetta for so long that your subconscious is saying now, "What kind of a person shall I revert to when she's gone? Shall I still be the Me I've become and know better than any other self?" It's a sort of identity crisis Patterson sometimes sees in widows – but they're *expected* to mourn their loss and take time to readjust, while you, poor love, have to put on a happy face.'

'But I *am* happy, Duncan. Truly. And Jennetta's certainly not the only person in my life.'

'You don't need to tell me that, darling. But she is your oldest root, the only real root. In a sense she was your mould too, and now the mould's breaking. Don't be afraid. I'm longing to meet the butterfly that emerges from the chrysalis. A whole new voyage of discovery with you. For a start, I've never been to bed with a mother-in-law.'

'Idiot!' Beth snorted with sudden laughter.

But she recognised the truth of much of what Duncan said about her close relationship with Jennetta. In some ways it had perhaps been too close. It was a measure of Duncan's generosity that he'd never been jealous. He was a truly good man, Beth acknowledged remorsefully to herself.

'All right, then, I'll go and see Patterson – but it sounds very much as though you two've put your heads together to set me up with a Catch-22 situation. If I deny his suggestion it's because my subconscious won't let me admit it, even to myself, because it's irrational. But if I express other fears, then they're unreasonable and again I'm being irrational.'

'No, you can't win,' Duncan laughed as he stood up to go. 'Just try and be your usual honest self with Patterson, that's all I ask. I know he can help.'

Duncan took Beth's letter with him to the post; considerate, but more precipitate than she'd intended. After some thought she phoned Jane, whose school run it was that afternoon.

'Why don't you and Jonquil stay on for an hour or so when you drop Penny off?' Beth invited, first clearing a few perfunctory civilities out of the way.

'Why, Beth, of course!' Jane's voice soared with surprise at this change of tack after the polite brush-offs during the past weeks. They hadn't met since a day or two after the Mallinsons' return from holiday, Beth realised. 'It's been ages!' Jane echoed her thoughts. 'I've been expecting to hear more about our *haute couture* crawl.'

'Yes, we must discuss that,' Beth murmured vaguely,

remembering the suggestion that Jane should help her choose her wedding outfit. 'See you after school, then.'

Jane's readiness to rally round was gratifying. Beth worked off her relief by preparing a picnic feast for the girls to guzzle out of earshot in the grounds, and a cake and an iced pitcher for Jane. It's a mistake to cut off your roots, she reminded herself of what Duncan had said, and she'd been in danger of doing just that again. Beth saw belatedly that whereas her retreat had once seemed to be the only route to self-preservation, now it would be a suicidal cutting of communications that could leave her out in the cold, socially, and out of touch. Intimacy with Jane had brought unexpected embarrassments in the undelicious shape of her aunt Grace, but only their continued intimacy could provide an antidote to the far greater embarrassments looming between the lines of David Morgan's letter.

'Make a stranger of Jane,' Beth warned herself aloud, 'and you simply won't know what's going on behind your back.'

'Seems to me you could do with a let-up.' Jane gazed clinically into Beth's face as later they settled themselves on the patio. 'Gamboge around the gills, my dear – An iced drink? What a heavenly idea!' She took the frosted glass Beth held out to her and drank gratefully. 'My God!' she gasped, awed. 'What *is* this?'

'My mother-in-law's recipe,' Beth smiled. 'She calls it Singapore Swamp, on account of the floating vegetation.' She poured a glass for herself. 'It's reasonably innocuous.'

'It's *absolute* ambrosia, Beth – and not all that innocuous. What's under the cover?'

'Your cake,' Beth murmured, uncovering the plate.

'Not *my* cake? *How* I've missed you!' Jane laughed.
'So. Last lap? Only just in time, I'd say. Aren't you
sleeping?'

'Much better now the heat's less,' Beth tried not to
sound irritated. Why did people imagine they showed
their concern best through bossy personal remarks? 'But
I had – rather a shock today,' she admitted, 'and I suppose I'm tired enough for it to show.'

Jane looked away towards the paddock where the
girls could be heard.

'Anything you can talk about?' she asked quietly.

'Oh, it's nothing private,' Beth assured her. 'Just –
unexpected. I had a letter from a solicitor asking about a
friend I was at school with in Fulham. There's a legacy,
apparently. Unfortunately I lost touch with her when I
was seventeen so I can't help. What stunned me, though,
was how he'd found *me* after all this time.' She glanced
uncomfortably at Jane. 'You know – a sort of Big
Brother sensation. Well, good heavens – I've changed
my name twice since then.'

'Hell, how unnerving!' Jane sympathised. 'But I'm
sure you've the right to ask how he managed it.'

'Well, he did say in passing – Are you ready for some
cake?'

'Need you ask?' Jane grinned.

Beth helped her to cake and sat back with her own
plate while Jane moaned appreciation.

'So what did the solicitor say?' she prompted thickly.

'Oh, he'd traced my friend to a hostel in south
London, a place called High Bank.' Beth munched tidily

264

on and ignored Jane's quiet exclamation. 'That's where I last knew of her myself. He turned up the woman in charge at the time and she put him on to me. You see, my friend – she was rather a livewire – just upped and left, so after a bit this woman returned my letters with a note to say what'd happened. I wrote to her a couple of times in case there was any news, but there never was. It seems she'd filed away my letters, signed in my maiden name, and they were enough for the solicitor to work on. Amazing, really.' Beth picked up the cake-knife and looked enquiringly at Jane; but Jane merely replaced her half-eaten cake on the table.

'When was it you lost touch with your friend?' she asked in a strained voice.

'About – about twenty years ago,' Beth gave her a puzzled stare. 'Jane, is something wrong with the cake?'

'No – Just let me think a minute. I mean – it's lovely. About 1969?' she muttered, calculating. 'Did this solicitor mention the Warden's name?' Beth shook her head wonderingly. 'Can you remember what she told you about your friend?'

'Er – that she'd gone to find work in East Anglia, as I recall. Look –'

'Did she tell you that your friend left with just the clothes on her back – after hitching a lift while she was visiting away from the hostel?' Jane leaned forward, her eyes intent.

'She was seeing her foster-sister,' Beth nodded, wondering how much detail Jane knew to fill in that outline. 'Elizabeth Ramsay. I knew her too. Every second girl of my Coronation generation was christened Elizabeth and called something different,' she smiled coolly. 'But –

you're talking as if this means something to you. It's as
– bothering as this morning's letter,' she added in bewilderment.

'Positively my last question.' Jane raised her hand as
though to forestall any more protests. 'What was your
friend's name?'

'Sandra Littlejohn.' Beth met Jane's incredulous
look. 'I feel,' she said carefully, 'as if I've said more than
I realise and convicted myself of something. *Am* I to
know more?'

Jane's inquisitorial manner collapsed in confusion.

'Beth, I'm sorry! But believe me, I'm quite shaken.
Crimson crikey – It really is *the* most in*cred*ible coincidence!' She shook her head in disbelief. 'You see – Aunt
Grace was the Warden at High Bank when your friend
gave them all the bag!'

'Your Aunt Grace?' Beth echoed numbly. It was plain
she had difficulty assimilating the news. 'Yes, I remember you telling me she worked in a hostel,' she said after
a moment. 'Good heavens. But – but you've more than
simply matched up the dates, haven't you. You seem to
know the whole story. Has your aunt mentioned the
solicitor's enquiries, then?' She held her breath.

'No, she hasn't – and that's queer too,' Jane reached
thoughtfully for her plate. 'But I have heard the story –
quite recently. It was your friend's remains Aunt Grace
was convinced they'd found.' For a second the words
rang sickeningly and Beth felt the blood rush from her
face.

'Oh – You mean on the day of the heath-fire,' she said
shakily. 'For a moment I thought – But for heaven's
sake! Why did your aunt assume *that*?'

266

'Because,' Jane replied a little consciously, 'she'd always supposed the worst. Your friend Sandra was never traced, you know. You weren't the only one to lose touch with her. And there was also apparently some doubt at the time as to the sex of the driver who picked her up.' Beth's bewilderment was obvious and Jane elaborated. 'Aunt Grace told us that it was at first thought to be a woman, but police enquiries indicated that it might've been a man – an assignation, even. That actually fitted with what Aunt Grace knew of Sandra – Sorry, Beth, but she doesn't seem to've had a high opinion of your friend. So it wouldn't have surprised her if Sandra'd never left the general area where she'd been picked up, on a dark winter's evening – and there were the bones. She jumped to the wrong conclusion, as it happens, but there was some method in her reasoning,' Jane ended defensively.

'Yes, I see,' Beth murmured, dazed. 'I knew nothing of all this. A – a hell of a coincidence, as you say. I feel utterly – stupefied.' She refilled her glass, apologised absent-mindedly and refilled Jane's. 'More cake?' She loaded Jane's plate without waiting for a reply. Jane silently berated herself for her tactlessness. They were, after all, discussing something more personal than a coincidence.

'I've written back to the solicitor,' Beth went on after an uncomfortable pause, 'and of course I've asked him to let me know if he ever finds Sandra. But obviously I must talk to your aunt. What's her address?' To Beth's surprise and immediate annoyance, Jane hesitated.

'Well – I don't know that'd achieve anything useful,' she said, self-consciously chasing crumbs on her plate.

'She can't know any more than I've passed on, or that solicitor wouldn't have followed you up.'

'She knows a darn sight more than she ever let on when *I* was asking for information,' Beth pointed out sharply. Jane glanced up. 'I want to know *why* it was supposed Sandra'd arranged to meet some man. She wasn't remotely interested in men.'

'Well – Maybe not in *that* sense, Beth,' Jane began worriedly. Beth's tone was quite unfamiliar. 'But what if he'd been someone who'd promised her a job – or even simply an opportunity to get well away – '

'Was there even a *hint* of such a man *before* Sandra ran off? You see? *That's* the sort of thing your aunt could tell me. And I'd also like to know if she's any idea what became of Sandra's foster-sister,' Beth challengingly trailed her coat. When Jane said nothing she continued more calmly.

'I was hurt when Sandra cut me off but she was on the run, after all, and that was that. Now I feel I've been – well, dragged back into her life only to hear that all these years there's been reason to suppose her dead. *Murdered*, Jane, if your aunt's reasoning's reliable. She's the only one I can ask for information. Can't you understand how I feel?' Beth appealed.

'My dear, I'm sure I'd feel exactly as you do,' Jane began helplessly, 'but it's Aunt Grace, you see – '

'You mean she wouldn't care for me to visit her? What's she got against me?' Beth snapped, reverting to her aggressive manner.

'Good God, nothing at all!' Jane protested strongly. 'How can you think that? But she's old, and she's – tired. It's not so long since she was thoroughly stirred up by those damn bones. Now, it seems, she's been approached by a total stranger who's raked up that old business once again. I'm worried she hasn't phoned to tell me of his visit. It could mean she's in a total tizz even now –'

'Or she's being tactful,' Beth pointed out. 'She can't have been in any doubt that you'd all had enough of the subject that day.'

'Oh, God, that's true – *poor* old thing!' Jane groaned remorsefully. 'But I daren't ring her to ask. If she's taken the solicitor's visit in her stride I'd rather let sleeping dogs lie. And if she hasn't – well, they'll get in touch with me soon enough. But you see what I mean? If *you* go asking questions as well – I can't risk her peace of mind, Beth.'

'And what about my peace of mind?' Beth demanded angrily. 'Your aunt's behaviour that day on the Downs could have been extremely unsettling for Penny – and no thanks to her it wasn't. Now I find that through her efforts I've been put through a traumatic day myself and you're refusing me the chance to – to exorcise it. For a pretty feeble reason, if you don't mind my saying so. She'd probably *relish* the opportunity of getting in a few more digs at Sandra.'

Jane's expression had grown more and more shocked as Beth talked, but although she made an obvious effort at appeasement she remained firm.

'Beth – look – I'm really terribly sorry I've upset you so much, but I feel *responsible* for Aunt Grace – '

'I believe she's told you she doesn't want me there,' Beth interrupted.

'But of course she hasn't,' Jane flapped her hands in

269

frustration. 'Why on *earth* should she? She won't have known that the old letters of enquiry from Sandra's friend would lead the solicitor to *you*. The coincidence would stagger her as much as it's staggered us – but I'm *not* prepared to test her with it. She may be a trying old thing at times, Beth, but she's my *family*.' An unusually hard light in Jane's eyes at last warned Beth she d pushed too far. She threw up her hands in capitulation.

'Of course. I understand and I'm sorry. I got things badly out of proportion. I – I seem to get hooked these days on making mountains out of molehills,' she added with a rueful look. 'Inventing problems. Have another Swamp and show I'm forgiven.' Beth forced a smile and picked up the jug.

'Better not,' Jane muttered awkwardly. She got to her feet and brushed down her skirt. 'I ought to get Jonquil home while my steering's still legal.' She looked anywhere but at Beth while she spoke. 'But it was a lovely tea – and thank you.' She's hoping to leave without mentioning the shopping expedition, Beth told herself.

'Glad you could both stay,' she said lightly. 'I'll get in touch about my outfit hunt when the consultant's fixed the date of my medical.'

'Medical?' Jane swung round, startled.

'Oh Lord, haven't I told you? Yes, merely – exploratory.' Beth shrugged and glanced away from the scrutiny. 'Come on down to the paddock and collect your young.' Jane followed unspeaking and Beth, her mild, undemanding self again, filled the silence with herbaceous prattle as they walked through the garden.

So it hadn't been an entirely successful get-together, Beth reflected as she cleared away the debris from tea, but it certainly could have gone worse. She'd been prepared to sacrifice some of her anonymity – unthinkable once, but she'd grown involuntarily more practised during recent months – in return for discovering what she wanted to know. With Jane still her friend and sympathetic, Beth expected her own close connection with Sandra and High Bank would remain confidential if she revealed it. After all, Jane herself was pretty cagey about her aunt's former profession. Only the unexpectedness of crossed paths had popped out that confidence. People can never resist making an outcry about coincidences, Beth mused. God knows why, when so many of them are humanly contrived.

She'd been half afraid these past few months that the aunt – bloody Nosy Parker in person – had picked up an echo in her memory connecting Jane's lunch-guest that day in June with High Bank. Beth hadn't recognised her then – how should she? – so she'd had no warning to be particularly wary. Only on the following day was she quite certain who the old woman was. The subsequent hysteria over the bones had seemed to indicate at least a train of thought set off by that lunch-party. If so, it was only a matter of time before Jane was told of her friend's early history. There might even follow a lachrymose reunion and a celebration of old times. Beth felt sick at the thought.

She'd avoided Jane after that; an illogical form of self-defence at the time and even more so after Jane proved her ignorance by her unchanged manner when they next met. Beth was quite sure Jane's attitude would change when she knew of her background. She'd seen it happen before. At best the knowledge would be mutually

271

embarrassing. Bad enough. At worst, all Beth's small deceits would be reviewed and magnified; there'd be delicate indications that Lady Mallinson no longer found her company 'suitable'. Beth couldn't have borne that.

It had taken David Morgan's letter to jolt some sense into her. Even a ghastly reunion seemed a chance worth taking for the sake of defusing this latest threat to her peace of mind. In the event she'd given away very little for learning that neither Jane nor her aunt had any idea of Beth's former identity. Nosy's suspicions hadn't led the solicitor to Beth Masters; he'd merely followed Beth Ramsay through official channels. In fact Beth had laid the trail herself. The Warden's last few letters had come to the flat, she remembered, so she must have mentioned her new address as well as her married name – an openness that would have been in character then. That's all David Morgan had learnt from Jane's aunt. It seemed unlikely too that either Jane or her aunt would raise the subject again.

So after all Beth had nothing to worry about *there*. Instead she'd let herself be thrown by the unexpected intrusion of a man into the story; by the suggestion that Sandra might even have been killed and dumped soon after she'd thumbed that lift. Beth had been too horrified to think carefully. Of course she'd wanted to know what grounds there'd been for Nosy's theories, but just as understandably her own lack of control had frightened Jane off any idea of a meeting. Considered coolly, there was of course no basis for the silly woman's dramatics, except that hitch-hikers did occasionally run into trouble. The saga of Sandra's disappearance had no

272

doubt been used at High Bank as an Awful Warning –
typically – until the warning had fossilised into fact in
the Warden's mind.

Beth cursed herself for over-reacting. She'd seriously offended even Jane's tolerant goodwill. She'd done
what she could at the time to repair the damage by hint-
ing at a mysterious condition that might excuse her manners. (And that committed her to an appointment with
the family GP. It would please Duncan at least, Beth
shrugged.) More importantly she'd better get her relationship with Jane back on its old footing. Viewed quite
cold-bloodedly, with or without the superfluous aunt,
the Mallinson connection was too good an investment to
whistle down the wind. She owed it to Penny, Beth nodded portentously, as well as to herself.

# Sixteen

Beth's interview with Dr Patterson was arranged for Saturday afternoon – 'So we needn't feel hurried,' he explained, and she was grateful to him for giving up his spare time. A standard physical examination, however, showed nothing out of order that a tonic wouldn't help. A physical reason for her condition – even the despised gynaecological one – would have been easier for Beth to accept than any psychological one.

But apart from that minor reassurance Beth felt she might just as well have consulted Penny's Sherry. She was as honest as Duncan had urged her to be in her replies to the doctor's questions about her history and her current fears, but she no more convinced the doctor than Duncan that if she needed treatment it was not for her dread of losing Jennetta.

Beth couldn't be satisfied, therefore, with the doctor's various explanations as to why she should be *acting* so uncharacteristically, the point that worried her most. She'd been frightened often enough before but hadn't let it show, except in her reclusiveness – a private reaction at least. Burblings of 'stress, inevitable in the marshalling of a big wedding and reception'; of vicious spirals of sleeplessness resulting in greater stress; of an over-active subconscious – all seemed as irrelevant as if he'd diagnosed chronic wind. Beth had coped with stress for years, prided herself on her cool in a crisis and on her organising ability. How else had she survived?

She expected to be able to cope, and alone, because that's how it had always been.

In the end she accepted a prescription for sleeping-pills, influenced by the doctor's insistence that it was possible to drive the body beyond the mind's capacity to keep pace. That might explain her occasional crippling headaches. But neither broken nights nor headaches could account for her personality change, Beth believed. 'What kind of a person shall I revert to?' Duncan had quoted her inner mind as wondering, never dreaming how horridly all the warning bells had rung for Beth.

The one new fact that emerged during the interview was that Beth had experienced none of these symptoms when she married Duncan. Surely if she was afraid of malicious intervention in her life from Nicholls or Ramsay connections, *then* had been the logical time. Dr Patterson made a point of that to try and convince Beth that such fears *now* were unreasonable and could therefore be resolved by his blanket 'psychosomatic' explanation. But Beth felt there had to be a more palatable answer and she drove her mind to find it.

It was true that by the time she married Duncan her confused expectations of what might follow Nick's death and her claustrophobic fears for Jennetta and herself were largely forgotten. Not a ripple had disturbed her smooth transition from Mrs Andrew Nicholls to Mrs Duncan Masters. David Morgan's letter proved how easily she could be traced more than eighteen years after Nick's death; how much more easily while she'd still lived in Purley. Yet she hadn't been approached.

So why should she *now* revive that obsessive fear of persecution – and worse, go over the top? That she consistently traced it back to the balding man's interest made no sense; for not only had his face meant nothing to her, if he was one of Nick's old friends he was at least ten years out of date. Then why couldn't she accept the blasted man's interest simply in Jennetta's 'bride-to-be radiance', as Anna had believed it to be? Jennetta was a lovely-looking girl. Men *did* stare at pretty girls.

The thought of Anna reminded Beth that the balding man wasn't the only one that day to be interested in her family. She'd gone back to Dickins & Jones with only faint expectations of seeing any of the three there again; but had the balding man appeared, thereby confirming that his interest was more than casual, Beth had meant to confront him and put him on the spot before all those witnesses.

But only Anna had been there, an admitted *habituée*. Anna. Anna, with her familiarity, her cosy cross-examination of Jennetta, her ready response to Beth's wave for attention. All Beth's senses seemed to freeze as she made the connections and came to a conclusion she fought to reject.

Anna had recognised Beth. No wonder she'd flashed her scarred hand about. That was a trap to see if she could surprise a recognition out of Beth. And Beth had recognised her, in a sense. But then she'd dismissed Anna too readily, stupidly fixated on the balding man. As if he were The Balding Man, instead of merely a 'transferred object of suspicion'. That was at least understandable, for the alternative was horrifying.

Now Beth was really frightened. She knew the true cause of her lesser fears now. Those had been merely exploratory, yet even so they'd affected her badly enough. Subconscious recognition, subconscious warnings. But now Beth really had something to be frightened about, and from a quarter she'd least expected.

As soon as she could get Jennetta alone she questioned her about her conversation with Anna that, in her preoccupation, Beth had let pass her by. It was a bitterly frustrating exercise that served only to rouse Jennetta's curiosity without producing answers. Jennetta couldn't remember if Anna had mentioned her surname, whereabouts she lived, or the name of her business; however, she thought she herself had probably told her where and when the wedding was to take place.

'What on earth *did* you talk about?' Beth asked impatiently.

'Well, she told me about her daughter's wedding and asked about mine, and what Alan did. Then she told me about this business school she runs – But what's all this about, Mum?'

'If you told her where the church is,' Beth murmured thoughtfully, 'she must assume that we live in Epsom. Did she hint for an invitation?'

'Of course not. Are you thinking of inviting her?' Jennetta asked in surprise. But Beth only glanced at her abstractedly and turned to the telephone directories.

The next hour or so was even more frustrating as Beth phoned business schools, staff-training bureaux and anything remotely similar all over London. A couple of false leads raised her hopes but in the end there was nothing. The mews flat Anna had spoken of indicated that she lived in London, but of course her business could be somewhere outside. And that was assuming she had spoken the truth about herself. Was that likely? Beth even rang Fleetwood & Partners on the sudden thought that David Morgan's letter was a suspicious coincidence, in the circumstances; but again, there was no Anna known on the staff.

It only remained for Beth to return once more to Dickins & Jones and wait for Anna there. She left the house after lunch on the following Saturday without saying a word, too preoccupied to think how such behaviour would appear to her family. It was unfortunate that Duncan had cancelled his weekend golf in order to be more available for Beth.

He came indoors after spending some time with Penny in the paddock and found only Jennetta and Alan discussing their packing and shipping arrangements. The absence of Beth's car finally convinced him she'd gone out.

'And she said nothing to you, either?' Duncan asked Jennetta. 'It's not like her to leave us all wondering.'

'She's had something on her mind, Dad. Something to do with a woman we met in Town the day we bought my wedding-dress.' Jennetta recounted the incident and her mother's recent questioning. 'Anna said she had tea at Dickins & Jones every Saturday. If Mum's car's at the station, I bet you'll find she's gone up to Town looking for her,' Jennetta ended, as puzzled as Duncan.

'It's not like your mother to interest herself in strangers,' he pointed out, 'and she hates Town.' But Beth's car was parked at the station and Duncan's surprise turned to serious concern. He caught the next train up.

Beth's plan to find Anna off-guard was frustrated by Duncan's arrival. There he was, without warning, stand-

279

ing beside her chair as if he'd catapulted up through a trap-door in the floor. For a bewildered moment she gaped at him, unable to make sense of what she saw.

'Darling for heaven's sake! Why didn't you say? I'd have come up with you.' It was Duncan's familiar voice, the all too familiar look of worry in his eyes. 'Tell me what this is all – ' Suddenly Beth was maddened by his uxorious concern. Frustration and resentment spilled over into fury. Life was becoming as closely supervised as it ever had been in care.

'What the *hell* are you doing, following me about? *Spying* on me!' Beth's voice as much as her words paralysed Duncan in the act of pulling out a chair to sit down. 'Leave me *alone,* can't you!'

'Beth – please!' He was shocked by this repetition of the terrible scene in the bedroom; doubly so after believing that Patterson had worked a soothing cure. But bitterly conscious though he was of how public the scene – the rasping quality of Beth's voice had carrying power – and how he must appear, it was Beth's self-exposure he dreaded and tried to cover. Duncan couldn't simply walk out and leave her. 'Come home, darling,' he urged, taking her by the elbow. Beth swung at him.

'*Get* your hands off!' Duncan stepped back, distraught. Satisfied that she'd routed him, Beth turned away and her eyes continued their restless roving among the tables.

The restaurant manager materialised at Duncan's side and murmured something he didn't catch but it nerved him to take the initiative.

'My wife hasn't been well,' he forced himself to speak calmly, mechanically reaching for his wallet. 'I'll

280

pay her bill and take her out.' What that might involve made him quail.

'There's nothing to pay, sir.' The manager was impressed by Duncan's dignity and anyway anxious to get rid of a troublemaker. 'Another of 'em caught out on the game,' he told his deputy later.

Beth's apparent unconcern during this exchange distressed Duncan as much as anything yet. He touched Beth's arm again and she reared round like a striking snake. He caught her wrist and held it, forcing himself to look calmly into her contorted face.

'The manager's entitled to call the police if you won't let me take you out,' Duncan warned firmly. 'Come on, Beth.' With relief he saw her eyes refocus, as if she was seeing him for the first time, and her features relaxed. He put his other arm around her and helped her to her feet. There was no resistance. He picked up Beth's bag and steered her out between the tables.

It was a silent journey home and Duncan was grateful for that much, given the crowded carriage, while he struggled to come to terms with the anguish of realisation. For Beth's condition was obviously more serious than Patterson had led him to believe.

Behind her bland expression Beth was consumed with anger, directed about equally at Duncan and herself. Duncan had aborted her mission but her own carelessness had brought that about. And she'd been careless too in her handling of the situation afterwards. She'd thrown aside, not lost, her sense of proportion for the luxury of anger and had realised almost too late how little she could afford it. Beth was still determined to confront Anna but now she saw that Duncan had to be taken

281

more into her confidence. She couldn't have him trailing her around. That would bitch it all again. It was ironic that the very qualities for which Beth admired Duncan, and with which she felt so comfortable, should now be so infuriating.

Jennetta and Alan had gone and Penny was safely oblivious in the paddock with Jonquil when they drove home in their separate cars from the station.

'You're home and you're safe now,' Duncan piloted Beth to an armchair. 'I'm afraid we must talk, Beth.' His face was set.

'I was hoping to avoid just that when I left without telling you,' Beth sighed wearily. 'It was a mistake not to warn you, but – it's so complicated, Duncan. It might be easier if you simply asked questions in order.'

'Thank you. I'd prefer to take this step by step. Very well, then. I'd like to know first why you went up to Town.'

'To try and find a woman Jennetta and I spoke to several weeks ago.' That at least bore out what Jennetta had suggested, to Duncan's relief. 'I'd seen her once before, when we all had tea there together. When you pointed out that balding man. I didn't actually recognise her on either occasion but she did seem familiar. I'm sure now she recognised me, yet she didn't make herself known. But now I know who she is. She's Sandra Littlejohn, the girl mentioned in David Morgan's letter. It's dawned on me too why she didn't remind me who she was. Because she's planning some mischief to get back at me for deserting her – like I told you. Jennetta mentioned where and when the wedding's to be and I'm certain she's intending to spoil it. She even hinted we'd meet again.'

Duncan had been growing more and more sceptical as Beth talked.

'But why should she bother after all this time?' he protested. 'And how can you be sure it's someone you knew only as a child? Beth, I think she's another of your "transferred guilt objects",' Duncan smiled understandingly. 'You're still on your self-persecution binge, aren't you?' Beth controlled her impatience with an effort.

'No, you're wrong. If you think, all this – trouble started that first day I saw her and thought her familiar. I must subconsciously have recognised her then, but it was David Morgan's letter that resurrected – that jogged my memory. Sandra had a scarred hand, you see, and so has this woman, Anna. Both Jennetta and I noticed it. Believe me, Duncan, I know. I went this afternoon to find out what she's up to.'

'Well, I'm not convinced,' Duncan announced heavily after a moment. 'But I *am* thoroughly worried. The trouble is –' he sighed and rubbed his hair up the wrong way – 'the trouble is that I don't want to upset you further, and that ties my hands. Beth, I wish you'd see Patterson again – and I'll come with you this time. Are you taking that medication he prescribed?'

'"Medication"!' Beth sneered, feeling her anger implode in stealthy perspiration. She went hastily to stand at the open patio doors to feel what little breeze there was. 'Sleeping-pills, that's all. And I'm to be grateful that he didn't offer me Valium for my jangled, middle-aged, female nerves. For weeks I've – sensed this threat but haven't been able to place it. Now I've finally pinned it down, you talk as though Patterson should've prescribed a strait-jacket three times after meals. He's an old fool and I *won't* go back to him.'

'Not a strait-jacket,' Duncan said quietly, coming up behind her, 'but a second opinion. I'm afraid this – obsessive fear of yours may affect your mind if we don't get proper treatment. If you could've seen – *heard* yourself this afternoon! I can only imagine you weren't fully aware of yourself. It's happened once before, darling.'

Beth drew a long, deep breath. By jostling her mental and physical balance together she could synchronise both at a single point, like a spinning top, for long enough to control her temper and her reactions. Sometimes these days the effort was too great. When she was certain of her poise, Beth turned to face Duncan.

'I know I need treatment – a holiday when the wedding's safely over. But of *course* I was fully aware of what I was doing this afternoon! I desperately needed to meet Sandra and I'd managed it so that I was alone. But for all I knew *she* wouldn't be. There were three of them together that first time I saw her. Then you burst in on my careful stake-out. I didn't want her warned or to see that I was accompanied by a hefty man. Remembering the way she spoke to Jennetta and me, she'd certainly have recognised you and faded away. I *had* to dislodge you quickly, Duncan. There wasn't time for this sort of explanation and you'd have demanded that, wouldn't you?' Beth asked with a half-smile. 'Of *course* the incident wasn't pleasant for either of us – *and* it failed to shift you – but I'm sure as I'm standing here that Anna is Sandra and that she means trouble. I may not've seen her for twenty-odd years but I knew her very well once, remember. She was always unpredictable and vengeful.

284

She simply *couldn't* resist this opportunity to get back at me.' And she had secrets in her head from which Duncan would never recover, were he ever to hear them.

He was at last convinced by Beth's manner, and willing to be. Her story was at least the lesser evil.

'You really think she may target the wedding?'

'Well, isn't it a marvellous opportunity for her? Just think!'

Duncan did so, with consternation.

'Then shouldn't we notify the police, darling? It's only a fortnight to the wedding. Perhaps we could apply for an injunction, or whatever, to – to prevent her from coming anywhere near us. I'll discuss it with Rob Mallinson –' But Beth was impatiently flapping her hands.

'Police involvement is hardly the best publicity for Jennetta's wedding! I don't want her or the Mallinsons – anyone – to know about this if it can possibly be avoided. Just imagine if the local rag gets wind of it – "Bride's Mother in Remand Home Blackmail Threat"!' Duncan blanched. 'No, let me try again to find Sandra next Saturday and deflect her. If I can't make any impression on her, *then* we'd better warn the police to look out for – for practical jokes at the church or the reception.'

Beth went back to her chair and collapsed into it. She was exhausted, but she'd won.

'Come with me next Saturday if you wish, Duncan, but it'll be a wash-out if we're seen together.'

'I really don't care for the idea of you tackling this business alone, but at least you've taken me into your confidence now and I don't feel so God-awful *lost*. If you're convinced about this woman then it's perhaps

285

best for you to see her alone – always supposing you're not barred from Dickins & Jones,' Duncan added as the shaming thought struck him. Beth saw that he viewed that disgrace as second only to her being convicted of immoral earnings. She fought down a manic cackle.

'As it was you who caused the trouble,' she pointed out with a tired smile, 'it's as well you've decided not to be there.'

However, Duncan had a point, Beth considered. A further visit might well be embarrassing. She cast around for another way of intercepting Anna – Beth found it hateful to think of her as Sandra. She returned to the suspicion that David Morgan's letter had been curiously well timed and that Anna herself had sent it to stir Beth up. In that case she must have some connection with Fleetwood & Partners to use their headed stationery. She wouldn't be known there as Anna; she wouldn't have told Beth the name she now lived by. And nor, of course, would she be known as Sandra.

On Monday Beth transferred the old snap from her handkerchief-case to her bag with some vague idea of using it to sweeten what was certain to be a bitter reunion with her foster sister, and drove to Bromley. She found the premises of Fleetwood & Partners in Bickley Road but it wasn't a firm of solicitors as she'd at first assumed; it was a computers and software consultancy. That didn't surprise her. Beth was already convinced that no one was looking for Sandra Littlejohn, with or without the lure of a legacy.

There was a snack-bar just across the road from the prosperous Fleetwood frontage, and further along there was a pub and a restaurant. The partners and their employees would no doubt spend their lunch-hour at any of the three places and Beth would have a clear view of their comings and goings.

For several hours she spun out the time with coffee and cakes, indifferent to the quality, turning over in her mind how best to approach Anna when she appeared. She almost certainly intended some form of blackmail. Beth Masters had far more to lose now than ever troubled Beth Ramsay if all the hidden details of the attic den at Number 30 were dragged out into the open, whether or not they were believed. Beth had a sudden vision of Tom's body lying in a litter of bloodied glass splinters and nausea tightened her guts. But Anna's strongest weapon was Jennetta's wedding. She'd know that Beth wouldn't call in the police before then, whatever else she did. And the later Anna left her demands, the more vulnerable to blackmail Beth would be. She daren't leave Anna with the initiative.

Beth needed to discover too whether she had an accomplice. She'd spoken of living alone, but there was her daughter – *if* she was Anna's daughter. At about twenty-five she was older than Beth might have expected. Jennetta, after all, wasn't yet nineteen. The alleged daughter was just the sort of unmemorable figure that was easily overlooked. She could have been trailing Beth for weeks and Beth simply wouldn't know her again.

She watched from the snack-bar window until nearly two o'clock, but there was no sign of Anna and the curious looks directed at herself had become too pointed to ignore. Beth decided that there must be a staff canteen on the premises that Anna had preferred to lunch at. She paid her bill and crossed the road to Fleetwood & Partners. She'd see this David Morgan whose name had been taken in vain and who must have puzzled over Beth's reply to his supposed letter. He might recognise Anna's description. Beth wouldn't let herself even wonder if there actually was a David Morgan. Because if there wasn't she'd have to start again at Dickins & Jones, losing another week and this element of surprise as well. But after haggling over Beth's lack of an appointment, the receptionist buzzed through her name and she was shown into an office.

Beth instantly recognised the man who waited to receive her, and she saw that he knew her. It was the balding man. Her brain refused to construe, but conventional social formulas cover most embarrassments. Beth heard the door shut behind her and she automatically crossed to the chair in front of the desk, her 'company' smile fixed in a rictus. It was as much as she could do. She stared blankly, unable to speak.

'I wasn't expecting a personal visit so soon after your very prompt reply to my letter, Mrs Masters,' David Morgan smiled perfunctorily. 'You've caught me – a little unprepared, as you see.' He had a light, pleasant voice, and his formal business suit was reassuring.

'I'm – I'm sorry if you're very busy,' Beth stammered. 'But – actually I came here thinking you were a solicitor.'

'That's what I meant. And now you see I'm not.' Light dawned. The computers consultancy was a front for a private enquiries agency. 'You don't recognise me, do you, Mrs Masters?'

'Oh, but I do.' Beth pulled her wits together. 'I saw

you in London one Saturday. My husband said you seemed to be interested in us. But why?' Beth saw that he was embarrassed for some reason. And why, anyway, should a private detective looking for Sandra Littlejohn be covertly interested in the Masters family, Beth wondered, beginning to think clearly. 'Why're you pretending to be a solicitor looking for Sandra?' she asked straightly.

'Because I didn't believe you'd – co-operate if you knew the truth.' He smiled thinly down at his desk.

'But isn't that false pretences?' His head jerked up. 'What is the truth – and who *are* you?' Beth demanded.

'The truth – is that I'm David Morgan. It's not an unusual combination of names. My father was Thomas Morgan, of 30, Churchill Avenue, Fulham.' Beth felt the blood drain from her face and her vision began to swim sickeningly. 'I see you know now who I am.' He gazed at her with the sort of deliberate interest that's usually permitted only to doctors.

Beth refused to drop her eyes. It was a physical effort to remain upright in her chair and concentrate, all her muscles and will-power at full stretch.

'I can only remember that there was such a person,' she spoke slowly, like a speech exercise, in her struggle not to falter. It was something that she could speak at all. 'I'm sorry, but – you were hardly ever home and – Sandra and I were children then. We left there in very unhappy circumstances,' she belatedly tried to excuse her joyless reactions at their reunion.

'But I remember you both quite well. I came to see you afterwards. After my father's funeral.'

'Did you?' Beth asked vaguely. 'So why're you trying

to find Sandra in such an underhand way?' He didn't like that either and took a moment to reply. Beth's confidence began to revive.

'Let me ask you a question first. Why did you come here?'

'Because after I'd answered your letter,' Beth said readily, 'I realised that in fact I had seen Sandra recently – twice. She calls herself Anna now.'

David Morgan smiled in a satisfied way that was vaguely offensive and Beth was puzzled again. 'So you knew who she was?' But that disconcerted him in turn.

'Are you admitting it?' he asked, and Beth was even more at a loss.

'That I've seen her? I've even spoken to her.'

Morgan stared at Beth from under his heavy brows.

'Let's start again,' he said curtly, 'and drop the holy innocents act'.

'I beg your pardon,' Beth stiffened. 'I assumed from your expression that I'd just confirmed what you believed. That the woman with her daughter whose table you shared in Dickins & Jones was Sandra.'

'Oh, I recognised Sandra there, all right,' Morgan's lip lifted over his teeth in a half smile. 'I recognised you. You're Sandra. Your little girl looks exactly as you did, yet your husband calls you Beth. That intrigued me very much.'

Beth's startled exclamation was forced out of her as though by a blow to her stomach. Morgan sat back in his chair, clearly enjoying her surprise.

'I got on the same train and watched you all get out at Epsom. The Social Services people very kindly looked up their records to help me find my foster-sisters and they put me on to the former Warden at the Hostel. She told me all I needed to know about you two. She's blind now but not stupid, and she's been closer to you than you've realised. You'd be surprised to know what humble connections some of your grand friends have!' he nodded with smug significance.

'She hadn't looked at your letters for years and she gladly gave them to me to read aloud to her. And what a coincidence! Her niece is friendly with a Beth Masters, whose elder daughter's surname is Nicholls. Could she really be the Beth Ramsay who married Andrew Nicholls all those years ago? Well, near enough she could be. I asked her not to say anything to her niece as I wanted to surprise you. And I have, haven't I? I looked up your address in the phone-book, but I haven't seen your house. No doubt it'll be grander than my father's poor semi that sheltered you when you had nothing and no one of your own. Oh, you've come up in the world since then, all right, and far more than you deserve!' For the first time his expression reminded Beth of his father.

She sat woodenly through this tirade, not looking directly at Morgan's hot eyes or his sneering mouth but concentrating on the end of his nose, which was globular and faintly spongy-looking. Only his deductions were surprising, after all, not his information. Even the shock of hearing how much the Warden now knew about her niece's friend was diminished by Morgan's announcement of his identity.

'You see, I expected you to be in touch with some tale of having seen "Sandra". She finally made life too uncomfortable for you, did she, with what she knew? You look stunned – and so you should.' Morgan's face flushed darkly as he reached his conclusion. Half rising from his chair he barked, 'I'm Nemesis, Sandra!'

Far from feeling stunned Beth was almost ready to laugh at his self-admiring revelations. He'd given her time to get over her initial shock and now she was icily angry. Beth too was quickly on her feet and leaning over his desk before Morgan finished speaking. She flipped the intercom switch.

'You are certainly dishonest and possibly a criminal, if not unhinged,' she said clearly. 'I came here in good faith' – Morgan turned off the machine with a convulsive movement of both hands and sank back in his chair – 'believing you to be legally interested in Sandra's whereabouts and with information that would've led you to her. I wouldn't now tell you the time of day.

'However,' Beth stripped off her gloves and opened her bag, 'this I will show you. I brought it in the hope that you might find it useful. Here,' she dropped the snap on the desk. 'You may see there the likeness you claim to recognise in my daughter, but you'll find it in both those faces. And that's how you remember us, and hardly bothered to tell us apart except that Sandra was smaller than I. So much for your supposed recognition of me now. You dishonestly hoped that in order to prove I'm not Sandra I'd tell you where to find her, that I'd "co-operate". The legacy is obviously a lie, so why do you want her?'

But Morgan only glanced up at Beth and then doubtfully back at the snap. Beth hit again.

'I see you prefer to explain that to the police. And also why you insist that I'm Sandra. She cut her hand very badly when your father had his accident, trying to help

292

him. I imagine you were told that at the time. Her right hand was left noticeably scarred, whereas mine,' Beth held out both her hands, palms up, 'are free of scars, as you can see.' She turned them over. Morgan's eyes glazed. He'd forgotten the cut hand, Beth saw.

'And now I'm leaving.' She replaced the snap in her bag, picked up her gloves and stalked to the door.

'Wait! Please –' Morgan suddenly came to life.

'You've been offensive enough. Anything more I'd prefer said before witnesses,' Beth snapped, and left.

# Seventeen

Beth walked stiffly back to her car and drove away without much thought for direction; more consciously away from Fleetwood's than back home. The identification of David Morgan as the balding man had been shock enough, never mind the rest, and the effort of surviving that and walking quietly away left Beth feeling shredded. She had shot her bolt. She finally came to, miles from anywhere she knew and wondering how she'd arrived there in one piece.

Beth checked the map-book that was always kept in her car and diverted to the M26 for the M25. Vaguely remembering it had been recommended, or at least mentioned not so long ago as a way home, she turned off for the A217 and the homeward road south of Sutton for Epsom. Her route crossed Banstead Downs, and as she drove Beth saw localised evidence of fire damage. It was years since she'd even driven across the Downs, but now on an impulse she parked and walked in the low evening sunlight as she tried to clear her head. There was hardly a soul about at that time of an October Monday.

It seemed to Beth that Anna and David Morgan were in league together. That was the worst of all possible combinations against her. It was surely too much of a coincidence that they were acting separately and simultaneously. Her sighting of them together at Dickins & Jones was conclusive, for although she'd failed to recognise Anna, events had proved that Morgan must have known perfectly well who she was. That was why he'd been so taken aback when Beth told him she'd seen him there, and why he'd concentrated on trying to bully and confuse her out of her certainty. A soured, envious man with a chip on his shoulder and Anna, who felt Beth had betrayed her, certainly added up to blackmail.

In the course of her wandering Beth came upon the fifteenth tee – where they'd had their picnic the day Sandra disappeared, she remembered. (So perhaps it hadn't been a simple impulse to walk, any more than it was chance that brought her home this way, she stared thoughtfully at the marker.) 'Here. We'll sit here. It's my lucky number,' Beth had said. An omen for her new job. She seemed to remember it being nearer the road then, though. Perhaps they'd changed things about since. The cropped turf was backed by a shrubbery windbreak like some of the others, where wild rose stems clung to hawthorns all aglow with their autumn crop of fruit. Only its number distinguished the tee. A path had cut across the course then, just a sandy track that had met the main road. They wouldn't have changed that. Beth vaguely remembered that it was a public footpath.

They'd rambled all over, talking and laughing; Beth in high spirits with excitement and anticipation, forgetting to be superior, and Sandra playing up to her. When their carrier-bags got too heavy they'd stopped for a blow-out. Then they'd walked back along the path in the late afternoon and came out where the main road was being patched, their crossing-point down to Mrs Peabody's. Beth wondered if she still lived there behind her wisteria.

In reminiscent mood, Beth searched for the sandy track and found it, the continuation of a residential road that ran up through Cheam and served houses overlooking the golf-course. They'd seemed palatial to them then. 'One day I shall live in something like that,' Beth had announced. 'And I shall have the one next door,' Sandra had laughed. 'We'll never be separated again.' Beth followed the track now between clumps of gorse and brambles and hawthorns, where the fire hadn't reached, past greens and bunkers until it threaded rougher ground near the main road. She became conscious of the traffic noise and the need to continue her journey home.

The path rounded a final mass of hawthorns and birch saplings raising their autumn-tinted tops over the inevitable tangle of briars humping over just as inevitable roadside rubbish. The vague shape of what might be an old barrel – perhaps even from the same roadworks Beth remembered – showed through a patch of thin cover. Exposed and unsightly, a tattered car-seat, a dump of rubble and plastic shreds trapped among the bushes witnessed to more human laziness. Beth walked on towards the road where her car was parked in a lay-by a hundred yards away.

She returned home to a household in turmoil. Beth had committed the unforgivable nuisance of forgetting that afternoon's school lift. The parents of the abandoned children – even Jane – had apparently phoned critical and questioning messages which her family couldn't satisfactorily answer. 'Where on earth have you *been*?' they demanded offendedly and Beth, though conscious

297

of her lapse, was too tired to care.

'Just – driving about,' she mumbled, with an equally uncharacteristic lack of conviction. Her attitude annoyed Jennetta.

'So was I – just driving about,' she said sharply. 'And I passed my test, if you're at all interested. Luckily I was able to borrow *Alan's* car.'

Beth was remorseful then, but was left uneasily groping after a feeling that there was something else about Jennetta she should be remembering. She could hardly think straight for a thumping headache and hoped the elusive fact wouldn't be too mortifyingly recalled to her attention.

Penny was shocked to have been 'forgotten', and her bewilderment showed in her head-down, monosyllabic unapproachability all through supper, Jennetta was too disgusted to bother hiding her feelings, and Duncan was as angry as Beth had ever known him. It was altogether a perfect evening for an early night. Half blinded by her headache, Beth dragged herself upstairs with a muttered apology soon after supper.

Her body felt as though it had been stretched all day on the rack, but her usually recuperative bath failed to relax her. Beth was still awake when Duncan came to bed.

'Where *did* you get to?' he asked, still tight-lipped.

'To David Morgan – to tell him about Anna being Sandra,' Beth murmured limply. 'But they're both in league against me.'

'Oh, my poor darling! You're *ill*! *Really* ill!' Duncan melted instantly and took Beth in his arms. She lay stiff and unresponsive. She didn't need telling she had a

298

headache, she needed help. 'Why on earth should this man, Morgan, be against you?' Duncan asked in the tones of one soothing a child's unreasonable fear.

'He was at the foster-home too.' Duncan was silenced and Beth too discouraged by his reactions to explain further or to ask for his help. Duncan was a write-off, talking only of butterflies or threatening her with the police. She lay resentfully against him, staring wide-eyed into the dark.

'Try and go to sleep, darling,' Duncan murmured after a while.

'I *am* trying. These damn sleeping-pills don't work fast enough.'

Duncan too lay awake, wrestling with a problem that wasn't Beth's alone. Her sense of guilt at her lack of a proper family background seemed to feed her obsessive fears about Jennetta's wedding, he reflected. Certainly the nearer the wedding came the worse Beth's fantasies about these characters from her past had grown, to show themselves in unpredictable – terrible – ways. They had made her ill. He could feel the heat of her body through his cotton pyjamas as if it was on fire with a raging fever.

Duncan inched away from Beth to give her space to sleep and wondered unhappily if – how – the wedding should be postponed. If Beth was even willing to consider such an idea, was there any guarantee that she wouldn't be just as unpredictable whenever Jennetta was married? A postponement would devastate Jennetta, especially when she knew the reason – that her own mother was more likely to ruin her wedding day than any of the imagined shades of her past. Now she'd invented yet another one and lumped him in with that foster-home she never liked to speak about. Duncan could no longer believe in Anna-Sandra. But Alan – When the circumstances were explained to Alan, might he not prefer an indefinite postponement? Duncan's heart bled for Jennetta.

Beth's breakdown – they used to call it a 'mental' breakdown – was temporary, of course, he reassured himself. Brought on by stress. But it must cast doubts on Jennetta's unknown heredity. One in – how many was it? He had sheets of tables at the office but figures comfortably ignored the personal anguish. One in however many suffered from some form of mental collapse. 'Nervous' breakdowns were better understood these days, but that didn't make Beth's any easier to bear – or for Alan to overlook.

The wedding was so close – dare he leave matters as they were and pray for the best, Duncan wondered. That might not be fair to Alan. It might be criminally unfair to Beth herself who, but for his silence, should perhaps be in residential care immediately. There seemed to be no limit, in Duncan's horrified imagination, to what Beth might do under this continued strain – go out one day and be found wandering with no memory nor knowledge of her identity; crash the car in one of her fits of abstraction that were becoming more common; wholesale shoplifting – anything. He couldn't watch her every hour of the day. And there was Penny to consider as well. It was no longer possible to think that Beth could never be violent.

Those were Duncan's last inconclusive thoughts before he lurched into an uneasy sleep, anxiously listening to Beth's relaxed breathing.

She might have been running from her nightmare or dispelling it, the sensations were alike. She was back on the golf-course, hunting again for the sandy track in the weak light of a rising moon. The street-lamps lit the verge – too clearly – but out on the course it was confusing. Landmarks looked alike and her small torch was useless except at close quarters – typical of nightmares. But she was otherwise well prepared, wearing boots, gardening gloves over her driving gloves and carrying a pair of secateurs; properly dressed for rough gardening. There were blackberries and roses to prune. There'd been a dream quality about her careful planning, a sense of make-believe. None of it was really true; she could always wake up and find herself back in bed.

Suddenly she came upon the opening between clumps of high cover. She flitted through it silently, as happened when dreams were going well, relieved to be on the level path at last and not stumbling into bunkers – that sensation of falling that jerked all her muscles awake. She'd heard someone behind her, of course, the hallmark of any nightmare, but she expected to lose them once she struck the path.

She'd have to hurry, however. Her boots were divers' boots, weighted with lead. The kelp grew thickly hereabouts and beckoned deceivingly. She made a false cast, felt a brief flare of panic as her efforts geared down to painful slow-motion. Escape seemed impossible. Then she found it, the wrecked car-seat beside a mass of young trees and undergrowth; but there was no time after all to sit and rest, although iron bands twisted painfully around her ribs and squeezed out her breath in tiny unrefreshing gasps.

She listened for a moment but there was only the inter-mittent sound of late-night traffic and the shushing of dying leaves above her head. Leaves – or waves that broke and threatened to engulf her. They beat on her ears like the pulse of her own lifeblood. She forged on, forc-ing her way through the tumble of briars and bushes, looking for the easiest approach by the light of her torch but careless of runners and branches that snagged at her Casharel slacks and plucked at her jacket. Vicious, envi-ous fingers and trip-wires for her feet. The more entwined, the more impatiently she tore free, using her gloved hands to break the creepers' grip rather than spend time with the secateurs. There *was* no time.

She knew she'd reached the middle of the clump when the going became easier. She could almost walk upright and the ground underfoot was soft with leaf-mould. Excellent for the garden, of course – but she'd forgotten to bring a sack. The blackberry tangles had thinned to sneaky, almost leafless runners weaving towards the light. Somewhere here – She flashed her torch and found the barrel's vague outline, half-buried under leaf-litter and untidily oversewn with bramble stems; a hump like a grave. She'd inspect its possibilities in a moment, but first she must rest. She cut and wrenched away the worst of the growth along one side of the barrel and lay down on the rough bed of leaves, breathless but secure.

It was a good hiding-place even in daylight. The trees and bushes met overhead and almost shut out the moon-light and the acid glow of the street-lighting. A few more weeks of autumn and the cover would be less, but it didn't matter. She'd have stopped running. It would be too late for discovery.

She'd seen long ago what a good hiding-place this would make. On the day of their picnic on the fifteenth tee. Sounded like a book or a film. 'Bunfight at the Fifteenth Tee', she laughed quietly. It hadn't been such hard work getting through then, for all she'd been rolling and dragging the barrel. That had been a dream within a dream, where everything was possible. She'd been high on excitement, of course, and the goad of 'now or never' had been urgent. Even anaesthetic – as it was now. She'd notice the cuts and tears only if she allowed herself to.

She pillowed her head more comfortably on her arms and thought about that day, the first day of her freedom. The barrels had been in the roadside ditch near where the men were working, chy-iking the girls as they'd started down the track with their bags of food and fizz. One of the barrels was battered and empty. She'd later stuffed Beth's body into it. It had seemed tailor-made for just that purpose.

Beth had stopped hereabouts for a pee on their way back. The workmen had gone, leaving their things tidy for the next day and their tools out of sight in the empty barrel. That had been a bonus. She'd intended to crump Beth with the cider-bottle. Nowadays they locked everything up in tin shelters. 'It's OK, they've gone,' she'd called back to Beth who was nervous – although earlier in the afternoon she'd hung around the men like a second-hand tart.

Then she whipped off her anorak, grabbed the shovel – it had Beth's name on it, you could say – and ran back and cracked Beth over the head with it while she still had her pants down. She'd owed Beth that. It bonged like Big Ben and Beth squawked and put her hands over her head. She got another crack, with the edge this time, as she fell forward into the bushes. Then another for luck. She'd run back for the barrel, tipped out the tools and trundled it down the track. Beth hadn't moved. She'd stuck one of the empty carrier-bags over her head and bundled her into the barrel – all floppy arms and legs, clumsy cow – and stood it on end to shake her down.

Another bonus – they'd left a heap of tarry stuff, still warm, under a weighted tarpaulin. She'd shovelled the stuff on to the tarp. and dragged it back down the path; scooped it in on top of Beth and rammed it down hard with the shovel. She hadn't enjoyed that bit, the smell and the chopping sensation. Typical of Beth to make her do something she didn't want to but had to. Beth had this hold over her. Finally she'd rolled up the tacky tarp and crammed it in like a cork and shoved the barrel into the open heart of the bushes. Then she'd dug leaves and clods of earth over it, hardly able to see by then.

She'd chucked the shovel among the other tools on her way back to old Fatty's – via the phone-booth for her call to the Warden. She'd enjoyed that conversation, paid for with Beth's money out of Beth's shoulder-bag, and creased herself listening to Nosy spluttering and damn near wetting herself at Sandra's Last Words. She'd ditched her gloves by then, one at a time. It was already beginning to rain, and it went on raining all weekend. Couldn't have been timed better.

And it couldn't have gone better either. She'd planned a rough outline while they'd wandered about exploring, but everything had conspired to make it perfect. There'd been people about on the course earlier but they'd cleared off when the afternoon clouded over and she'd been left undisturbed. She'd seen straightaway that the golf-course had possibilities and had originally simply intended to leave Beth well hidden and then scram; but when Fatbags mistook her for Beth before they went out she'd got the idea of changing places. Why should she make herself uncomfortable on the run?

She'd worked out all sorts of plans for months beforehand, ready for the opportunity when it came. The exercise had kept her sane. In the end what offered was quite different but simpler and better. All the same, those old plans had been practice in a way. She'd had a chance to decide what not to do this time round. Not to make too much noise or too much mess. And to have a really good story ready, a choice of several, in fact, to fit any occasion. She used to send herself to sleep thinking them up.

Yes, she'd been sickened by the mess at Number 30, and even now the memory of it turned her stomach. That was a spur of the moment job, of course. She hadn't thought beyond the simple shove of the step-ladder down the stairs – she'd hidden in the bedroom doorway and toppled him as he'd started down – and then to get outside again as fast as she could, as if she'd been there all the time. He was almost at the bottom by the first bounce. One bashed eye was already closing by the time she'd reached him but the other had swivelled about at her. He was making disgusting snorting noises and obscenely clashing his broken dentures. She'd acted by instinct then. And suddenly there was Beth squealing like a scalded pig at the back door – !

When her chance finally came with Beth it had worked out much better than that first time. It was nearer the road than she'd have liked, but it had to be close to

305

the roadworks because the barrel was so obviously meant. Never look a gift-horse in the mouth. And nearer the road the barrel wouldn't look out of place if it was spotted in the months to come. That's how she knew she'd got the right place now – near the road and just off the track.

But her luck hadn't stopped there. She was a fair mess by the time she got back to the digs, but Fatty was watching her telly behind drawn curtains and she'd sneaked up to Beth's room without being seen. She'd changed into Beth's clean jeans and tidied herself up a bit. She couldn't do anything about the bramble-scratches on her face but they'd proved to be unexpectedly good value after all. Then she'd socked Fatty with the story of Sandra's hitch. By then, even if she could have seen them both together she couldn't have sworn which was who. And anyway, she was too busy passing the buck. That's when they remembered their responsibilities, those people – when it was someone else's.

So, if Beth had been found she'd have been Sandra. It was a bit spooky at first knowing herself to be dead, especially when Fatty discussed the chances of Sandra making out and even being recovered. And it might have been a bit complicated if she had been found too soon, since Sandra had supposedly got a lift with a woman – the description a cross between Nosy and Fatty, she grinned to herself. But the fact of a woman-driver seemed less likely to call all hands to panic stations and the last thing she wanted was the Warden conscientiously twitching her whiskers around Banstead. She'd kept a look-out for her car and some money handy for a quick get-away just in case.

And actually, as it happened, she'd been over-optimistic about Beth's body being written-off as Sandra's; she hadn't then known about dental identification. She knew about fingerprints, but theirs weren't on record. She hadn't discovered about teeth until Nick was killed, and it did nothing for her peace of mind at the time.

Anyway, she'd resisted going back to check that the barrel remained undisturbed. There was always the chance she was being watched in case Sandra got in touch, so she hadn't gone near the Downs for ages. But as the weeks went by she could relax, and with the months Beth became Anybody. Sandra, rather. Sandra became Anybody – but for meeting someone who could have told them apart. Or, because of her damn teeth, if anyone linked the body to the girl who'd absconded from thereabouts. Jane's Aunt Grace had given her a nasty few days in that connection. She was another who'd lived too long and made too much mischief.

But after the disappearance of Sandra she'd done all the things expected of Beth, even to crying all over the phone that night. She hadn't realised 'til then how shagged-out she was, how keyed-up. She'd come down like a ton of bricks afterwards and slept that night as if she'd fallen unconscious. The best night's sleep she'd ever had, no planning, no worrying, no looking back on the day's failures. She'd ingratiated herself with Fatty just as Beth would have done, and that wasn't difficult, either. Dead easy.

Beth's character had become a dead bore, though, sanctimonious little bitch. She'd had to give up fags, for a start. But she was stuck with it. *And* it added another eighteen months to her age. She'd taken over Beth's birth certificate, of course, as well as that bloody sampler that had gone everywhere. Fatty'd admired it and she'd made her one something like it for a Christmas present. And naturally she'd taken over Beth's Savings book. Her signature at least didn't take much working at. That too had become hers and she'd loathed it every time she wrote it. It was like banging another nail into her own coffin. Luckily the letter of appointment to the clerking job was among Beth's things, or she'd have had the embarrassment of not knowing where to report for duty that first Monday. The snap was there too.

Beth had deserved knocking off for her character alone – and she'd had no idea just how shitty it was until she came to live it for her. But there were other reasons, of course. She'd never have been safe while Beth was alive. She might have kept her trap shut, but Beth had ways of reminding her how she could bust her any time. She'd signed her own obituary the first day she used Number 30 as a threat. All that looking after 'poor little traumatised Sandra' – Beth picked up the jargon, always – all that sisterly closeness was just to use her for her own amusement. Her own ego. Beth even took to calling her 'Sandy', *knowing* what it meant to her and tickled pink to see her squirm. It was as bad as life at Number 30.

So she'd asked for it and she had it coming to her. Beth didn't know, dumb bitch – and God, she was dumb! Thick as pig-shit. But *she'd* known there'd come a time and she'd recognise it when it did. It had come that November day and she'd made it work for her again. The *effort* of playing along 'til then – ! She'd worked her pants off impressing everyone with her 'improvement', patronising sods, to keep close to Beth. As hard as she'd worked at Number 30.

Beth had grown big-headed about her 'influence for good' that made such a hit with the staff, but *she'd* never forgotten how Beth had come by that influence and she'd sweated to stay near Beth. Even so, it was touch and go she'd miss catching up with her at the Hostel. Her chance might never have come once Beth had moved on. And right to the end she'd had to work at it – practically *spell* it out to Beth to have her along for the day she left the Hostel. Brain-dead cluck. Only one of them was going free that day. In the end it had all worked out even better than she could have imagined. It was obviously *meant*.

Except for that stinking turd, David Morgan. She'd kept coming back to him, too, without realising why. She'd been cheated. She'd been got at through *Beth,* of all things. Beth, who should have been dead safe. Who could have guessed her Prince Charming would drop out of the blue and cock up all she'd worked for?

Morgan had never counted, yet he'd guessed enough to frighten her shitless. She gave a sudden caw of laughter at the memory of her stupefaction in his office that morning. If it had been a – a talking moose goggling at her across his desk she couldn't have been more taken aback. He'd been too cautious to spell out everything he suspected, but he'd been right about her reason for off-loading Beth and he guessed she'd actually done it when that *bloody* Parker woman told him about Sandra absconding. And who'd have dreamt she'd turn up again too, and so close. Bloody 'Aunt Grace'!

It wasn't surprising she hadn't recognised her at Jane's, but when she did realise who she was she shouldn't have written her off so lightly. She knew that now – too late. The old fool had shopped her without even trying. Had stabbed her in the back when she'd thought she was harmless. All *Beth's* bloody fault again.

But Morgan must have been suspicious about his father's accident all this time. Maybe she'd blown it that day at Dover House when he'd slapped her face and had cause to remember her. Then put two and two together when he'd found that randy old bastard's attic den. Guessed it had been her and not that streak of piety, Beth, who'd sprung the 'accident'. He couldn't do anything about it before because of the worms he'd stir up. *Now* he could launch a crusade on behalf of his missing foster sister and get at her that way. Just because he'd recognised her through Penny. And heard Duncan call her 'Beth'. It was always the same, betrayed again – but this time by her own family.

There was nothing Morgan could do, though. She'd spiked his guns. She'd certainly shaken him even if she hadn't entirely convinced him he was mistaken. In the end she had the birth certificate to prove who she was, and even the scars on her hand had blended among the natural creases. It would take a palmist to distinguish them.

If he'd been really certain he'd have boasted about that as well as about his *amazing* detective powers. Luck, that's all it was. Motivated by nasty, malicious envy. He should stay quietly thankful his father hadn't been publicly disgraced. If he'd *known* anything he'd have threatened her with the police before she'd threatened him. No, he was guessing and hoped she'd betray herself if he frightened her enough. *That* was never the

310

way. But the police – they were the real threat. They could order a dental check. It had been the possibility of police investigation after Nick's death that had terrified her then; when her Mrs Nicholls persona via Beth Ramsay was still insecure. Well, she'd thrown Morgan Anna. Let him get side-tracked by her if she was only an innocent Anna Nobody. But what if she weren't? What if Morgan was in league with Anna as seemed likely?

What if Anna was Beth? True, she hadn't recognised Anna as Beth, she'd merely recognised the evidence: the scars on her hand and her head. Marks where the shovel had fallen? Not hard enough. Had Beth struggled out, got herself picked up and taken to hospital? Without an identity, without perhaps much of a memory until Morgan had somehow come across her and worked on her. Yet she hadn't seen any mention of an attack in the local paper twenty years ago, for all her careful reading. But if Anna was Beth and Morgan in league with her, then Morgan knew all there was to be known. They hadn't gone to the police, because they intended black-mail. 'Oh, you've come up in the world, all right.' No thanks to *his* bloody family.

There was one sure-fire way of finding out if she had anything to fear from Beth – from either of them – and that's why she'd come. Morgan without Beth was nothing. Better get on with it or they'd find her asleep on the job. She should've checked straight away while the adrenalin was still flowing. Now she felt sapped. She wasn't looking forward to it anyway – hadn't wanted to do it alone, but Duncan was as much use as a hole in the head. He expected too much of her these days.

# Eighteen

However, she was forced to lie still as feet thudded along the path and bushes rustled. She'd been vaguely aware of movement to and fro while she allowed herself the rare luxury of examining her own cunning, but the sounds were nothing to do with her. There were too many more convenient places for a quick jump, she knew, to tempt couples to fight their way into where she lay.

When it was quiet again she felt through the creeping growth around the barrel and found its open end. She cut away the brambles and scrabbled out dead leaves and damp loam that had sifted inside. Only when her hands touched the folds of petrified material could she be really certain that she'd found the right barrel. Not because she'd seen others among the detritus – she hadn't; but because it was amazing that the one she looked for should be recognisable after all the years. Things were still working out for her.

The metal had rusted and flaked around the opening and much of the underside, now sunk in the earth, was a wreck; but the barrel's general shape and its upper part had been saved from collapse by the wad of asphalt she'd shovelled in. It had set like rock. No one had squirmed their way out of *that*, she told herself with satisfaction as her fingers pried around the sealed, resisting folds of the tarpaulin. Beth, who was also Sandra, was safe in her secret place like a fossil, and Anna was just

Anna after all; some innocent, ageing tart. And Morgan was on his own. She scooped back the soil and leaves and spent a little time artistically draping a few bramble runners over the opening.

When she checked the closed end, however, she found the metal less well preserved, and in fact that end was far from closed now. Stems and suckers rambled in and out, as if the folded body inside had prevented the asphalt from working right through. From being concerned to know that the remains were still entombed, she became anxious to make sure they were safe from any chance discovery. There was nothing innocuous plugging this vulnerable end. She should have tipped some rubble in first, she supposed – but hell! you can't think of everything. She began pulling at the intrusive trailers, annoyed to see how easily fragments of the barrel came away with them.

In the distance a voice called eerily, 'Beth!' and she grinned to herself, suddenly amused. Beth couldn't hear. They couldn't frighten *Beth* with ghosts. Only nightmare possibilities that turned into probabilities could frighten Beth – and hadn't she just proved that they no longer existed? There was no ghost, and only Beth's nuisance value remained.

Propped on one elbow she shone the torch through the ragged holes. Just a black mass inside. So, the asphalt *had* encased the body. She put in her gloved hand, touched something yielding and recoiled sharply. Some bloody animal had made its nest in there. She peered in again but there was no sign of movement.

Outside it was different. Footsteps, snapping twigs. She turned out her torch as the voice called again, closer to hand. *Piss* off. Hadn't they homes to go to? The blundering footsteps receded.

She couldn't leave the creature in the barrel. God knew what it might drag into the open, burrowing and gnawing; bits of Sandra uncovered by its bloody interference. And if she simply blocked that end with rubble and earth now – which was a distasteful idea anyway – it would only whinge or try to dig its way out, drawing attention to what lay inside. Grimly hoping it was a hibernating hedgehog or dormouse and not lurking rats, she took off her right-hand gloves for a better purchase, reached in and grabbed.

Cloth. She found only a handful of cloth, a little slimy to the touch. Not the tarp. That was still corking the other end. Bemused, she cautiously eased her hand out and shone the torch. Cloth should have rotted after all these years, surely. But here it was; black material, slightly damp from the sweating loam. She'd worn nothing black that day, though – Beth had worn nothing black, she corrected herself impatiently. This was the *wrong* bloody barrel after all. Angrily she tugged out more of the material – it had no business to be there – enough to make out faint traces of quilting. An old anorak? Beth's navy nylon anorak, standard Dover House issue. But – empty? Bloody hell, she'd left it behind to make-believe she was still inside, the devious bitch!

Half in panic, half in fury, she got to her knees and wrenched savagely at the material. More of the barrel fell away. She had almost the entire sleeve out in the open. From the tattered remains of a cuff there fell a tumble of small, discoloured bones, like dice from a shaker. *Disgusting*! She gagged and fell back, dropping her

315

torch among the leaves.

After a while she heard the murmur of familiar voices and she lay still, listening. It seemed important not to interrupt the dispassionate discussion.

'At least I know she's there.'

'You knew that the moment you found the tarp. still in place. Why the fuck couldn't you leave well alone? You're your own worst enemy, Sandra. You've broken the barrel now and you'll lose your pocket-money.'

'It's only an old barrel. Just shove the – the gunk back inside and cover it up for the moment. I'll come back later with a spade and tidy up. Everything's all right.' She nodded in silent agreement.

'My poor darling! You're *ill*!' *Who* said that? For a moment her optimism faltered. Recent scenes tapped at the misted panes of her memory. It was true; she was ill. They were sticking needles into her – all over. And the bed smelled – like earth. The stench of her grave. Not needles, worms – already burrowing into her flesh. Ugly maggots of corruption gnawing inside her skull. She reared up convulsively, tearing herself free of the clawing brambles.

'Beth? Is that you?' the pestering voice called again and once more feet pounded along the track. Her head thudded, keeping in step. So, Beth *was* alive. It wasn't Beth who was dead. She was alive and somewhere close by, or he wouldn't be calling her. Or perhaps he didn't know yet that Beth was dead, she sniggered softly. *She* knew, though, and knowledge is power. What? What did she know? For a moment she wasn't certain. She tried to grasp at the tail of an idea that billowed and re-formed like washing on a line. Then she remembered. It was

Sandra who'd died. Dead and buried deep years ago, but somehow she'd kept that secret and got her reward. Tears ran down her face as she remembered Sandra, smothered by a creeping lust. Honour thy father and thy brother, little children, to come unto thee and forbid them not –

'Beth!'

'Hallo?' It was a man's voice that answered. Confusing. She dropped to all fours, her head weaving blindly as she tried to peer through the bushes to the track.

'Have you seen – I'm looking for someone. My wife. I lost her among these damn bushes half an hour ago –' Duncan. Calling for *Beth*? Of course. Duncan loved *Beth*. So had Nick, for a while. Everyone loved Beth. Sometimes she despised them for it. She'd gone on hating Beth for it long after she was dead. They wouldn't find her so lovable now, if they could see her! But Duncan was giving the game away. She couldn't trust anyone. They were all in it together, all conspiring against her. 'She's got to be somewhere around – her car's still parked by the road. I've been hanging about there waiting for her to come back to it. She hasn't been well, you see, and I'm afraid –' And suddenly so was she.

'I'll help you look for her.'

'Oh God, I'd be so grateful!' The fool! The bloody, *bloody* fool!

'Haven't you got a torch? Stay with me, then. I have.'

A powerful beam leapt out of the night and raked the bushes. It shimmered through the leaves of her den like flashes of the gunfire that thundered in her ears. She felt

317

the bullets scream through her skull leaving worms of pain like cigarette-burns on a table. They pierced her safety with tiny holes of light until they ripped a great, bright tear in her darkness.

David Morgan. Suddenly she was fully and blindingly aware. It had been his voice so considerately offering to search for Beth. She recognised the excitement in it. The high. He knew his chance had come. He'd known from what that bloody Parker woman told him of Sandra's disappearance that the body would be somewhere here.

*That's* when she'd started losing her grip, long before the Dickins & Jones incident – when that fat old toad had turned up at the Mallinsons'. It had seemed then that the poison from the past she still trailed with her was safely dispersed, but the infection had festered. She hadn't realised it but it was that weekend which had unhitched her tether, whipped up her panic reactions and sent them bolting out of control from mere ghosts. But for that, Morgan's letter wouldn't have worried her and she'd never have followed it up with a visit. He'd have been stumped. But for that she wouldn't be here now.

He'd taken his chance and made it work, just as she'd done. He'd seen her frightened and that was enough. All he'd done was watch the house – and *she'd* led out a procession of witnesses to a corpse preserved like a fly in amber.

She rolled up into a foetal ball and wrapped her arms around her head, waiting for the shovel to fall.